Praise for the Authors

LuAnn McLane

"[A] fun and flirty contemporary romance." —Fresh Fiction

"Lighthearted comedy and steamy romance . . . a delightful tale."
—Romance Junkies

"A hoot! The pages fly in this sexy, hilarious romp."
—Romance Reviews Today

"Charmingly entertaining . . . a truly pleasurable read."
—*Romantic Times*

Susanna Carr

"Sizzling and charming." —Romance Junkies

"Witty and sexy . . . what a huge amount of fun!"
—Just Erotic Romance Reviews

"The sexual tension is unbelievable!"
—*New York Times* bestselling author Sabrina Jeffries

"Delivers exactly what readers want." —TwoLips Reviews

Janice Maynard

"Romantic, entertaining, and sexy enough to leave you wanting
more!" —*New York Times* bestselling author Lori Foster

"If you . . . like your romance lovin' hot, emotion driven, and often,
Maynard delivers in spades." —myLifetime.com

"Smart, sexy, and so hot it singes the pages."
—*New York Times* bestselling author JoAnn Ross

"A must read. A true scorcher." —Romance Junkies

Wicked WONDERLAND

LuAnn McLane

Susanna Carr

Janice Maynard

A SIGNET ECLIPSE BOOK

SIGNET ECLIPSE
Published by New American Library,
a division of Penguin Group (USA) Inc.,
375 Hudson Street, New York, New York 10014, USA
Penguin Group (Canada), 90 Eglinton Avenue East, Suite 700, Toronto,
Ontario M4P 2Y3, Canada (a division of Pearson Penguin Canada Inc.)
Penguin Books Ltd., 80 Strand, London WC2R 0RL, England
Penguin Ireland, 25 St. Stephen's Green, Dublin 2,
Ireland (a division of Penguin Books Ltd.)
Penguin Group (Australia), 250 Camberwell Road, Camberwell,
Victoria 3124, Australia (a division of Pearson Australia Group Pty. Ltd.)
Penguin Books India Pvt. Ltd., 11 Community Centre,
Panchsheel Park, New Delhi - 110 017, India
Penguin Group (NZ), 67 Apollo Drive, Rosedale, North Shore 0632,
New Zealand (a division of Pearson New Zealand Ltd.)
Penguin Books (South Africa) (Pty.) Ltd., 24 Sturdee Avenue,
Rosebank, Johannesburg 2196, South Africa

Penguin Books Ltd., Registered Offices:
80 Strand, London WC2R 0RL, England

First published by Signet Eclipse, an imprint of New American Library,
a division of Penguin Group (USA) Inc.

First Printing, November 2010
1   3   5   7   9   10   8   6   4   2

Contents

Hot Whisper

Hot for the Holidays

Hot Arctic Nights

Hot Whisper

LuAnn McLane

Chapter One

Claire paused and put a hand to her chest before picking up an exquisitely carved statue of Santa Claus. She ran her French-tipped fingernail over the smooth wood surface and sighed. The attention to detail made the jolly old elf appear so lifelike that she could almost hear him give her a deep *Ho, ho, ho!*

"Oh, this is perfect!" Claire said with a happy sigh. Her mother collected Santa figurines from all over the world, so Claire had seen countless Clauses over the years, yet none had captivated her quite like this one. Who would have thought she would have found a Christmas gift for her impossible-to-buy-for mother at a tiny train depot in . . . Where was she? After glancing up, Claire spotted an artfully painted sign behind the register and nodded slowly. "Whisper, Colorado."

What a soothing name, she thought as she clutched the Santa to her chest. A little bit of her earlier tension eased from her neck and shoulders. The weeklong convention in Denver had been exhausting, and she longed to get home for the holidays. Flying back to Atlanta would have been quicker, but after a terrifyingly turbulent flight a few years ago, Claire now had a cold-sweat-inducing fear of ever boarding another airplane. Truthfully, the train ride had turned out to be a quiet, laid-back alternative that Claire had thoroughly enjoyed. Her demanding job as a senior stylist at a high-end Atlanta salon left Claire little downtime, so the cross-country trek had been a welcome excursion. And for a girl born and raised in the city, seeing miles upon miles of farmland sprinkled with small towns here and there had been quite an eye-opener.

"Hand carved by Jesse Marshall," Claire read from a glossy brochure lying next to the display. A self-confessed shopaholic, Claire had managed to find a fun little trinket in each and every train station, but these Santa statues were an unexpected delight and a bargain at thirty-five dollars. "Hm, local artist," she murmured.

"Um, miss, we're closing."

"Oh!" Claire glanced over at the young clerk and smiled in apology while wondering why he appeared so skittish. "Sorry, I was having a difficult time choosing, but I think I'll take this one." She held up the Santa and started walking toward the front of the store. "Wow!" Claire looked out the window in surprise. "When did it start snowing?" Fat flakes twirled in a gusty wind and were coming down hard.

"A few minutes ago, and the weatherman said we're in for quite a winter storm. I don't mean to rush you, but I'd like to close up and get home."

"I don't blame you. I'm from Atlanta, so we don't deal with

this much down there, but I've seen enough snow to know that I'm scared to drive in it."

"Me, too, when it's coming down like this. Whiteouts are the worst," he confessed, but then angled his head while giving her business suit an odd once-over. Claire had boarded the train after an early-morning workshop and didn't have time to change into more casual clothes. "Wait!" he said slowly. "Were you on the train?"

"Yes." Claire jammed her thumb over her shoulder. "I'm heading back to Atlanta."

The clerk's eyes widened. "Lady, the train left the station, like, ten minutes ago."

Claire felt the color drain from her face, and she clutched the Santa in a death grip. "Wh-what?" She swallowed hard and then slowly turned around, hoping to see the sleek silver train sitting on the tracks. "Oh. My. *God!*" She whipped her head back around so fast that her long auburn hair fanned out like helicopter blades and then settled back down. "They left without me?"

"When they blow the whistle, that means you have to board. I was in the back room doing inventory with my iPod cranked up or I would have said something to you," he admitted with a wince.

"W-well, it's not fair, because I didn't hear it," she protested, but then frowned in thought. Okay, maybe she *did* hear it, but she became distracted by the Santa display. "Well, they've got to come back! Call them or something! Surely they haven't gone far, right? They could just back up. Or maybe I could catch up to the train." Claire pictured herself running and then jumping on board like a scene from a Harrison Ford flick. "I could totally do it. I work out three times a week," she continued in a fast-paced, high-pitched, panicked tone that made her sound a lot like Miss Piggy. She knew she was babbling ridiculous nonsense but could not even begin to stop herself.

"It doesn't work that way," the clerk answered slowly, as if addressing a two-year-old. "You'll have to wait for another train to come through Whisper."

In an effort to calm down, Claire inhaled a deep breath. It didn't help. She looked at the clerk's name tag and tried to stop channeling Miss Piggy. "Okay, Danny, when might that be?" Her smile trembled. "In a few hours, perhaps?"

Danny shook his head slowly from side to side instead of the hoped-for up and down.

"Tomorrow?" she asked in a tiny, tearful tone.

"Next Saturday," Danny answered in a hesitant voice, as if realizing he had a nearly hysterical female on his hands.

"Next *Saturday*?" Miss Piggy came back full force. "But . . . but . . . Christmas is Thursday!"

He responded with a wide-eyed, silent shrug.

"Could I rent a car?" It would be a long drive, but she could make it home in time for Christmas Eve. Well, if she didn't get lost, which she was prone to do.

After another anxious glance at the swiftly falling snow he said, "Sorry, but there's no car rental in Whisper."

"Oh . . . maybe I could hitch a ride with someone," she murmured, but then remembered she was in the middle of nowhere and pictured herself in a big rig, sitting in the bed of a truck with bales of hay and animals, or in an RV with strangers. . . . "A hotel?" she asked brightly, even though her heart was beating like a jackhammer.

"There are a couple of bed-and-breakfasts over on Main Street, but both had No Vacancy signs out this morning. The closest hotel is a good twenty miles away, and with the snow coming down like this, you'd be hard-pressed to get there."

"Especially without a car," Claire responded glumly, and then looked down at her red dress shoes and wished they were boots.

"Look, I really have to close up. Is there someone you can call?"

Claire raised her head slowly. "Danny, I'm hundreds of miles from my home with no place to stay. All I have is the clothes on my back and my purse."

"And a snowstorm is swiftly approaching," he reminded her with a sympathetic but pointed look.

"What am I going to do?" she asked more to herself than to him, and then thought with sudden dark Christmas humor: *I'm scrooged.*

While Claire stood there silently trying to wrap her brain around her predicament, a jingle of bells was followed by a sudden blast of cold air that blew her hair from her shoulders. She shivered, dearly wishing she had her parka, which was on the train. At the time, shrugging into her big coat had seemed pointless, since it was only a short walk to the gift shop. Oh, how wrong she had been. . . .

She and Danny both turned to see who had entered, but the soft tinkle was in sharp contrast to the large man who stepped into the shop.

While looking down, he stamped on the welcome mat, shaking snow off his boots before brushing a layer of white off his impossibly wide shoulders. A navy sock hat trimmed in yellow covered his head, but dark wavy hair curled from beneath the edge and rubbed against the collar of his blue coat. A heavy growth of dark stubble obscured the bottom half of his face, but as a cosmetologist Claire had studied bone structure enough to know that beneath the beard was a handsome man.

"Hello, Jesse," Danny said, clearly happy to see an adult who might be able to take control of the situation.

"Hey, Danny," Jesse answered in a deep, tired tone as he straightened. Then his gaze landed on Claire and remained.

"Are you here to pick up the rest of your inventory?"

While Jesse nodded absently, Claire felt the full impact of his attention. She had to look up, which was unusual since in heels she exceeded six feet tall. Having grown up all knees and elbows with a mop of unruly red hair, freckles, and crooked teeth, Claire still couldn't get used to male approval even though she was pushing thirty. Her shyness was most often mistaken for aloofness and in fact had become her armor when she felt ill at ease. So when Jesse assessed her with his intense blue eyes, Claire lifted her chin a challenging notch and added the arch of one eyebrow for good measure. She might have pulled it off, but she shivered in her suit and her lips might have trembled just a tiny bit.

"The train left her," Danny announced bluntly, and looked at Jesse, hopeful for a solution.

"What?" Jesse gave Claire a stormy stare that suggested she was a complete and utter fool. "When they blow the whistle, they mean business."

"Apparently," Claire answered with a small smile, even though she wanted to march over and kick him in the shin. She refrained because it might scuff her heels, plus Jesse the lumberjack could quite possibly be her only hope for rescue, so she widened her smile and wished she were better at flirting. She did a little hair flip and realized she was channeling Miss Piggy again. *God . . .*

Danny cleared his throat, drawing Claire's attention. "Are you going to buy that?" he asked, and pointed to the Santa she still clutched in her hand.

"Oh . . . yes, I might as well, even though I don't know how I'm getting it home for Christmas," she said as she handed Danny the figurine. "Would you wrap it in tissue paper? My mother is going to love it. She collects Santas from all over the world, and this one is just exquisite, don't you think?"

Danny nodded and shot Jesse a glance.

Claire knew she was rambling on again, but the gravity of her situation was sinking in and it was either babble, cry, or quite possibly crumble into a crazy combination of both, which would certainly not help her cause. With that in mind, she ground her teeth and refused to give in. "So, is there a taxi service here in Whisper?" Claire asked in a deceptively calm voice while she paid for her purchase.

Danny gave her the expected side-to-side shake of his head. "Sorry."

Snow was coming down ever harder. Danny handed her a cute bag. "Thanks. Although this little Santa was the reason I missed the train. I must have been so caught up in browsing that I didn't hear the whistle." She shrugged. "When I shop, I can get into a zone, you know?"

Danny gave her a look that clearly stated that he *didn't* know, and then looked past her. "Jesse, you need a box? There are only a few left. The angels went fast."

"Oh, there were angels?" Claire asked in a forlorn voice. "That's what I collect," she added, but neither Jesse nor Danny seemed to care.

"Yeah, a box would be great," Jesse responded in his deep rumble of a voice. When he walked up to the register, Claire noticed that he smelled like a manly combination of pinewood and spicy aftershave. "Thanks," he said, and took the box. "I'll just be a minute."

"Good, I need to get going. My mom's called, like, five times telling me the roads are getting slick."

Claire stood there uncertainly, wondering what to do. Danny was leaving. Jesse the lumberjack was packing up the Santa carvings. *Wait.* . . . Her eyes widened and a lightbulb went off in her head. "You're Jesse Marshall?" It was hard to believe that a man of his stature could create such delicate pieces of art.

"Yes," he answered while packing up the few remaining carvings.

"Well, I am honored." Claire felt hope blossom in her chest. "Truly," she added a bit louder when he didn't seem to be paying attention. The brochure had tossed around phrases like "award winning" and "world renowned." The fact that he was well-known and respected made him seem safe. . . .

He was her only hope.

Claire squared her shoulders and was about to ask for Jesse's help when Danny opened the front door, letting in another blast of cold air. Claire's teeth chattered and she tried but couldn't suppress a violent shudder.

"We're coming, Danny," Jesse said a bit tersely. "Just hold on a minute."

Danny obediently closed the door.

"We?" Claire asked hopefully.

He gave her another stormy look as he started unbuttoning his coat. After he shrugged out of it, he handed the vested parka to her. "Put this on," he said, then bent to pick up his box. After he straightened, he added, "Stay here."

"Okay." Clutching the coat, Claire nodded, but then took a step forward and tugged on Jesse's flannel sleeve. "Wait, does this mean you're taking me with you?"

"Do you seriously think I was going to leave you stranded in the bitter cold?" Jesse asked, but before Claire could answer, he pivoted and walked out the door.

"I'll take that as a yes," she called out to him. After carefully putting her purse and package down, Claire pushed her arms into the big coat. It felt warm from Jesse's body heat and smelled woodsy and masculine. Claire sighed with feminine appreciation, drawing a look from Danny that brought heat to her cheeks. "He's not exactly Mr. Congeniality, is he?"

Danny shrugged. "Jesse works all year-round to stock up on his carvings, but this time of year he's at it day and night. He hates to disappoint someone who wants one of his Santas, and this year his angels have been just as popular. But I'm sure he's bummed because the airport is shut down. Jesse always leaves for someplace tropical right about now."

"Wait." Claire raised her eyebrows in wonder. "He brings

Christmas joy to so many people but then leaves for the actual holiday?" For some reason that struck her as sad. "I wonder why."

Danny shrugged again but looked away as if he knew more than he was willing to say. One of the aspects Claire enjoyed about being a hairstylist was hearing everyone's story and so her curiosity was piqued. But before Claire could pry, Jesse returned.

Danny held the door open for them to exit. "See you, Jesse. Hope you have a nice holiday," he said, and then turned to Claire. "And I hope you make it home to Atlanta," he added, much more friendly now that she was no longer his problem.

"Thanks, Danny," Claire said. "I'm sure I will."

Danny nodded again, but the look he gave Jesse clearly said that it wasn't likely to happen.

"No you don't," Jesse said when Claire stepped forward.

"What do you mean?" She shot him a confused frown.

"Not in those ridiculous shoes."

"These red shoes aren't ridiculous! They add a pop of color to my navy suit."

"Do I seriously look like the fashion police?" Jesse gave her a slight grin. "I mean you won't make it down the slick steps."

"Oh." She glanced at Jesse's sturdy boots and felt heat in her cheeks. "Well, what choice do I have?" Claire asked, but wrinkled her nose at the snow-covered ground.

"As of now, none," Jesse replied, and then without warning scooped her up into his arms.

Claire gasped in surprise. She was tall and built *solidly*, according to her mother, who was petite and reed thin. Next to her mom and sister, Claire had always felt big and clunky. "What are you doing?"

"I think that's obvious," he replied drily, giving Claire hope that beneath that dark beard lurked a hidden sense of humor. Claire had never been carried by a guy before and never thought she would be—well, at least not without a grunt or a stagger, but to her relief Jesse carried her with apparent ease.

Gusty wind whipped across the parking lot and Claire felt guilty about wearing Jesse's coat, but he gave no indication of being cold even though he had to be. Snowflakes swirled and twirled, landing lightly on Claire's upturned face, making her giggle in spite of the crazy situation she had somehow managed to get herself into. Or perhaps it was hysteria bubbling to the surface.

"What could you possibly be laughing about?"

"The snowflakes tickle."

Chapter Two

"*T*ickle?" When Jesse looked down at the gorgeous red-head's upturned face, he marveled that despite her predicament she managed to take delight in something as simple as snow. At first glance her statuesque beauty had screamed high-maintenance ice queen, but the soft vulnerability in her expressive green eyes suggested otherwise.

"Yes, light and feathery little tickles." A fat flake landed on a cute nose sprinkled with nutmeg-colored freckles that she probably hated but he found surprisingly adorable, which was amazing given the fact that he was exhausted and in a horrible mood. Right about now he should be chilling on the beach with a cold beer in his hand, but last-minute orders coupled with the impending storm made his vacation plans go to hell in a handbasket. The very last thing he needed was to be saddled with a stranded stranger for God knew how long. And he sure as hell didn't need to complicate matters by offering her anything more than shelter, which he realized was going to be damned difficult, since he already had the sudden insane urge to lean in and kiss that full mouth of hers.

Not good.

"Isn't it pretty?"

"Whatever." Jesse knew he played the role of the broody badass very well and decided that would be the easiest way to keep her at arm's length. Given his disheveled appearance, he thought he could pull it off without a hitch. With that in mind, he put his best scowl in place and was trying to think of something surly to say when she opened her mouth and captured a snowflake on the tip of her tongue. Jesse watched, mesmerized, and with a groan melted right along with it.

"Oh, I knew it!" Her smile immediately faded and her green eyes widened. "Put me down!"

"What?" Jeez, could she read his mind? "Hey! Hold on!" When she tried to wiggle her way out of his grasp, Jesse staggered backward and luckily landed against his truck or he would have fallen, taking her right along with him. "What are you doing?" Maybe she was high maintenance after all. Or crazy. It wouldn't be the first time he had been dead wrong about a woman.

"I should have known better!" she cried, and pushed against his chest. As she managed to dislodge one of her endless legs, she flipped one of her silly shoes up in the air. She yelped when her toes sank into the snow. Her package dangled from her other hand, and her purse slipped to the ground with a thump.

"Would you just stop it?"

Her answer was to wiggle harder. "No, I'm going to give you a . . . a hernia or something."

"What?"

"I'm too heavy."

"Why would you say that?"

"You grunted!"

"Grunted?"

"Yes!"

He looked at her in question. *Oh . . . the groan.* "No, I didn't." Jesse slipped his hand beneath her leg to lift her freezing foot out of the snow.

"You didn't?"

When she squirmed to look at him more closely, Jesse shifted his feet and hit a slick spot. "Whoa!" They both almost went down, and he had to scoot his hand upward to balance her weight.

"See!"

Jesse shook his head slowly. "It's because you're squirming." He had somehow managed to get his hand beneath her skirt fairly close to her ass, and even though she didn't seem to notice, he sure as hell did. "For the record, I didn't grunt."

"But I heard you."

Jesse sighed. "What's your name?" he asked softly.

"Claire Collins."

"Well, Claire Collins, I could carry you for miles without grunting even once."

"You could?"

"Okay, now you're hurting my ego."

"I'm very sorry," she said so sincerely that she nearly made him laugh. "It's just that I'm a big girl," she added, and lowered her lashes.

Big girl? Jesse felt a flash of anger at the society that made curvy women feel unattractive. Claire was drop-dead gorgeous and didn't seem to realize it. His feelings must have shown on his face because her eyes widened and she put one hand on his cheek. It was a sweet, simple gesture but touched him in places that hadn't felt emotion in a long time. If the truck hadn't been behind him he might have staggered again.

"Really, Jesse, I didn't mean to insult you," she insisted, mistaking his reason for scowling. "It's just that most men would have struggled dealing with my weight."

Jesse got the impression that she meant it in more ways than one. "I'm not most men." He wanted to say more but didn't.

"I get that. *Most* men wouldn't open their home to a complete stranger."

"And I need to get you there. It's freezing."

"Right . . . ," she said with a smile, but then her eyes rounded. "Hey, your hand is on my . . . *butt*." When the word "butt" came out a high-pitched whisper, Jesse had to suppress another grin. He wasn't a grinning kind of guy. What was she doing to him?

"It wasn't intentional. I swear."

"That's what they all say."

"And you're wearing a lacy little bit of nothing. Ah, my own little Christmas miracle," Jesse surprised himself by saying, and smiled up at the sky.

By rights Claire could have been angry at his comment, but instead she tilted her chin up and laughed, causing the hood to slip from her head. A gust of wind blew her long hair forward, brushing against Jesse's cheeks and bringing the light floral scent of perfume his way. The warmth of their breath mingled, then frosted as snowflakes danced all around them.

And their eyes met. Held.

Jesse didn't think he had a romantic bone in his body, but time suddenly seemed suspended and in all of his thirty-five years he had never longed to kiss a woman more than at that particular moment. But a sudden blast of arctic air brought him back to the reality of her situation. "We need to get you inside out of the cold." He meant for his voice to be all business, but what came out of his mouth sounded low with some swagger. "I warmed it up for you," he added, and then nearly groaned. "You know, the truck." Why was everything he said sounding like a cheap pickup line?

"Thanks," she answered politely, as if one of his hands weren't cupping her nearly bare bottom and they hadn't just almost kissed. Luckily they were on the passenger side of his truck, so Jesse eased away from the fender, turned, and opened the door. Claire slid into the heated leather seat with a little moan.

"Better?" Jesse asked as he handed her purse to her.

"Much!"

"Good," he said, but then spotted her bare foot, which was glowing pink from the exposure. It bothered him way more than it should have that she was uncomfortable, and after closing her door, he retrieved his gym bag from the back cab and located some clean socks. After turning around, he spotted her delicate red shoe lying in sharp contrast with the fluffy white snow. He cocked one eyebrow as he leaned over and scooped it up with one finger. "Women," he mumbled with a shake of his head. He had to admit, though, that the shoe was pretty damned sexy.

Claire is damned sexy.

Don't even go there, Jesse sternly reminded himself as he walked around to the front of the truck. Claire was depending on him for shelter and safety, and to take advantage of her vulnerable state would be wrong. Luckily his log cabin was big enough that if he put her in the guest wing, she could wait out this storm in complete privacy, and if by some miracle the airport cleared airplanes for takeoff, he could get her home for the holidays and he would be bound for the beach.

After climbing into his truck, Jesse handed Claire the socks. "Here—they're clean and will keep your feet warm."

"Thank you." She accepted them with a shy smile. "Look, I know this is a huge inconvenience for you," she said as she slipped her other shoe off and tugged on his socks. "I just hope there's some way I can repay you."

About a dozen different ways immediately popped into Jesse's mind, but he kept them to himself. "Can you cook?" he asked as he carefully pulled out onto the main road. Snow was coming down hard.

"Not . . . so much." Her smile faded. "My mother is an interior designer and my father is a lawyer for a big Atlanta law firm. When Patty, our housekeeper, didn't cook, we had takeout," she explained sadly, but then brightened. "But I like the whole *idea* of cooking." She raised her hands in expression. "And I watch the Food Network. I'd be happy to assist you. I'll just need some supervision."

"Close supervision?" He meant it as a joke, but a sudden vision of them preparing a meal together seemed intimate and sensual. When Jesse glanced her way, she wrinkled her cute nose at him.

"Um, *yeah.*" She smiled, but the slight tremble let him know that she was still nervous, and who could blame her?

"Well, I like to cook, so you're in luck. But, hey," he said in his best reassuring tone, and his earlier thoughts of intimidating her flew out the window. "I know I have dark circles under my eyes, I'm unshaven, and my hair is a mess, but I'm a decent guy and won't let any harm come to you. My cabin is clean and warm and I just got finished grocery shopping with all of the other crazy people fighting for the last loaf of bread." He shook his head and then chuckled. "I got caught up in the moment and bought stuff I normally don't even look at, but I felt compelled to fill my cart. You'd think we were going to be snowed in for the winter instead of for a few days."

"A few days?" Her face fell.

Jesse could have bitten his tongue. "At least, I'm afraid."

She looked down at her folded hands. "I'm not getting home for Christmas, am I?"

"Possibly." Jesse slowed down to turn onto the road leading up to his home and then looked over at her. "But, Claire, I'll be honest. It's not likely."

"If I didn't have this stupid fear of flying, I'd already be home."

"So that's why you were on the train?"

She nodded glumly. "I've never been away from my family

on Christmas Day." She brushed at a tear but then swallowed hard. "I'm sorry."

"It's okay. Believe me, I understand."

She gave him a trembling smile. "Well, you know what they say?"

"I have a feeling you're going to tell me."

"When life gives you lemons," she said, and then lifted her chin, "add vodka."

"Now you're talking!" Jesse laughed so hard at her unexpected comment that he lost his concentration and fishtailed on the slick road.

"Whoa!" Claire's eyes widened, but then she laughed. "That was fun. Do it again!"

"Really?" He shot her a glance to be sure.

"Yes!" she shouted, looking so cute all bundled up in his big coat.

"Hang on, girl!"

"Okay!"

Jesse gave the truck some gas and then jerked the steering wheel, sending them into a donut. While clinging to the armrest, Claire braced her other hand against the ceiling and squealed with delight. When he sent them sliding the opposite direction, she shrieked but then laughed harder, making Jesse laugh right along with her. He hadn't done anything this spontaneous in a long time and it felt amazing.

When he came to a stop, Claire leaned back against the headrest with her hands to her chest and then turned to him with a smile. "That was crazy fun."

"Yeah, it was." She had a warm smile and pretty eyes that drew him in.

"I have a snowmobile, and I could take you on a wild ride if you're interested."

"You know what? Why the hell not?" She shot him a grin that made him laugh again . . . something he normally didn't do this time of year.

"Your attitude keeps getting better and better," he told her, and then thought with surprise, *So does mine.* This morning he'd been ready to bite the head off anyone who came near him, and now he was laughing. Amazing. At first glance, Claire Collins might appear to have big-city sophistication, to be the type of woman he would never approach . . . and yet he felt drawn to her in more ways than one.

"So, what do you do for a living?"

"I'm a hairstylist at Sweet Indulgence Salon and Day Spa."

He glanced her way. "Sounds fancy."

"It is. I was at a conference in Denver for hair extensions."

"Okay, what are hair extensions?"

"Human hair that is weaved into your own. It can be very damaging, and this company has a new process that's state-of-the-art."

He raised his eyebrows, then pointed to his head. "Wait, someone *else's* real hair? People really do that?"

"Yep."

He looked at her beautiful auburn hair with a frown.

"It's mine," she assured him with a chuckle. "Wow, it's really coming down. How can you even see?"

"I know the area like the back of my hand. But the good news is that we're almost to my cabin."

She nodded and looked out the window at the tall pine trees dripping with freshly fallen snow. "It's beautiful here."

"That it is." But before long it would be pitch-black . . . much different from in the city. Instead of sirens and honking horns, Claire would be hearing the sounds of nature.

As if reading his mind, Claire turned and said, "I'm thinking I'm in for quite a Christmas adventure."

Jesse arched one eyebrow in agreement. "Yes, my little Southern city slicker, I believe you're right." Just as he pulled into the clearing where his cabin stood, three deer scampered across his front yard.

Claire's eyes rounded and she put a hand up to her chest and stared out the window. "Oh, look!"

"That's common. There's a lake out back. I see deer all the time." Among other animals that he would warn her about later, but if she was this freaked-out about deer, he had his work cut out for him.

"No . . . I mean, *that's* your so-called log cabin?" She turned and looked at him. "You've got to be kidding me."

Chapter Three

"What do you mean?" Jesse asked as he killed the engine.

"Um, Jesse, this isn't a log cabin."

"Well, technically, it's a log and timber hybrid with stone accents."

Claire shook her head. "No, I mean, cabins are little." She made a small square with her fingers. "This is a . . . a lodge."

Jesse shrugged. "It was my family home and my mother loved to entertain, especially—," he began, but paused. "Anyway, she wanted plenty of guest rooms. My parents were both artists and designed it from the ground up. It's more than I need, but I'll never sell it."

Claire looked out of the window through the swirling snow. "Wow, it's magnificent, Jesse. I don't blame you one bit. With the pine trees and the mountains . . . wow, it looks like a scene inside a snow globe." She turned to look at him. "So your parents don't live here anymore?"

A shadow passed over his face as he removed the keys from the ignition. "No."

Claire wanted to ask more, but he abruptly turned and opened his door. A moment later he was at her side. "Oh . . ." She looked down at her sock feet and winced.

"We've established that I can carry you," he reminded her with a wry smile. "Just link your arms around my neck and hold on, okay?"

"But—"

"Claire, just promise not to wiggle and we'll be fine."

After a brief hesitation she said, "Okay, I promise."

"Good. Now, just relax. I'll come back later for the packages and supplies."

Claire felt a bit shy about linking her arms around him, but after she nodded, he scooped her up and lifted her from the truck. He trudged through the deepening snow and, as promised, carried her with apparent ease up wide steps to a wraparound porch. The entryway was a beautiful arch of multicolored stone surrounding wooden double doors.

"Can you lean over and let us in?" Jesse asked.

"Sure." Claire nodded and held her hand out.

"What?"

"I'll need the key."

"It's unlocked."

She raised her eyebrows. "You're joking!"

"The crime rate up here is . . . well, *low* unless you count raccoons stealing garbage and deer eating acorns."

"No, that doesn't count." Claire laughed but then thought about the alarm system on her apartment in the city and shook her head in wonder. "It must be nice not to have that worry."

"Yeah, well, there's a downside. Pizza isn't delivered either."

"Oh, well, that sure has to suck!"

"Yeah, but it has made me a pretty good cook." He chuckled and looked down at her.

Wow, his eyes are blue.

"Yeah, sometimes it sucks. I guess you can't imagine living without fast food."

"Sometimes I need me some Starbucks."

Jesse grinned. "Like about now?"

"Um . . . yeah."

"Sorry about your bad luck."

"I seem to be having a string of it." After she opened the door, Jesse eased Claire to her feet and flicked on overhead lights. "Wow!" *Perhaps my luck is changing.* She padded in her stocking feet across the gleaming hardwood floor into a massive great room. A floor-to-ceiling fieldstone fireplace was the focal point, and although the room was large, leather furniture accented with plump pillows in jewel tones made the space feel warm and inviting. Many of the furnishings seemed to spring from nature, including a glass-topped tree trunk that served as a coffee table, and a wine rack made of antlers, giving the room a rustic charm that managed to maintain a touch of elegance.

Claire turned around to face Jesse, who remained standing on the braided rug in the foyer. "Your so-called cabin is breathtaking. I can't wait to see the rest of it." She thought the lack of Christmas decorations was a bit sad, but she kept her questions to herself.

"Make yourself at home while I bring in the supplies. My bedroom is on the first floor, but you can choose any of the guest rooms upstairs. Oh, and help yourself to anything in the fridge. The kitchen is to your left. Grab a beer if you want one. Don't be shy."

"Thanks. I might grab one in a bit," Claire replied calmly, but after Jesse headed out the door, she hung his parka on a nearby coatrack and then made a beeline for the kitchen. Okay, it might not be happy hour yet, but she was stranded with a complete stranger in the middle of Colorado with little more than the clothes on her back. . . . Yeah, she could use a little liquid courage. She flicked a switch that turned on recessed lighting, but before snagging a beer, she had to pause to admire the gourmet kitchen. "Oh . . . my," she said breathily. Stainless-steel appliances gleamed against the walls, while a granite center island surrounded by tall stools seemed to invite her to sit down. Cherry cabinets added elegance to the sleek look, but the slate gray tile floor brought a touch of the rustic feel back into the room. It was gorgeous.

"Hey, are you okay?"

Claire turned at the sound of Jesse's deep voice and felt a little embarrassed that she stood in the middle of the room with her hands crossed on her chest. "Oh, yes, I was just admiring your kitchen. It makes me want to learn to cook."

"Up here, you have to. The only takeout comes from the freezer."

"It's always good to have a backup plan," Claire agreed.

"That's my motto. How about you?"

Claire looked down at her sock feet and then back at him. "What's your guess?"

"I'm guessing . . . no." Jesse grinned as he set several bags of groceries onto the center island.

"Then you must be a good guesser."

"Mmm, not so much, actually. I didn't have you pegged at all."

"Care to elaborate?"

"Not really." He took his hat off, revealing thick, jet-black, wavy hair that he probably took for granted and any woman she knew would die for. When he reached up and ran his fingers through it, Claire had the sudden urge to walk over to him and do the same thing. You know, as a professional, she tried to tell herself. "Well, I have plenty of supplies to work with and we've got nothing but time on our hands."

"Ah . . . so you really are a backup-plan kinda guy?"

"I try to be prepared."

"Well, where's the fun in that?"

He looked at her as if not knowing whether to take her seriously or not. She often got that same look from her parents.

"Can I help you put things away?"

"Sure," he replied, and started unpacking the bags.

Claire noticed with approval that they were reusable mesh but had to giggle when she pulled out a whole pineapple. "What? Were you thinking of having a luau?"

He grinned. "I told you I got caught up in the moment. It was chaos in the grocery store. I swear people were grabbing random things off the shelves, and I jumped right into the fray.

I actually like to cook, but I'm a typical buy-only-what-you-need kind of guy. The pineapple was a rare impulse purchase. Maybe I was lamenting the loss of my tropical vacation." He placed ground beef, an onion, peppers, and a packet of chili spices on the counter. "See, the ingredients for chili. No more, no less." He looked at Claire with male satisfaction. "What? Why are you grinning?"

She lifted a carton out of the bag. "Eggnog?"

"My one Christmas indulgence," he explained.

"Orange juice, butter, sub rolls, lunch meat." She nodded. "Pretty normal," she continued, but then grinned when she unveiled a pint of strawberries, one apple, two oranges. "You are such a girl," she teased.

"Hey, we were going to be snowed in. I didn't want to get scurvy."

She peered back into the bag and giggled.

"What now?"

"Really?" She lifted up a container of chocolate fruit dip. She wiggled her fingers. "Hand over your man card."

Jesse shrugged and raked his fingers through his hair. "I don't know—I guess I was wondering what I was going to do with all of that useless fruit, so I felt compelled to purchase that." He raised his eyebrows. "Hey, let's try it." He opened the carton of strawberries and rinsed them off. After handing her a plump one, he took the lid off the dip.

"Don't mind if I do." Claire dunked her strawberry in the dip and took a juicy bite. "Oh, mmm, yeah." She nodded. "Good stuff."

Jesse grinned, then followed suit. "See, I knew what I was

doing," he told her and, after dipping his strawberry into the chocolate, he took a generous bite and groaned.

Claire had a comeback on the tip of her tongue, but when Jesse licked a bit of chocolate from his bottom lip, she completely forgot what she was about to say. For someone so big and strong he had a sensual grace about him that made her want to sigh . . . and so she did.

"You're right—good stuff," he said, mistaking her reason for sighing. "Want more?"

"Oh, you better believe it," Claire answered instantly, but then felt heat creep into her cheeks. "I mean, yes, please." When Claire accepted another strawberry, the brush of his fingertips against hers sent a warm tingle up her arm. Her eyes widened in surprise and she wondered if he was feeling the same way. She took a nibble of the strawberry and toyed with the button on her suit while she tried to regain her composure.

"You look uncomfortable," he commented.

"Well . . . this is a bit of a situation I've gotten myself into."

Jesse gave her a slight grin. "No, I meant you look uncomfortable in that suit."

She lifted her shoulders. "It's all I have, remember?"

He leaned forward and rested his hands on the granite island and then looked at her thoughtfully. "Well, I don't have any female clothing on hand, but go on into my bedroom and rummage around. You can make do with rolling up some sweats, or long underwear might be a better fit since they're tighter. Grab a flannel shirt or whatever you want. It's all clean."

Claire's eyes widened. "I can't dig around in your drawers!" She shook her head. "Wait, that didn't come out right."

Jesse's low rumble of laughter did warm, fluttery things to her stomach. "You are one funny chick."

"I get that a lot, but I don't really try."

"I'm bone tired and in a bad mood. And yet you're able to make me laugh. What's up with that?"

"Maybe Santa sent me."

Jesse angled his head and gave her a hot look that almost made her slither to the floor. "I'm thinking he did."

"Well then, you must be at the top of the naughty list."

Jesse chuckled again, but the word "naughty" seemed to hang in the air between them. "Speaking of naughty . . ." He arched one dark eyebrow and then pulled out a six-pack of beer followed by a bottle of bourbon. "See? I have guy things, too."

"Oh, now you're talkin'. Mmm, I'd love me some bourbon in the eggnog."

"Yep." He nodded. "One of the few Christmas traditions I can't resist," he admitted, but his smile seemed a bit forced.

Claire angled her head in question, but when he failed to elaborate, she didn't want to pry and let his comment slide.

"Let's forget the beer and go for the good stuff. You in?"

"Does a bear shit in the woods?"

Jesse put the heel of his hand to his forehead and cracked up. "I know firsthand that the answer is yes. God, you are something else."

"Sorry, I was just getting into log cabin character. I can't believe I just said that. My mother would be mortified."

Jesse shook his head slowly. "Don't be sorry. I haven't laughed this hard in ages." He shooed her with his hands. "Now, go and dig around in my drawers. When you come back, I'll have some Christmas cheer ready for you." When she hesitated, he said, "Claire, if you don't, I'll have to put on a suit to make you feel better. And I hate suits."

"It's not that."

"What, then?" he asked as he uncapped the bourbon.

"Can I take a drink with me?" She caught her bottom lip between her teeth and gave him a wishful look.

"Absolutely. I understand. It's been a tough day." He gave her a slow smile. "Coming right up."

Claire felt another flutter in her stomach and suddenly felt the need to sit down. She watched him move with quiet efficiency and a fluid grace that was at odds with his size. When Jesse reached up to retrieve two glass tumblers from the cabinet, she admired the fit of his jeans and the stretch of flannel across his wide shoulders. She was used to seeing guys in designer clothes, but his Wranglers somehow seemed so much sexier. He had rolled up the sleeves of his shirt, revealing corded muscles in his forearms, and Claire guessed his thick, muscled body came from physical work rather than oiled machines in a sleek, modern gym. That thought brought an image of him shirtless, chopping wood. . . .

Oh my.

"Here you go," Jesse announced, and slid the glass across the shiny surface.

Claire took a healthy sip of the sweet creamy eggnog laced with a generous bite of bourbon. "Oh, wow."

"Taste okay?"

"Excellent." She took another swallow and then licked the

sweetness from her bottom lip. "Oh yeah, this is hitting the spot big-time," she commented, but then felt warmth creep up her neck once again. Why did everything she was saying seem to have sexual overtones? She watched Jesse's long fingers drop ice cubes into his own glass and knew the answer. The man defined big, brawny masculinity, and yet there was an air of keen intelligence about him. The fact that he was a talented artist added another layer and created a fascination that she had never experienced until right now. There was also a sense of sadness lurking in the depths of his eyes . . . a vulnerable edge that he tried to keep hidden, but Claire could feel it and wanted to chase it away.

"Why are you looking at me so intently?" he asked, then grinned. "I bet you're itching to cut my crazy long hair."

When he reached up and shoved his fingers through it, Claire took another long pull on her drink. "I am."

"A cut is long overdue, but I've been too busy to worry about it. Maybe you can shape it up for me?"

"Earn my keep? Good thing you didn't ask me to sing for my supper because I suck."

"I didn't mean it that way." Jesse shook his head. "You're my guest."

At first she thought he was teasing, but when he really appeared a little offended, Claire reached across the counter and put her hand over his. "I was only teasing. Guess it's my big-city attitude coming out. I'd be happy to run my fingers through your hair." *Oh God.* "And cut it." She reached over and demonstrated. "You know, like this. Lift, snip, lift, snip." *Wow, his hair is soft.* "Lift . . . um . . . *snip.*"

"Claire, I know I don't look like it, but I have had my hair cut before."

"Right." She pulled her hand back and pressed her lips together. "Um, I'll go change into your clothes now. I might as well keep the humiliation rolling right along."

"You want me to change into yours to make you feel better?"

"You'd do that for me?" She clasped her hands to her chest and batted her eyes.

"Of course," he replied, playing along.

"After all, what's Christmas without a little cross-dressing?"

"I think you meant a little corn-bread dressing. . . ."

"Oh." Claire slapped a hand to her forehead. "My bad. Wow, I've gotten that wrong for years." Claire picked up her drink and headed out of the room but said over her shoulder, "I just hope you like thongs. . . ."

Chapter Four

$\mathcal{A}$fter Claire left the kitchen, Jesse put his cold glass to his forehead and groaned. "Damn . . ." It might be snowing outside, but he sure as hell was burning up. The more Claire let her guard down, the more attracted he was to her, and that last casual comment about her thong nearly did him in. He shook his head. She was a fascinating combination of shy and bold, making him wonder what she would be like in bed.

"Don't even go there," he reminded himself. He took another healthy swallow of his spiked eggnog and tried to gather his scattered wits, but when he spotted her slinky red sandals sitting on the black granite, he had a sudden vision of Claire lying on his bed wearing nothing but those sexy heels.

Not *going there* really wasn't working out for him. With a deep sigh he absently added some bourbon and a splash of eggnog into his glass. "Okay, that was supposed to be the other way around," he said under his breath, but then shrugged. He downed half of it while putting away the rest of his groceries and trying without much success not to think about Claire getting naked. At least she was going to be swimming in his big clothes and hiding her sweet curves. That should help matters a little, anyway.

Maybe.

"Okay, maybe not," he mumbled softly when she walked into the kitchen.

"Excuse me?"

"I said you look hot," he answered as if joking, except he wasn't. His green plaid flannel shirt was an amazing shade on her with her deep red hair and moss-colored eyes. She had used her own belt to cinch it at her waist and wore snug-fitting long johns underneath.

"Right." She wrinkled up her nose and looked down at her outfit. "Could I have a teensy bit more of your eggnog?" She held her thumb and index finger an inch apart and then pushed her glass his way. "It was de-lish."

"Absolutely," Jesse answered, and then refreshed her drink. After sliding it her way, he said, "Feel free to explore the cabin or watch television. I'm going to take a cold—I mean hot—shower if you don't mind."

"Oh, no, go right ahead."

"Thanks." He picked up his drink but then paused. "If you get hungry, there are a few snacks. We'll cook dinner later, okay?"

She looked at him over the rim of her glass. "*You'll* cook dinner. I'll just sit here and look . . . pretty in flannel."

When she stuck a pose as a joke, Jesse walked over and said softly in her ear, "My shirt never looked so good." He didn't look to see her reaction but heard her slight gasp and continued walking. It blew his mind that she didn't know how hot she was, so he paused in the doorway and said, "Hey, that wasn't supposed to be a cheap pickup line."

Her cheeks were pink, but she gave him a smile. "We've already established that you can pick me up, remember?"

"You are correct," he replied, but then looked down at her feet. "We will have to do something about shoes. That might be a little tougher."

"I'm sure we can come up with something if we put our heads together."

"Yeah, we'll think of something," Jesse answered, but envisioned a much more physical reason for putting their heads together, like kissing, for instance. "Damn," Jesse whispered as he entered his bedroom. There was no way he could take advantage of the situation, he thought while he unbuttoned his shirt and then shucked his jeans.

"It wouldn't be right," he muttered as he turned on the multiple showerheads and then stepped into the walk-in stone-sided stall that he had remodeled the past summer. In honor of his parents he had left the essence of the cabin untouched, but over the past five years he had made changes to fit his own tastes. Updating the decor also muted the memories that were embedded in every square inch of the cabin.

The hot pulsating spray against his tired body should have been soothing, but all he could think about was how incredible it would be to have Claire sharing the steamy space with him, and his body instantly reacted. He looked down at his raging erection and groaned. "Look, I know she's got a bangin' body, but she's vulnerable and she's been drinking," he said as he soaped up his chest, but his dick remained stubbornly erect. "Yeah, I know, buddy—it's been a long time, but it just wouldn't be right," he lamented with a sad chuckle. As he lathered up his hair, he remembered the feel of Claire's fingers against his scalp. With a groan he closed his eyes and turned his face up to the waterfall showerhead, rinsing the soap from his body. "This isn't going to be easy."

But as Jesse was toweling dry, the answer to his moral dilemma suddenly hit him. What if Claire came on to him? He smiled slowly. Yeah, he wouldn't make any sexual advances toward *her*, but if Claire initiated something, well then, all bets were off. She couldn't be hurt or pissed off then, right? With that thought in mind, he started shaving. When the beard was gone, he splashed on a bit of spicy aftershave and then headed to his walk-in closet. Not wanting to be too obvious, he tugged on another pair of jeans but opted for a body-hugging long-sleeved black T-shirt instead of his usual flannel. He felt kind of silly dressing to show off his physique, but this was his game plan and he was sticking to it.

After taking a deep breath, he ran his fingers through his too-long hair and then headed to the kitchen, but she was no longer sitting at the island. She must have gone exploring. "Claire?" he called, but all he got was silence in return. He walked into the great room and then spotted her sleeping on the sofa. For a moment he simply stood there and looked at her, and then he smiled softly. She had instantly brought a vibrant spark back into his life that had been missing for a long time. Yes, Claire Collins had stirred something deeper than just sexual desire, and Jesse felt a sharp pang of sadness that she was only passing through. In a few days she would be gone from his life. Jesse shook his head. He was overreacting to a woman he had just met and yet he couldn't shake the feeling.

Flickering light from the fireplace cast a golden glow over her features, and Jesse grinned when he spotted the starter remote still clutched in her hand. Claire slept on her side with her head on a throw pillow, her long hair slipped over her shoulder, making Jesse long to run his fingers through it to see if the deep red tresses were as silky as they appeared. Her lips were slightly parted and she appeared so peaceful that he decided to start dinner preparations while allowing her to sleep.

But as he turned to leave, he must have made a sound because she shifted and somehow tugged open the first button of his big shirt. A generous amount of a black lacy bra appeared along with some mouthwatering cleavage. Jesse knew that it was impolite to stare and that he should turn away, but he simply could not. Instead, he took a step closer, telling himself he needed to cover her with the throw on the back of the easy chair when in reality he knew the heat from the fire was more than enough. What he needed was to touch her. . . .

Jesse was about to drape the cover over Claire, but his foot hit the edge of the sofa, making just enough noise to jar her awake. She blinked, and when the remote slipped from her grasp, she leaned over to grab it, rolling off the sofa to land face-first with a thump and a yelp.

Jesse dropped to his knees. "Oh damn, Claire, are you okay?"

"Define okay," she said, and then rolled over to her back.

"Okay as in nothing is smashed or bleeding?"

"Luckily the floor broke my fall," she replied, but then reached up and gingerly touched her nose.

"That had to hurt like hell," Jesse commented, and then gently brushed her hair out of the way. "Are you really okay?"

"Yeah." She nodded but then sat up and flexed her left wrist.

"Let me see." Frowning, Jesse took her hand in his and gently examined it.

"I'm fine," she insisted. "I just hope I didn't break your television remote."

"The remote is for the gas fireplace."

"Okay, that explains a lot," she said with a low rumble of laughter. "I was getting frustrated and pushed a lot of buttons on that thing. Wait, with all of the trees in your backyard, you use fake logs?"

"It's better for the environment, puts out plenty of warmth. I think it's just as aesthetically pleasing, not to mention convenient. Saves some trees."

She nodded. "Makes sense, but yet you use trees to make your carvings?"

"Much of what I use comes from recycled Christmas tree trunks."

"Really?" She raised her eyebrows, and it pleased him that she seemed interested.

"I'll tell you about that later. Now, be honest, are you really all right?" He rubbed the pad of his thumb over the top of her wrist and looked into her eyes.

"I've always been big and clumsy, so I'm used to bumps

and bruises," she admitted with a small smile, but then glanced away.

"You're not big and clumsy," he told her firmly.

She turned her head to look at him. "Oh, you ain't seen nothin' yet," she warned him with the arch of an eyebrow. "I tend to talk with my hands, and with these long arms I knock things over. You have no idea how many times I have fallen victim to 'You break it, you buy it.' There's just way too much of me. . . ."

Her comment brought his attention to her exposed cleavage. "Um, I have to disagree."

"What?" She followed the direction of his gaze and gasped. "Were you ever going to tell me that my . . . that I was hanging out all over?" She buttoned up and then looked at him accusingly.

"Of course!"

"Your nose is growing."

Jesse inclined his head. "Guilty."

"I'd tell you if your zipper was down." Claire gave his chest a shove but laughed.

"What can I say? I'm a guy."

"Point taken."

"But, Claire?"

"Yeah?"

"I have to tell you that you're absolutely dead wrong."

Her smile faded and she looked at him with those expressive eyes that got to him somewhere around his solar plexus. "About what?"

Jesse leaned forward and whispered in her ear. "There is

definitely *not* way too much of you." God, how he wanted to kiss her, but he stuck to his plan and somehow refrained. "Let me help you to your feet."

"Thanks." Claire nodded absently after Jesse stood up and offered his hands. But when he tugged her to her feet, she lost her balance and fell forward into his arms.

"Whoa there." Jesse grabbed her around her waist to steady her but then left his grasp there way longer than needed.

"See, I told you I was clumsy." Claire splayed her hands on his chest but then turned her gaze toward the floor.

"Hey, that was my fault." Jesse tilted her chin up and gazed at her mouth. He really wanted to kiss her. All he needed was for her to make that first move. . . .

Chapter Five

The heat in Jesse's eyes made Claire's heart beat wildly. "Wow, I was right," she said softly.

"Really? Because you haven't been right yet," he reminded her as he rubbed his thumb across her chin.

Claire reached up and traced one fingertip over Jesse's cheekbone and then down his jawline. "I knew that beneath that beard was amazing bone structure."

"Oh, so you are right for once." When Jesse cocked his head slightly and smiled, the sudden movement made one of Claire's fingers fall against his mouth.

Claire's breath caught at the feel of his moist, warm lips, and perhaps it was the bourbon that made her bold, but instead of pulling away, she ran her fingertip over the bottom fullness. "You have a mouth made for kissing."

"Right again."

Claire lifted one shoulder and rubbed her finger back and forth. "I'm just sayin'. . . ."

"You might want to put that observation to the test." When he spoke, her finger touched his tongue, and he inhaled sharply.

Claire eased her fingertip in just a bit, and when he licked lightly, Claire felt a sharp sizzle of desire curl all the way to her toes. "Excellent idea." With a little moan she leaned in and replaced her fingertip with her mouth. *Oh my.* His lips were firm but silky soft, pliant, and oh so warm. The kiss began gently, sweetly, but when her tongue met his, she opened her mouth, eager for more . . . and he gave it. Claire leaned against him, savoring the hard feel of his chest against her breasts. And when she threaded her fingers through his thick hair, he wrapped his arms around her, pressing closely, kissing deeply.

Firelight flickered and danced all around them while the kiss went on and on, making her wild with wanting him. Needing to feel his skin, Claire tugged his T-shirt from his jeans and slid her hands up his bare back. When she lightly raked her fingernails over his shoulder blades, he moaned and lowered his hands to cup her ass and press her even closer. She could feel the steely hardness of his arousal and responded by flattening her palms against his back so that her breasts rubbed against him.

"You are driving me crazy." When he pulled back and began kissing her neck, a slow tingle blossomed and traveled south.

"You are so soft and smell so damned good," he whispered hotly into her ear. "I want you to come with me."

Nodding, Claire took his hand and would have followed him anywhere . . . into the storm, up the mountain . . . but luckily he drew her over to a soft fuzzy rug in front of the fire. When he knelt down, she followed his lead, but then, instead of touching her, he seemed to be waiting for her to make the next move. She found this role reversal incredibly hot, and while watching him intently, she unbuttoned the first three buttons of her shirt.

Jesse looked at her with heavy-lidded eyes and swallowed. "Seeing that black bra beneath my flannel shirt is just nuts."

"Touch me," she whispered.

"Gladly." His low, sexy tone felt like a physical caress. When he trailed the pad of his thumb over her exposed skin, Claire's breath caught and her eyes fluttered shut. "Like this?"

"Yes . . ."

Encouraged, Jesse slid her shirt off one shoulder, and then, after brushing her hair to the side, he started a trail of hot kisses over her collarbone to her neck. Claire tilted her head, giving him better access, and when he gently tugged on her earlobe with his teeth, she had to reach out and cling to his shoulders for support. While nuzzling her neck, he made quick work of her belt and kissed her exposed skin as he slowly unbuttoned the rest of the shirt.

"I want to see you. All of you." But when he leaned back to gaze at her, Claire hesitated. While she knew she was toned and fit, she was a big girl and had never really felt . . . ultrafeminine or very sexy. But the desire in Jesse's eyes told a different story, so she shrugged slightly, allowing the shirt to slip from her shoulders to the rug. She had rolled the big long johns down to her hips and while watching him, she tugged them down a few inches, showing him that she hadn't been teasing about the thong. "I wear them to avoid panty lines," she felt compelled to tell him.

"Well, don't wear them if you want to avoid me," he whispered, and reached out to trail one finger from her navel to the top edge of the black lace and satin. When he rubbed his finger back and forth, heat pooled between her thighs and with a breathy sigh she sank down onto the rug. Her hair fanned out all around her and she let him look his fill. The heat in his gaze made her feel gorgeous instead of self-conscious. "Let me take off your clothes."

Claire arched her hips so he could peel off the long johns. He tossed them to the side and then looked at her lying on the rug in nothing but her scanty underwear. The fact that Jesse was little more than a stranger skittered across Claire's brain, but she shoved it away. For whatever reason, she felt safe with him and this seemed so surreal . . . magical, and she was way beyond being able to stop.

"Take off your shirt," she said, and then watched him tug the T-shirt over his head. He was thickly muscled with defined pecs and washboard abs. A mat of dark chest hair narrowed to an enticing happy line leading to the top of his jeans. "No wonder you carried me with ease," she murmured, and then put a hand over her mouth. "I said that out loud, didn't I?"

With a low rumble of laughter he shook his head.

"I know—I talk too much."

"I marvel that you can make me laugh, especially this time of year."

Her smile faded. "You said that out loud, too," she told him softly.

Jesse gave her a long and steady look. "Claire, you're making me say and feel things I haven't for a long time."

"I'm not making you, Jesse." She sat up and touched his bare chest. "I am allowing you." She swallowed the sudden emotion clogging her throat.

"Hey . . ." He cupped her chin and searched her face for answers. "You don't have to do any of this."

"So it's not your house, your rules?"

Jesse chuckled softly but then continued to look at her closely as if to make sure. "You're my guest. You rule."

"Look," she assured him, "I don't know why fate brought us together, but here we are."

"Claire, I'll be honest. We live hundreds of miles apart and live very different lifestyles. And I'm a loner. I can't promise you anything beyond the next few days."

"I'm not asking for anything more than right here and now," Claire answered, and then reached behind her back. She shed her bra, allowing her breasts to tumble free, but then suddenly felt self-conscious and covered herself with her palms. She caught her bottom lip between her teeth and shyly looked at him through half-lidded eyes.

"Dear God . . . how can you think you are anything less than perfection?" When she raised those incredible green eyes to gaze at him, Jesse felt a bead of sweat roll down his chest, and it had nothing to do with the heat from the fireplace. Her dainty French-tipped fingers barely covered her full breasts, making her pose more provocative than if she were completely nude. The flickering flames seemed to lick at her skin and highlight her hair, and he could see just a hint of the black thong between her thighs. He wanted to bury his face there and taste her sweet body before having her endless legs wrapped around him.

"I think you're a tad overdressed," she told him in a throaty voice that aroused him even more. When she reached over and unzipped his jeans, the brush of her fingers against his skin sent a hot shiver down his spine.

"Right again." He hadn't bothered with boxers and sighed when his erection was free of constriction. After kicking his jeans out of the way, he came back to his knees and then started a trail of kisses up her calf. When he got to the inside of her thigh, he heard her sharp intake of breath. She stiffened slightly when he kissed the black silk triangle and, even though he was dying to taste her, he knew she wasn't ready, so he moved upward to her navel while using his finger to toy with her thong.

Claire gasped and braced her palms on the rug when he slid his finger beneath the silk to find her slick heat. Her head fell to the side and she arched her back, leaving her breasts exposed for his eager gaze. The glorious sight made him steely hard, but he wanted her crazy for him, so he caressed her with his finger, watching her in the firelight. She bit her bottom lip, and when he plunged back inside, she gasped and fisted her fingers in the rug. Jesse leaned in and took one rosy nipple into his mouth, first circling it with his tongue and then sucking. When she moaned, mindless with need, Jesse fingered her swollen clit while he lightly nipped her nipple. He rose up and kissed her . . . loving the feel of her heat, the taste of her mouth. She had a natural sensuality that didn't seem practiced or forced but simply real.

"Oh . . ." When she arched her hips, Jesse leaned back so he could watch her climax and then slid his finger in one more time, finding her sweet spot. Her lips parted, her back arched, and she moaned in that throaty voice of hers that drove him crazy. A moment later she cried out with pleasure before falling back to the rug.

Her cheeks were flushed a rosy pink, and with her hair fanned out all around her, wearing nothing but the tiny thong, Jesse swore he had never witnessed a more erotic sight. While she was breathing hard, her eyes remained closed, and unable not to, Jesse leaned in and kissed her moist lips softly. "I'll be right back," he said in her ear. "Don't go anywhere."

"Like I could walk," she murmured with a slight smile, but kept her eyes shut.

After tugging on his jeans, Jesse grabbed the throw off the sofa and draped it over Claire before heading to his bathroom for protection. He needed to cool down before he did something foolish . . . like make love to her without a condom. Besides, they had all night, and he wanted to make this last. But before heading back to the great room, he made two sub sandwiches and tossed some chips on two plates. He piled them on top of each other, stuck a corkscrew in his pocket, tucked a bottle of Merlot beneath one arm, and snagged two wineglasses. It was a balancing act, but he had big hands, so he managed.

"Hey, I could have helped," Claire offered. She had sat up and wrapped her curvy body in the blanket.

"I've got it," Jesse said, but just as he made it to the rug, everything started to slide. With a low giggle Claire caught the wine and reached for the glasses, causing the blanket to slip from her shoulders just as Jesse sat down. When she blushed and grabbed the edges of the blanket, Jesse wanted to remind her he had seen just about every inch of her delicious body but refrained. Women were silly creatures.

"I wanted to make something more elaborate, but hunger made me go for cold cuts. I hope you don't mind."

"Not at all," she replied, and tried to reach for the plate but couldn't with the blanket clutched around her. Jesse smiled and then reached for the shirt lying on the rug.

"Here," he offered, and turned to uncork the wine while she shrugged into it.

"Except for the strawberries, I haven't eaten since breakfast, so I'm famished. I think that's why the eggnog hit me so hard."

"Probably." Jesse glanced her way while he poured the Merlot and knew that Claire was trying to blame what just happened on the bourbon. But if she thought she looked less sexy in nothing but his shirt, she was oh so wrong. Wanting to put her at ease once more, he handed her the glass and then stood up.

"I probably shouldn't drink this," she said while looking up at him.

"Just relax, Claire," he requested, and had to smile when this time she hesitated, but when he extended his hand, she took it. "Hey, follow me." He guided her over to the floor-to-ceiling windows. "Look." When he flicked on an outside light, the blowing snow seemed to sparkle like glitter. Fat flakes were floating down fast, adding to the white inches already piled up on the big deck. Tall shadowy pine trees seemed to glow in the background.

"Oh, wow," Claire said as she stood there and looked through the glass. "It's beautiful." She took a sip of wine and stared out at the winter wonderland.

"I agree, and it's not going to stop anytime soon. We are officially snowed in."

She took another sip of her wine but remained quiet.

"Claire, we're going to be spending several days together. I don't want you to wake up tomorrow with regret."

She nodded slowly and cradled the glass in her hand.

"This was so unexpected for us both. It's like something out of place and time." He shrugged and then said, "I guess that sounded weird."

"No, I was thinking the same thing earlier. It's like we're in a Hallmark holiday movie," she said, but then shook her head and chuckled. "Well, the unrated version."

Jesse laughed. God, he liked being with her. But then his smile faded. "But odds are that after the storm . . . ," he began, but for some reason the rest of the sentence stuck in his throat.

"We'll never see each other again," she finished softly.

This time Jesse remained quiet.

Her eyes widened slightly. "That's why you let me take the lead . . . why you stopped."

"Claire, it would have been wrong to take advantage of the situation, but I'm only human. If I have you naked in my arms again, I won't be able to stop." He shoved his fingers through his hair and blew out a sigh.

"I get it. Before was spontaneous. This time we are making a conscious choice."

He turned and looked at Claire. "So, what are your thoughts?" He held his breath and waited.

Claire nibbled on the inside of her cheek for a minute and then said, "Jesse, maybe we're overthinking this."

Jesse wanted to raise his fist in triumph while doing a little jig—even though he had never done a jig in his life—but he cleared his throat and, as calmly as he could, said, "You think so?"

"Yes." Claire angled her head, causing her hair to slide over her shoulder. "Here's what I propose. . . ."

Chapter Six

"*L*et's turn on some music, sit in front of the fire, and eat our sandwiches."

"Okay," Jesse responded with a slight smile.

"We can talk."

"Sure. Yeah, talking is good."

"Get to know each other."

"Absolutely." He nodded firmly, but his disappointment was so evident that Claire felt both sexy and desired. Jesse Marshall was big enough and man enough to make her feel feminine and fragile. This newfound sex appeal gave her a heady boost of confidence, and she loved the feeling.

Claire placed one hand on his bare chest and said, "After we eat dinner, I want you . . ." She really wanted to say *for dessert* but knew she wouldn't manage that without blushing or giggling, so she said, "To kiss me."

"Okay," he calmly agreed, but Claire could feel the rapid beat of his heart beneath her palm. "Then let's eat." He picked up another remote, and after he pushed a button, soft bluesy music played from discreetly placed speakers.

Claire looked at the four remotes on his coffee table and shook her head. "I would never be able to keep those straight."

"Pretty high-tech for a backwoodsman," he responded with a grin.

"Little bit," Claire replied, but she already knew there was much more to Jesse Marshall than she had first thought. They settled back onto the rug and between bites carried on a conversation about favorite movies, books, sports, and their work. Claire chattered on about her family, but Jesse avoided the subject and she didn't feel as if she should pry, even though she was amazed at how comfortable she felt with a man she barely knew.

"Do your parents know you are stranded here in Whisper?" Jesse asked.

Claire shook her head. "I'm not due home yet, and they knew that cell phone reception on the train was going to be sketchy, so they're not expecting many calls. I decided not to give the bad news until I have to. My mother is a bit of a Southern diva, and I want to spare my father for as long as I can. Besides, there's still an outside chance that I will make it home."

"Makes sense, I suppose," Jesse agreed. "But I still think you should call soon."

"I know, but I can't stand the thought of ruining their Christmas," she admitted, and then took a sip of wine. "This will be the first Christmas I've ever missed with my family," she added softly, and ran the tip of her finger over the rim of her glass. "I'm sorry for getting so emotional. Don't mind me."

"No, I understand perfectly." Something of a shadow passed over his features once again, but then he seemed to shake it off. "I'm sorry, you're right—don't think about it right now. I shouldn't have brought it up, but I didn't want them to worry."

Claire reached over and put her hand over his. "You're a good man, Jesse Marshall."

"I was raised well." He smiled but then frowned down at his own glass, but not before Claire caught a flash of hurt in his eyes, making her want to wrap her arms around him and ease whatever was the cause of his pain.

Needing to see his smile return, Claire sat up and asked brightly, "Okay, when are you going to take me on your snowmobile?"

Jesse arched one eyebrow. "Have you ever been on one, little city slicker?"

"No."

"Do you scare easily?"

She waved a hand through the air. "I live in the heart of the city. Do you seriously think I scare easily?"

"We'll find out."

"I'm tough as nails," she boasted, then gave her hair a flip for good measure. "You can't scare me," she insisted, and as if on cue, a loud howl could be heard from outside. Her eyes rounded, and she asked, "What was that?"

When Jesse laughed, Claire leaned forward and gave his chest a shove. He fell back onto one elbow, causing her to tumble forward with him. She slowly pushed up from his chest, letting her fingers trail over his warm skin.

The promise of the kiss had simmered between them the entire time. Also, it didn't help that her black bra was lying on the rug or that he was shirtless with the top snap of his jeans undone. If there had been a pop quiz at the end of the conversation, she wouldn't have passed because all that filled her brain was the need to have her body pressed against his.

Claire busied herself taking the last bite of her sandwich. "That was delicious." She dusted her hands together, but when she licked a bit of spicy mustard from her bottom lip, Jesse watched her intently, and so she lingered longer than necessary. "Thank you."

"I promise you'll wake up to a hot meal for breakfast."

"Do you get up . . . *wake up* early?" she asked, and then felt heat from her cheeks to her toes.

His lips twitched, but he left her comment alone. "I'm normally an early riser," he responded, but his eyes remained on her mouth. "But I'm on vacation, so I'll get up whenever the spirit moves me." He moved the plates out of the way and stretched out his long legs. "Are you a morning person?"

When he leaned back on his elbows, his muscles rippled in the firelight, making Claire totally lose her train of thought once again. She leaned forward and said, "I . . . uh, what did you just ask me?"

"Does it really matter?"

"No."

"Then get over here and give me my after-dinner kiss," he requested in a deep low tone.

"Okay." Claire leaned in and bestowed him with a chaste kiss on the cheek.

"You have got to be kidding me."

"Yeah . . . I was." With her heart pounding, Claire swung her leg over him to straddle his hips. She leaned in and, bracing herself with her hands on his shoulders, slowly licked his bottom lip. Taking the lead wasn't like her, but hot passion quickly melted her inhibitions. When he groaned, she nibbled lightly, sucked, and toyed until she finally slanted her mouth over his and kissed him slowly, sweetly, licking . . . savoring, and then going deeper, hotter. He tasted like red wine and hot man, and she could not get enough.

Claire rocked against his erection, driving them both nuts when his denim-covered shaft slid against the silky thong. After a breathy little moan she started a trail of kisses down his chest, pausing at his nipple to lick and bite before going lower . . . and lower still while letting her hair trail over his chest.

When Claire unzipped his jeans, she heard his sharp intake of breath and smiled. His penis sprang forward, big, bold, and ready. She curled her hand around it, amazed that the skin was so soft and yet he was so very hard.

"God, Claire," Jesse said, and his abs tightened. She ran the tip of her tongue up his shaft and then swirled it over his head before tugging his jeans over his hips and pulling them off.

Claire came up to her knees and looked him over, getting her fill. He was thickly muscled, gloriously hard, and his skin appeared golden in the firelight. The crackling heat caused a fine sheen of sweat across his chest, making Claire want to reach out and touch him, lick him everywhere . . .

but for the moment she simply stared. "You are a sight to behold."

"Then behold me," he tried to joke, but his voice was thick with passion.

Claire's laughter came out a low rumble. "I think I'm rubbing off on you."

"Please . . . do."

"My pleasure . . ." While on her knees Claire placed her hands on his chest and rubbed back and forth, but her laughter trailed off at the feel of his warm moist skin beneath her palms. "You feel . . . nice." She curled her fingers and raked her nails lightly through his chest hair and down to his groin, just grazing the tip of his penis. "I take that back. You feel amazing."

Jesse stirred, groaned, but just when she was about to take him into her mouth, he sucked in a breath and pushed up to a sitting position. "Not yet. I need to see you." Claire watched while his long fingers slowly unbuttoned her shirt and slid it over her shoulders. "Wow."

It was Claire's turn to suck in a breath when Jesse cupped her breasts in his big hands. "I can't say it enough. You are simply gorgeous." He circled his thumbs over her nipples, and when he leaned in and sucked her into his mouth, a hot shiver slid down Claire's spine. She shoved her fingers into his hair, arching her back, holding him close while he tasted, sucked, and played. His hands caressed and kneaded her bare ass cheeks, and without warning he suddenly slid his fingers beneath the sides of the thong and yanked the scrap of silk over her hips. Then, cupping her cheeks, he buried his head between her thighs, kissing her, devouring her, until her knees trembled.

"Here, baby . . ." He lowered her to the rug, eased her legs apart, and licked her oh so lightly, making Claire shiver and arch her back, wanting . . . needing more. He continued tiny quick-as-lightning licks until her fingers fisted into the rug. Her breathing became shallow gasps as her pleasure began to build, climb. . . . It was too much.

It wasn't enough.

But just when Claire was about to climax, he slowed down. "No . . ." Her throaty plea got her nowhere, and he nibbled on her inner thighs, teasing, toying, keeping relief just out of her reach until she was crazy with need. "Jesse!" When she arched her hips, he slid his hands beneath her ass and licked her faster, harder, until pure exquisite pleasure burst forward and exploded. Claire arched up against his hot mouth and pushed her shoulders into the rug. Her body turned to liquid heat while wave after wave washed over her. "That was amazing . . . ," she managed to say, even though her heart thudded wildly and she felt as if she were melting into the rug.

"Merry Christmas."

"It's . . . um, not Christmas yet." She tried to raise her head but couldn't.

"Good, because I'm just getting started," he warned her, and was rewarded with throaty laughter, but her eyes remained closed, and when she sucked her bottom lip between her teeth, Jesse knew she was acutely aware that he was drinking in the sight of her nakedness. With her beautiful body bathed in the glow of the fire and her hair fanned out over the rug, Jesse understood her earlier comment. She was a sight to behold.

"Jesse?" she asked in a soft purr, sounding chock-full of satisfaction.

"Hmm?"

"I know 'tis the season for giving, but I think it's about time for you to receive."

When she opened up her eyes and gave him a shy but sensual smile, Jesse felt something stir inside of him that went beyond passion. Once again it hit him hard that his time with her was limited, and he knew that this moment would be forever etched in his memory. He didn't want her to remember this as casual sex but didn't know how to voice his feelings.

"Just kiss me, Jesse," Claire whispered, and the emotion in her eyes told him that she understood.

"Gladly." Jesse knew that she was sated, and even though he was dying to make love to her, he wanted to bring her back to full arousal first, and so he leaned in and slowly slid his hand up her thigh, caressing her lightly. Her breath caught, but instead of closing her eyes, she rose up to her elbows, kept them open, and watched the path of his hand. "Your skin is like satin," he said as he moved upward, pausing to explore.

"Thank you," she replied in a breathless voice that told Jesse she was becoming aroused once more.

"I'm sorry that my hands are rough and calloused."

"No . . . I like it," she said, and when he slid both palms up to cup her breasts, her head tilted and her eyes fluttered shut. "I like your hands on me."

"Me, too." Jesse smiled. In her suit she had appeared all city sophistication, but there was a fresh honesty about her that he hadn't expected, making her even more enticing. He circled her nipples with his thumbs and then leaned in and kissed her soft, moist mouth before turning to quickly put on protection.

Jesse couldn't remember when he had wanted a woman more and he knew it was going to be a struggle not to climax quickly, so he spread her thighs, entering her inch by inch. She inhaled a deep breath and threaded her fingers through his hair. God, she was hot, wet, *tight* . . . and when he was buried deep, he had to pause in order to gain his composure. He began with slow, easy strokes, holding back when he wanted to pump hard. She rocked with him, kissing his chest, and when her breath started coming in short gasps, he knew she was getting close, and he stroked her harder, faster. She arched her back, tilted her hips as if needing more of him.

"Wrap your legs around me," Jesse requested in her ear, and when she did, he slid his hands beneath her ass. When she fisted her hands on the rug, he asked, "Are you okay?"

"Yes . . . oh yes," she answered, and nodded, and that was all he needed. She matched his rhythm and then some, making Jesse realize how great it was to have a woman who could handle his size. They were a perfect fit and he loved it. At this angle he filled her completely and was able to watch the play of passion on her face while he made love to her. Her lips were plump and moist, and her cheeks flushed a pretty shade of rose. That glorious mane of hair was starting to curl at the ends and when she opened her mouth and gasped, it pushed Jesse over the edge and he thrust deep, climaxing in a hot rush of pleasure while bringing her right along with him. He held her there for a long moment, savoring the feeling of being inside of her heat while she came.

Jesse lowered her hips to the floor, and after brushing her hair back from her face, he leaned down and gave her a lingering kiss. When Claire wrapped her arms around him and sighed, he felt the same bittersweet ache reach within and claw at his carefully guarded heart. After easing down beside her, he drew her close and for a while neither of them spoke. The soothing sound of jazz music played in the background, and the warmth of the fire had Jesse's eyes feeling heavy. She felt so good in his arms and he longed to have her tucked in his bed. "Hey, I'm fading fast."

"Me, too," she answered in a drowsy tone.

Not wanting to fall asleep on the floor, he kissed the top of Claire's head and said, "Are you ready for bed?"

"Yes," she answered hesitantly. "I'm exhausted. I hope I can make it up the stairs."

The stairs? Jesse wanted her to sleep with him, but given the circumstances, he didn't know if he should ask. But the cabin would seem dark and eerie, and sounds of nocturnal wildlife might leave her spooked in the middle of the night.

"Do you have a suggestion as to which room I should choose?"

Mine . . . , he almost said, but stopped himself, and yet the thought of her wide-awake and frightened bothered him more than he wanted it to. He had never felt this way about a woman so quickly, but he told himself it was the unusual set of circumstances and his unstable emotions during the holidays that was messing with his head. He reminded himself that she would soon be gone from his life and having her curled up next to him all night long was too intimate. They had already traveled into dangerous emotional territory. Even though he wanted her next to him, she should sleep in a guest room for both their sakes. "The one directly at the top of the stairs has a big bathroom that connects to it. There are extra toiletries in the medicine cabinet, hopefully including a new toothbrush, so help yourself to anything you might need. Fresh towels are in the linen closet."

"Thanks," she answered softly, and damn if there wasn't a hint of a catch in her voice. When she sat up and reached for her shirt, Jesse wanted to drag her back against him and hold her close. With her back to him he couldn't help but admire the delicate grace in the slope of her shoulders and the curve of her hips, and he had the strongest urge to brush her hair aside and kiss her neck. Jesse looked at her through the eyes of an artist, deciding that he would love to do a nude sketch of her. He had done so much woodworking that a charcoal drawing would be a welcome change of pace. Not that he would have the nerve to ask . . .

After Claire tugged on the long johns, she stood up and Jesse dragged the cover over himself since the sight of her had him getting aroused all over again. *Amazing*, he thought, since he was bone tired and seriously spent. When she glanced at the dishes, he shook his head. "I'll take care of that. You just head on up and get settled. The light switch is on the left."

Claire nodded. "Okay."

When she started walking toward the steps, he said, "If you need anything at all, just give me a holler."

She paused and turned around. "I will. Thank you, Jesse," she replied, but in the shadows she appeared a little uncertain.

"Claire . . . ," he began, but she shook her head.

"Don't," she said softly. "This is for the best."

Jesse watched her walk over to pick up her purse and then up the steps and had to grind his teeth in an effort not to go after her. When she disappeared from view, he leaned back on his elbows and inhaled a deep breath, but just when he thought he had himself under control, he looked down and spotted her black thong lying on the white rug. With a groan he closed his eyes, but the image stayed there.

Damn.

He looked up the stairs and reconsidered. . . .

Chapter Seven

*C*laire flicked on the light in the bedroom and sucked in
a breath. "Oh, wow." A stunning tarnished-copper bed looked
elegant next to the rustic log walls. A fluffy snow-white comforter invited Claire to snuggle, and stacks of dark blue pillows
added a burst of color that matched the dust ruffle brushing up
against the hardwood floor. Draperies of the same shade hung
from copper curtain rods that matched the ornate headboard. A
nightstand with log legs drew Claire's attention and she discovered that the rustic wooden armoire was actually an entertain-
ment center hiding a television. The pieces were rough-hewn
but artfully designed, making Claire wonder if Jesse also hand-
crafted furniture. The dresser drawers were empty, not that it
mattered, she thought with a wry grin.

After placing her purse on the nightstand, Claire opened
the door to the bathroom and smiled again. Everything was
modern but vintage-style, from the pedestal sink to the high-
tank toilet. But when she turned and spotted the double-slipper

claw-foot bathtub, she put her hands to her chest. "Oh, absolutely amazing!" She hurried over to the freestanding faucet and admired the porcelain details on the hand shower and immediately felt the desire for a long, soothing bubble bath with soft music and flickering candles. She wondered whether she should ask Jesse if he had any votives, but as soon as his name skittered through her brain, she envisioned him lounging in the tub, cowboy hat tilted back, a longneck dangling from his fingers, and the need for his back to be scrubbed, and then maybe his chest, and then . . .

"Oh, stop!" Closing her eyes, Claire inhaled a deep breath and blew it out. Just thinking about Jesse brought a heated flush to her face, and she put her cool hands on her warm cheeks and groaned. Leave it to *her* to finally find a man who could make her melt like butter on a hot biscuit and have him live hundreds of miles away.

But she pushed that thought aside and, as promised, found everything she needed in the medicine cabinet. After washing her face and brushing her teeth, she headed back into the bedroom, clicking on the cute little lamp perched on the nightstand before she turned off the overhead light. She slipped beneath the crisp sheet and pulled the cozy down comforter up to her chin and sighed. "The day started off pretty normal," she murmured, and then shook her head in wonder. Although her work as a stylist was fast-paced and hectic, her social life was pretty low-key. Stuff like this just didn't happen to her. Claire smiled slowly. It was about time she added an adventure to her predictable life. But her smile faded when she looked at her purse and thought about her cell phone tucked inside.

Claire considered calling her sister, Chloe, but then sighed. She had talked to Chloe and her mother just this morning, so they wouldn't be worried as of yet. But soon she would have to break her snowbound news to them all. "That is not going to be fun."

Another sigh escaped Claire as she leaned her head back against the squishy feather pillow. She folded her hands above the blanket and glanced around. She simply could not tell her protective parents that she was stranded in a remote mountain cabin with a complete stranger. Claire imagined the National Guard swarming in helicopters or a SWAT team perched in the trees. *Oh, this isn't going to be good.* While nibbling on her inner cheek, Claire contemplated the situation and then suddenly snapped her fingers. She was sleeping in a bed and Jesse promised a hot breakfast. . . . She was staying at a bed-and-breakfast! "Yes!" she said, and in the still of the night her voice seemed to ring out. "Oh no," she squeaked with a wince, and put a hand over her mouth, hoping Jesse didn't hear her silly outburst. With that thought, she quickly turned off the light. "Oh . . . no," she repeated in a much lower tone. It was dark. No, not just dark.

Pitch. Black. *Dark.*

And oh so very quiet.

Claire swallowed hard and brought the blanket all the way up to her nose, as if the fluffy feather comforter would somehow shield her from things that go bump in the night. . . .

Ahhhhhhhooooooh!

Oh crap—*correction.* Things that *howl* in the night and maybe go bump, too. When another *ahhhhhhohhhh* rang out into the night, Claire swallowed and with a weak laugh sang, "Werewolves of London." Tugging the covers nearly up to her eyeballs, she said, "I'm Team Jacob, so please don't eat me." She shook her head, thinking this was feeling more like a B horror movie than R-rated Hallmark. "R-Rated Hallmark is way better," she mumbled, and was very close to calling out for Jesse but refrained. *It's just the wilderness, you little city slicker.*

"Okay, calm down and just relax." Claire attempted to fall asleep, but she realized that although it was so very, *very* dark, her eyes were wide-open. After a few minutes her vision adjusted, but then the previously lovely furniture seemed to be lurking in the shadows ready to pounce. Feeling absolutely absurd for being so scared, she pressed her lips together and squeezed her eyes shut.

Realizing she would never fall asleep being this tense, she willed her limbs to relax one by one as if in the cooldown part of her Pilates class. After a while her method began to work and she started to drift off to sleep. . . .

And then she heard it. Scratching at her window! Her eyes opened wide and she strained to see what was trying to come in and get her, but could see nothing but shadows. Her heart pounded double-time, but when all she heard was silence, she blew out her held breath and had to start the whole Pilates thing all over again. She was only to her thighs when the scratching began and then quickly accelerated to banging.

Dear God!

Claire wanted to shout for Jesse, but with every ounce of courage in her body she eased from the protection of the comforter and then leaned over and turned on the lamp, wanting to see her would-be attacker in the light. Swallowing hard, she crept over to the window, shoved back the drapes, and, fully expecting to see some sort of eerie, beady-eyed creature of the night, sucked in a breath, ready to let out a bloodcurdling B-movie-worthy scream for Jesse to come to her rescue.

"A tree branch!" Claire whispered hotly, and allowed the drape to fall back in place. "Well!" Totally ticked at her scared-silly self, she stomped over to the bed and slid under the covers. Still grumbling beneath her breath, she snapped off the light and slammed her eyes shut. "It was only a stupid tree branch," she muttered darkly, but then thanked her lucky stars that she hadn't made a fool of herself by screaming. A girl could take only so much humiliation in one day. She yawned and this time made it all the way up to tensing and then relaxing her butt before falling fast asleep.

The aroma of bacon frying filtered into Claire's brain before she was fully awake, causing a dreamy smile before she snuggled back into the soft, squishy bedding. She really needed to invest in some feather pillows. Must be the hotel restaurant making breakfast, she thought with a sleepy sigh. She inhaled deeply and was delighted to smell coffee brewing as well. Still, she opted for more sleep, but her stomach rumbled in protest. With a groan she slowly lifted her eyelids while stretching and wondering why her muscles protested in odd places.

"Ohmigod." It suddenly all came flooding back to her befuddled brain. She was in Jesse Marshall's cabin in Whisper, Colorado, with nothing but the clothes on her back. She peeked beneath the covers. "Okay, make that *his* clothes on my back." Oh yeah, and she had made passionate love to him on a rug in front of his fireplace.

And now she had to go down there and face him.

Claire closed her eyes and inhaled a deep breath. *No biggie; we're adults*, she reminded herself with a firm nod. *This sort of thing happens all the time. . . .*

Just not to her.

Claire's stomach rumbled again and she rolled her eyes. She was going to have to face the music sometime, so it might as well be now. With a short determined nod she tossed back the covers and padded in Jesse's big socks into the bathroom. "Oh, dear God, where are my panties?" she asked in a high-squeaked whisper. She reached up and felt her breasts. "And my bra?" And while washing her hands, she looked into the oval mirror and winced. What was usually carefully flatironed hair had become a bed-head-starting-to-curl mess, and with her makeup washed off, her freckles stood out prominently and her eyelashes were spiky ginger instead of jet-black. The impact of not having her luggage was really starting to settle in.

Claire shoved her fingers through her hair, but it didn't really help at all and she suddenly felt a little bit like crying. She opened the medicine cabinet and prayed to find mascara, foundation, and eyeliner. "Damn!" She stared at her bare-naked freckled face and wild hair and shook her head. Handsome-as-sin Jesse Marshall was about to have a Coyote Ugly morning. . . .

But over the years Claire had become adept at hiding her insecurities, and so she squared her shoulders and headed down the stairs. Although her heart was hammering, she entered the kitchen with a big smile. "I smell coffee."

Jesse turned around from the refrigerator with a carton of eggs in his hand. "Did you sleep well?"

"Yes, thanks," she replied, and willed herself not to blush. Redheads were experts at blushing and she was no exception.

"Not scared, I hope."

She waved a hand sideways and managed not to reach up and try to tame her hair. "Not at all. I found the complete and utter darkness and absolute quiet very peaceful."

Jesse arched one dark eyebrow as if trying to decide whether she was serious. She got that a lot. "Really?" Unlike her, he looked devilishly handsome with messy hair and wore his low-slung gray sweatpants well. A long-sleeved red T-shirt stretched across his shoulders and hugged his biceps. She was further distracted when he bent over and retrieved a carton of orange juice from the fridge. She angled her head and gawked. Wow, he had the best butt ever. He straightened and gazed at her expectantly. "You weren't?"

She jerked her head back up and blinked at him. Wait, what did he ask? "Weren't . . . what?"

"Frightened."

"Bffft . . . no," she scoffed, and then added, "That werewolf scratching at my window turned out to be a mere tree branch."

Jesse set the eggs down onto the island and chuckled. "So you heard the howling?"

"Um . . . yeah." She nodded, and Jesse thought she looked completely cute standing there uncertainly in his big floppy socks and her bottom lip sucked between her teeth. Without her makeup she was a fresh-faced natural beauty, and her warm, bed-rumpled appearance made him want to walk over there and kiss her senseless. But although she managed to smile and joke, Jesse sensed a bit of uneasiness and he wanted to squash it.

"Have a seat. Just tell me whatever you want," he offered, and when her eyes widened slightly, he realized his comment sounded suggestive and he could have bitten his tongue. "For breakfast," he added lamely, and noticed her blush. "But first come on over and grab a mug of coffee. There's cream and sugar."

"Thanks. I could use some."

Oh, so could he, but he wasn't thinking about breakfast. Seeing Claire in his clothes was somehow so damned hot, and knowing that her bra and panties were lying on the sofa was getting him going. He was just about to turn away when she stumbled in his too-big socks and fell forward. Jesse reached out to catch her and with his arms around her took two steps back, landing against the edge of the counter. He felt the full impact of her braless breasts and groaned.

"I'm sorry! Are you okay?"

"Yeah," he said, but his voice sounded strained.

"I am such a train wreck!"

"Yeah, but a cute train wreck."

"Those two things don't go together," she said.

"With you, they do."

She frowned. "I'm trying to decide whether that was a compliment . . . and hey, your hands are on my ass."

"I know. This time I meant to do that," he admitted with a grin, but then sobered. "Claire, I couldn't sleep last night."

"B–because of the howling?"

He reached up and tucked his hand beneath her chin. "No, because all I could think about was you."

She laughed softly and pushed away from him. "Yeah, you had your eggnog goggles on." She lifted both palms in the air. "Now look at me. Freckle-faced, wild-haired Amazon chick." She lifted a lock of her hair from her shoulder. "When I wash this mane without product and a flatiron, it will be a crazy mass of curls."

Jesse shook his head slowly, thinking that she just didn't get it. "I want to sketch you."

"Sketch me?"

"Yes, you need to see how truly beautiful you are."

She angled her head. "I have a mirror. I know what I look like."

"Not through my eyes." Jesse wasn't sure whether he truly meant to say that out loud, but now it was out there, so he persisted, "Will you pose for me, Claire?"

Her mouth opened and then shut, and Jesse could sense her fear but also curiosity. She looked down at his shirt and then said, "You mean in my business suit?"

Jesse shook his head from side to side. "Not that suit."

"You mean . . ." Her eyes widened. "Oh!" Her cheeks turned a deep shade of rose.

"Please?" For some reason this suddenly became important to him. He took a step closer and put his hands on her shoulders. "No pressure, but just so you know, this isn't a smarmy come-on. I'm an artist and I have an eye for beauty."

"But I'm not—"

He put a fingertip to her mouth. "You are. *Beautiful*."

She moved his finger from her mouth and put her hands to his cheeks. "You already make me feel beautiful, Jesse."

Claire gazed at him with stark honesty and once again her quiet admission reached inside and grabbed Jesse in places that had remained dormant for a long time. When her smile trembled, he simply had to lean in and press his mouth to hers. He kissed her tenderly and then said in her ear, "Ah, but I want you to know it. Own it." He nuzzled her neck and then asked, "Will you do it?"

When she looked at him for a long, silent moment, Jesse thought she was going to refuse, but then she put a gentle hand on his chest and nodded slowly. "Yes," she answered softly, "I will."

"Excellent." Jesse let out the breath he had been holding and felt a surge of joy. He kissed her lightly on the lips and said, "Okay, now, how do you like your eggs?"

Chapter Eight

*A*fter a big breakfast of fluffy scrambled eggs, crisp bacon, and hot biscuits, Claire enjoyed a long soak in the luxurious bathtub. Jesse had refused to allow her to help clean up the kitchen and told her to take her time before coming down for the sitting. He needed to gather his equipment and said he would let her know when he was ready. After toweling dry, she located some lotion and smoothed it over her skin while trying not to think about walking downstairs in nothing but Jesse's big robe. She squeezed all the excess water from her hair and wished she had some product. Blow-drying without a diffuser would make her hair a big frizzy ball, so she wiggled her fingers through the waves and let her hair air-dry.

She entered the bedroom and sat on the bed, then reached for her purse. She dumped out the contents, hoping to find some makeup. Her cell phone thumped onto the comforter and seemed to scream, "Call your mother!"

"Oh, okay!" Claire picked it up but couldn't muster up

the courage to listen to her parents' disappointment when they found out she wasn't going to make it home for the holidays. Maybe she could just send a text message.

She looked at the time, and since she shouldn't be arriving in Atlanta for several hours, she decided to leave that emotional task until later. "Yes!" she said when she spotted a sample tube of mascara, a pressed-powder compact, and sheer coral lip gloss. Perfume! Sweet! She dearly missed her eyeliner and foundation, but this stash at least gave her a bit of polish, so she opened the compact and applied what little she had. With a happy smile she picked up her small spray bottle of perfume. After untying her robe, she slipped it from her shoulders and sprayed some on and in the process caught a glimpse of herself in the oval mirror standing in the far corner of the room. With a pounding heart she walked over and gazed at her naked reflection.

Like a prizefighter dancing in a ring, every little imperfection seemed to reach out and take quick jabs at her confidence. Her breasts were too full, her hips were too rounded, and her thighs too thick. She reached up and touched the riot of unruly curls tumbling over her shoulders and eyed her freckled face with a frown.

"What in the world was I thinking?" she whispered, and reached for the robe and secured the sash tightly. After sitting down on the edge of the bed, she inhaled a deep breath. "I can't do this."

Claire sat there for a few minutes with her hands folded. She was wondering what to say to Jesse when she heard a soft rap on her door. "Come in."

"Hey there." He filled the doorway looking so handsome

that she wanted to throw a pillow at him. Or maybe kiss him. "I brought you a glass of wine."

"Jesse, it's not even noon."

He shrugged his lumberjack shoulders. "No clocks, no schedule. This is my vacation," he replied with a grin that was way too sexy. He took two steps into the room and extended the glass to her.

"It's called a staycation."

"It's not what I had in mind, but it's working for me. All I know is that I woke up this morning wanting to relax and not worry about a damned thing." He reached over and put a fingertip between her eyebrows. "Get rid of that frown."

"Are you always this cheerful when you're snowed in?"

Something like surprise passed over his face. "Funny, but I've never been what you would call cheerful." But when Claire started to comment, he said, "Listen, I'm all set up downstairs, but if you don't want to do this, it's perfectly okay."

"I want to."

"Good."

"I just . . . can't."

"Then I'll sketch you with the robe on."

She raised her eyebrows. "Really?" She should have been relieved but instead felt an unexpected shot of disappointment.

He nodded and then extended his arm toward her. "If that's what you prefer. Come with me."

Claire slipped her hand into his and immediately felt a little feminine flutter. She had been single for so long and seeing couples holding hands always hit her hard with longing. There was just something so sweet, so romantic about it, and his hand was so big, so masculine, that he once again made her feel delicate . . . girly.

"Make yourself comfortable on the rug in front of the fire."

Claire nodded but felt heat in her cheeks when visions of what they did there last night filtered into her brain.

"I wanted you someplace warm," he explained as if guessing her thoughts.

An easel was set up a few feet away and Claire noticed a coffee can full of various-sized pencils and erasers. Despite a sudden wave of nerves she was curious about Jesse Marshall the artist. After taking a sip of her wine, she asked, "So you do more than just the Santa carvings?"

He nodded. "My father taught me wood carving at an early age. I developed a deep appreciation of art from my parents. It's something that's in my blood," he added, and Claire hoped he would elaborate, but he frowned for a second and then seemed to shake off whatever was bothering him. "The statues are my bread and butter, but I enjoy many forms of art, from watercolor to pottery, but charcoal has always been a favorite medium." He grinned. "I might not look like it, but I have a master's degree."

"Now, why would you say that?"

"Be honest, Claire." He angled his head at her. "When I walked into the train station, did I look as if I should be painting landscapes or chopping down trees?"

"Chopping down trees," she answered, and took another sip of the red wine. "What did I look like?"

"High maintenance. Haughty."

"Haughty?" She snorted. "I'm anything but . . ."

"I know that now." With a roll of masking tape in his hand, he walked over to where she sat on the rug.

"What are you going to do with that?"

"Tape you down so you can't run away."

"Right . . ."

"After I position you, I'll mark it off, so if you have to take a break, we know just where you were sitting."

"Oh, makes sense," Claire commented, and tried to ignore the tingle she felt when he took her ankle and put it where he wanted. His hands were warm . . . strong. She wanted to reach out and touch him . . . run her fingers through his hair.

"Charcoal is all about lighting and shading, so I want you to face the fireplace at an angle and sort of look over your shoulder. It's overcast outside, so there will be some amazing shadows to work with." He took her chin in his hand and, after turning her head at an angle, pushed her mass of curls over her shoulder. He seemed so serious that Claire allowed him to position her the way he wanted without any more questions. He walked over to the easel, looked at her for a moment, and then came back and marked her feet off with the masking tape. She was so very glad that she had just had a pedicure and that her toenails were a glossy red against the off-white rug. "Can you hold that pose for a while?"

"Yes," she replied, but was careful to remain still.

"Good, but it's more difficult than it seems, so just let me know if you need a break."

"Okay," she replied, and then watched him go to work. He seemed so intense and the heat in his eyes when he studied her made her suddenly wonder what it would have been like to be posing nude.

He sketched broad strokes with a fat pencil and then came over and slightly repositioned her chin, her shoulders, and then her ankle. "You holding up okay?" he asked, and then gave her a drink of her wine. "Warm enough?" When Claire nodded, the robe slipped from one shoulder, but when she reached up to put it back, he said, "Will you leave it? The slope of your shoulder is incredibly graceful."

Claire nodded, and with a frown on his handsome face, Jesse drew, put his thumb forward with one eye open as if measuring, and then went back to big, sweeping strokes. Claire watched, mesmerized, not realizing that she was barely breathing. When she took a deep breath, the robe slid from her other shoulder, leaving her back and the curve of her left breast exposed. Her heart pounded, but when he continued to sketch, she didn't want to disturb his concentration and left the robe pooled at her waist. A few moments later he came over to her, tilted her head a fraction, and then while holding her gaze reached down and loosened the belt on the robe. Neither of them spoke, but when his fingers barely grazed her body, she felt a jolt of sexual heat and didn't protest when he parted the terry cloth and pushed it from her body.

As Jesse sketched, his sweeping strokes became more refined and he reached for different pencils. He angled his head, studied her with a quiet intensity that felt like a physical touch. At one point he picked up a rag and swiped it back and forth across the paper and then began sketching once more. His hands became blackened from the charcoal and he smudged a bit on his nose and cheek but didn't seem to notice or care.

The passion in Jesse's eyes felt hot and caused Claire's nipples to tighten and heat to pool between her thighs.

Jesse chewed on the inside of his lip and shoved his fingers through his hair. He had sketched plenty of nudes in college but never a woman whom he had made love to; this was an amazingly sensual experience. He was literally putting passion on the page. Every stroke of the pencil on the velvety surface felt as if he were caressing her curves, and he become more and more aroused. Claire's over-the-shoulder pose was almost coy, and yet the heat in her eyes told a much different story. She was sweet, smoky heat, and he wanted to kiss her, touch her, lick her all over . . . *everywhere,* and then make love to her until she cried out his name again and again, and by the time he was finished with the drawing, he was crazy with wanting her.

Jesse looked at the drawing, angled his head at Claire, and had to steady his trembling fingers before adding a few details. He stepped back and smiled slowly. He had done it . . . captured her natural beauty, her sensuality, and yet her eyes held a sense of humor and her mouth a touch of vulnerability.

Claire Collins.

Through his eyes she was sheer perfection, and his Christmas gift to her was for her to *know* that she was a gorgeous, sexy woman.

"May I see it?" Her voice was husky, sexy, and her eyes were full of passion.

"Yes," Jesse answered. "Come here." When she reached for the robe, he shook his head. "Leave it."

She licked her lips and hesitated but then stood up and

walked over to the easel. She stood in front of Jesse, and his heart pounded while she gazed at the drawing. "Oh, my . . . ," she said breathily, and put a hand to her chest. "Oh, Jesse, it's stunning. Perfect!" She tilted her head and studied the sketch. "But . . . that's not . . . *I'm not* . . . That can't be . . . *me.*"

Jesse put his hands on her shoulders and looked at the sketch with her. "Oh, yes it is," he whispered in her ear. "And this is what I see when I look at you." He let her drink that in, then added, "You are beautiful. Alluring." He slid his hands up and sank his fingers into her silky curls. "You're sensual, but you somehow maintain an air of innocence . . . honesty. Claire, you're gorgeous from the inside out." He slid his hands down and squeezed her shoulders. "Don't ever doubt yourself, okay?"

She stood there for a minute looking at the sketch, and when she reached up and swiped at her cheek, Jesse felt as if the hard ball of anger that he had been carrying inside since the death of his parents was finally starting to melt. After years of cutting himself off from soft emotion, she was making him feel again, laugh again. . . .

Live again.

Claire turned and cupped his cheeks between her palms and then kissed him tenderly. "Thank you, Jesse."

Emotion clogged Jesse's throat and he had to pause before he said, "You're welcome." And then, without warning, he bent down and scooped Claire up into his arms.

After a little squeal she asked, "What are you doing?"

"Taking you to my bed."

"Ah, I guess it's time for an afternoon nap. . . ."

"Guess again."

Chapter Nine

$\mathcal{J}$esse zigzagged and spun in circles, making Claire hang on for dear life but laugh with delight. She felt carefree and light as air in his strong arms, but when he entered his bedroom, she sucked in a breath. "Oh, Jesse, this room is magnificent."

"Thank you."

High beamed cathedral ceilings allowed room for the massive four-poster king-sized bed against the back wall. The rustic furniture appeared strong and sturdy but again managed to have a smooth artsy elegance that invited touch. Deep maroon covered the bed and accented the windows, and a lovely Oriental rug added a splash of additional color against the hardwood floor. Light spilled in from the A-framed exit leading to a back deck with a lovely view of the woods. A stone fireplace was tucked in the far corner with a leather chaise lounge that called for a good book and a mug of hot chocolate.

But instead of placing Claire on the bed, Jesse walked through double doors leading to a master bath. "I have charcoal all over my hands and I managed to get it all over you. Mind if we wash off?"

Claire shook her head. "Of course not," she answered, and as he put her gently on her feet, she tried to avoid looking at her naked reflection. She thought about reaching for a white fluffy towel but didn't want to get charcoal on it, so she stood there while he started soaping up his hands. But when she started to turn the faucet on her sink, he shook his head. "What?"

"Come closer," he requested while he washed his hands. He chuckled when he removed the smudges from his face, but after tugging off his shirt, he turned to Claire. "Since I'm the one who did this to you, it's only fair that I clean you up. Don't you agree?" he asked, but without waiting for her reply, he started soaping her breasts.

"There wasn't any charcoal there."

"Really?" he asked innocently, and then turned her so that he stood behind her and she faced the mirror. "My bad . . ." He soaked a washcloth in warm water and took his sweet time wiping the soap from her nipples. There was heat in his eyes but something playful that wasn't there before, and she loved seeing this side of him. When she felt that the time was right, she was going to find out what had happened that took away his Christmas joy.

"There's some," he said, and slowly washed a dark streak away from her ribs. The warm rough material felt amazing on her sensitive skin, and he continued dipping the cloth in the water and washing her long after the charcoal was gone. Her skin glowed, tingled. With a moan he suddenly dropped the cloth and caressed her with his bare hands. When he dipped his dark head and kissed her shoulder, she leaned back against his chest and watched. Claire sucked in a breath when he cupped her breasts, lifting, toying, while he rubbed the pads of his thumbs over her nipples. While he began a trail of warm kisses up her neck, his hands traveled lower, and when he slid a finger lightly over her mound, her breath hitched, caught. He parted her folds while kissing her neck and then touched her clit just as he nibbled on her earlobe.

Claire felt as if she were heavy and yet floating at the same time, and when he sucked her earlobe into his hot mouth, he rubbed her intimately, dipping and then swirling. Her heart pounded and she fought the urge to close her eyes as she watched his hands work magic. When her breath became shallow, gasping, he raised his head and met her eyes in the mirror just before she climaxed. She pressed her shoulders against his chest and thrust her breasts forward when the sharp, exquisite feeling climbed higher . . . reaching . . . and then burst open with pleasure. "Jesse!"

He wrapped one strong arm around her waist for support when she sank limply against him. His other hand remained between her thighs, and when she closed her eyes, Jesse said, "No, baby, look."

And so she did.

Her hair curled wildly over her shoulders and her eyes were dilated with passion. Her lips were wet and her cheeks were flushed a deep rose. Looking down, she gazed at her full breasts, the curve of her hips, and the flare of her thighs.

"Tell me—what do you see?"

Beauty.

"Say it."

"I can't."

"You can," he urged, and when her gaze locked with his in the mirror, she saw it in his eyes.

"I'm beautiful," she said barely above a whisper.

"Don't forget it," he reiterated, and she was hit with a touch of sadness. He wanted her to say it and believe it after she left here. Left him.

Jesse looked at her and smiled, but his eyes seemed to echo her thoughts. But not wanting to waste a minute of their borrowed time, she said, "The charcoal is gone. Take me to your bed." When he scooped her up again, she whooped and then laughed. "Show-off!"

"Is it working?"

"Absolutely."

For the rest of the afternoon they used every square foot of the bed and explored every square inch of skin. Out of sheer necessity they paused to eat, but Jesse's tray of finger foods and flutes of mimosa led to their feeding each other.

"Mmmm," Claire moaned when Jesse sank a plump strawberry into chocolate dip and then slipped it into her mouth. She closed her eyes and licked her lips, then arched up off the bed when she felt a cold sensation on her nipple quickly followed by the moist heat of his tongue. "Um . . . Jesse, that chocolate dip is for the fruit."

"Okay," he replied, and then swiped a thick streak of chocolate down her torso.

"Jesse . . ." Claire rose to her elbows, but her protest died on her lips when he took a juicy piece of pineapple and slid it slowly through the chocolate on her skin and then fed it to her. He did the same thing near her navel and then painted a happy face on the inside of her thigh before licking it off. Claire giggled, but then sucked in a breath when his chocolate-dipped finger moved to her mound. He took a cool, smooth slice of apple through the chocolate and then dipped lower, parting her folds. The apple felt even colder next to her moist heat, and when he slipped it over her swollen bud, Claire gasped. She was sensitive and almost sore from the day before, but when he rubbed it back and forth, the ache was painfully sweet. She fisted her hands in the sheet, thinking that he couldn't make her come yet again. Her heart thudded. Her chest rose and fell. She leaned back on her elbows and closed her eyes and tried to protest when the cool apple was suddenly gone. . . .

But was replaced by his warm, silky mouth.

He licked her with soothing strokes as if savoring her taste, her scent . . . her body. She bent her knees and then threaded her fingers through his hair while he gently made love to her with his mouth. When she climaxed, it felt suspended, blossoming slowly but lasting forever. She opened her mouth but failed to utter a sound, then fell back against the pillows.

Claire felt the heat of his body above her, and when he threaded his fingers with hers and kissed her with a lingering sweetness, she knew that she was falling hard and fast for Jesse Marshall.

He rolled over, pulled her against him, and then tugged the covers up over their bodies. Claire sighed and snuggled into his embrace. She couldn't begin to recall when she'd felt so satisfied, so relaxed, or this content. She smiled when he kissed her shoulder and then the back of her head, and within seconds they were both sound asleep.

Chapter Ten

*W*hen Jesse woke up, the sun was beginning to set. Claire was still sleeping soundly, and he considered staying beneath the covers, but his stomach rumbled in protest. He grinned while shaking his head. He had worked up quite an appetite. As silently as possible, he crept from the bed, slipped on his sweatpants, and headed to the kitchen to throw together a pot of chili and some corn bread. After so many meals alone, it felt good to have someone to eat with.

After the chili was simmering on the stove, Jesse made two mugs of herbal tea and headed back to the bedroom. He set Claire's mug on the nightstand and then stood there and looked down at her sleeping form. The flickering light from the fireplace coupled with the wedge of light from the hallway cast a warm glow in the otherwise dark room. Claire stirred slightly, causing the cover to slip and expose one creamy shoulder. He was amazed that after making love to her all day long, he was already getting aroused. He could reason that it was because he hadn't been with a woman for such a long time or the emotion of the holiday season or the snowbound circumstances. He could tell himself the amazing lovemaking was due to the erotic aftermath of sketching her nude, but he would be fooling himself. In spite of his resolve not to, he was already falling for Claire Collins.

I could get used to this, he thought with a smile, but then cold hard reality reared its ugly head and brought his thoughts back out of the clouds. Claire would be leaving in just a few days, and he would more than likely never see her again. Jesse ground his teeth together and swallowed hard. This was the last thing he wanted to happen. He should have kept his distance. The idea of her leaving already tore at his gut—a hurt that was different from losing his parents but pain nonetheless, and something he had vowed to avoid until now.

With an angry intake of breath he turned away and managed to slosh hot tea on his bare chest. "Damn!" he growled.

"Hey, are you okay?" she asked in a sleepy voice that sounded like crushed velvet.

"Yeah, I just splashed some tea on my chest. No big deal. I didn't mean to wake you." He knew he sounded terse but turned to leave anyway.

"Then why did you bring me some tea?" she asked in a confused tone.

"I thought you might be awake, but when you weren't, I decided to let you sleep."

"Oh." When he remained silent, she said, "Something sure smells good."

"Chili," he responded, and took a few steps toward the

door. He knew he was being an ass and confusing the hell out of her, but he was suddenly so pissed at himself that he couldn't see straight. What in the hell had he been thinking?

"What's wrong, Jesse?" The hurt in her voice stopped him in his tracks and he slowly turned around. She looked up at him with those big vulnerable eyes and angled her head at him. "Did I do something wrong?"

"No, you didn't do anything wrong," he assured her while feeling even more like an ass. After a brief hesitation he walked over and sat down on the edge of the bed. "Christmas is a tough time for me." He cradled the warm mug in his hands and stared down at the brown liquid. "My parents were killed in a car wreck five years ago just a week before Christmas."

"I'm so sorry."

He nodded but didn't look up. "My parents, especially my mother, loved the holidays. Every inch of this cabin would be decorated, and it was an excuse to have the place packed with people. My mother always wanted a large family, and after several miscarriages she finally had me." He smiled softly. "My parents were both small people and always marveled at how they could have produced a big dude like me. Anyway, I was born on Christmas Eve and that made the holidays even more of a celebration for my mother. She always said that I was her best Christmas gift ever." He shook his head slowly.

"So that's why you leave."

"Yeah. It's hard enough carving those damned Santas all year long. I can't ever escape Christmas until I get the hell out of here for a couple of weeks."

"Why do you continue to carve them if it's so painful?"

He looked at her then. "My father taught me as a kid. It's his legacy and all I have left of him."

"Oh . . . Jesse." When she gazed at him as if she wanted to hug him, Jesse glanced away, but she would have none of it. "And you finally let your guard down with me. Allowed yourself to feel again." She hesitated and then added, "And you're angry with me because of that."

"No, I'm pissed at myself. I don't have to state the obvious. We've started something that has no chance of going beyond these few days."

"It doesn't have to be that way."

Jesse raised his eyebrows. "Really? You don't even fly, Claire. Are you going to take a three-day train ride when you want to come for a visit?" Tears welled up in her eyes, but he persisted. "This started with the eggnog and I apologize for that. And I thought if I let you make the first move that I wouldn't feel like a heel having a holiday fling. That you wouldn't be looking at me like you're looking at me now."

"So that's what this is to you?" she asked in a small voice.

"I wish—," Jesse began, but before he could explain what he meant, his cell phone rang. "I'm sorry." He set down his mug and then held up one finger. "Excuse me."

Claire watched him pull the phone from his pocket with annoyance, but after raising his eyebrows at the caller, he answered, "Hello? Yeah? Really?" He glanced her way and then said, "You're kidding. No. Yeah, sure. I'll tell her. Thanks, Danny." After hanging up, Jesse looked at her as if not knowing just what to say but then cleared his throat. "That was Danny from the train station. Because of the backup at the airports, there's going to be a train coming through here tomorrow morning to Denver. I can catch it and fly out from there."

"What about the one for Atlanta?"

Jesse shook his head. "Not until Saturday." He hesitated and then said, "But you could catch a flight out of Denver, too."

"Jesse, I don't fly—remember?"

"But if you did, you could make it home in time for Christmas Eve. You're strong-willed. I'm sure you could do it. Take a pill or something."

She frowned and plucked at the bedsheet with her fingers. The mere thought of getting onto an airplane made her sweat. "If it were that easy, I would." Her sigh shook with emotion. "But look, I know how much you want to get out of here, and I don't want to hold you back. I'll take the train to Denver and wait there until I can catch the one back to Atlanta. I can book a room and buy some essentials."

"You're sure? But you'll be alone for Christmas."

"It's no big deal." Claire pressed her lips together in an effort not to cry but somehow managed to nod and then waved her hand through the air. "I'm a big girl. I'll survive."

Jesse raked his fingers through his hair and seemed to be deep in thought for a moment, and she held her breath with hope. "Claire, I didn't mean to sound flippant when I called this a holiday fling. What I meant was—"

"Jesse, don't worry," she interrupted. "I was just as much to blame."

"I wasn't trying to place blame."

Claire forced a smile. "Well, just think, tomorrow this time you'll be sitting on a sandy beach with a cold fruity drink in your hand. This little fling will just be a fond memory."

"Claire—"

"I should get out of your hair and let you pack. What time should I be ready in the morning?"

He frowned. "Let's go on out and eat the chili. We can talk about it over dinner. Maybe—"

"Thanks, but I'm still tired. I think I'm going to take a soak in that magnificent claw-foot tub. You go ahead and eat. If I get hungry, I'll come down and help myself." When he hesitated, she said, "Plus, I really have to call my parents and let them know what's going on. Just wake me up in the morning."

"Are you sure?"

She nodded. "After a hot bath I'm likely to fall asleep."

He was silent for a moment, making her heart thud. "Okay, but if you need anything, let me know. I'm going to head outside and clear the road with my Bobcat. But I'll have my cell phone on me. I'll write my number down for you."

Claire nodded but waited for him to leave the room before reaching for her clothes. Not wanting him to see the tears that she was trying desperately to hold back, she waited until she heard the door shut before she came out. She avoided looking at the easel or the fireplace, and the spicy aroma of the chili made her stomach do a little flip-flop.

"Well, this day sure ended up sucking," she muttered, trying to cling to her sense of humor but failing. She angrily swiped at a tear and then sniffed loudly. She reminded herself that she barely knew Jesse Marshall, but then again, it sure didn't feel that way and she just couldn't wrap her brain around never seeing him again. In a very short amount of time they had managed to have such an intense connection on so many different levels, and yet Jesse didn't seem to have a problem heading to the beach and right out of her life.

Claire flipped on the light and then flopped down onto the bed. She stared up at the ceiling and wondered what to do while dreaded tears leaked out of her eyes. If this really were a Hallmark movie, at the last minute she would chase him down at the airport. Or better yet be sitting on the beach waiting for him when he arrived . . . "Where? I don't even know where he's going, and maybe he wants to keep it that way."

Don't be that girl, she thought. With an angry groan she pushed up to a sitting position and shoved her hair out of her eyes. "Get your sorry-ass self under control!" she muttered, and was thinking about that soak in the tub that she had lied to Jesse about when her phone rang. *Mom?* she thought with a wince, and then dug in her purse and glanced at the caller display.

"Chloe," Claire said, relieved that it was her sister calling instead of her frantic mother.

"Where in the hell are you?"

Okay, maybe she wasn't relieved. "Whisper, Colorado."

"What?"

"Chloe, calm down."

"Calm down? I arrived at the train station a little while ago to pick you up, and all that arrived was your suitcases!"

"Have you told Mom and Dad?"

"No! But I was very close to calling the police! Claire!

Dear God, my heart is hammering out of my chest! If you hadn't answered . . ."

"Chloe, I'm sorry. I forgot that I had asked you to pick me up."

"And you apparently forgot how to use a cell phone! What in the world is going on?"

"You have to promise not to say anything to anyone about this."

"Claire!"

"Promise, Chloe. You cannot blab this to a soul!"

"Are you in trouble?"

Claire snorted. "No! I'm the good one. You're the trouble-maker, remember?"

"Blah, blah, blah. Now spill."

"I'm serious."

"You're never serious."

"I am this time," she insisted, and when her voice cracked, her sister finally remained quiet.

"Oh, Sis, tell me what's going on. I promise not to leak a word to anyone."

"Not even your current dude?"

"I don't have a current dude."

"But what about—"

"Stop! Just tell me why you're in Whisper, Wyoming."

"Colorado."

"Whatever!"

Claire knew she had stalled long enough. "I missed the train."

"What!" Chloe shrieked.

"I was shopping," she explained.

"Oh," Chloe commented in a lower tone and with a bit more understanding. Shopping was in her blood also. "Go on."

"I am going to tell you everything because I want your advice. Try not to interject too much and just listen, okay?"

"I won't," Chloe promised even though she was the queen of interrupters.

Claire settled back against the pillows. She started with the Santa statue and ended with the mug of tea, leaving out the details of their lovemaking but letting Chloe know that she had been intimate with a man she barely knew . . . but that it still somehow seemed a healing process that they both needed.

"Claire, you can't let Jesse slip through your fingers. This is like a holiday love story. Hallmark . . . no, wait, Fa-la-la-la Lifetime. Those are steamier."

Claire laughed without real humor. "More like a Nicholas Sparks novel . . . no happy ending."

"But, Claire, you're in charge of this ending."

Claire closed her eyes and blew out a sigh. "If only it were that easy. We live so far away from each other and have totally different lifestyles. This is silly. I need to just give it up."

"What, people don't need their hair cut in . . . where are you again?"

"Whisper."

"Why?"

"No, that's where I'm at."

"Gotcha." Chloe laughed.

Claire smiled in spite of herself. "I miss you. How could I ever move away from my family? My work? And why am I even talking about this? He made it clear that this was just a holiday fling."

"Duh, because he's as scared and confused as you are."

"Don't ever say 'duh' again."

"Duh," Chloe repeated just as Claire knew she would. "Look, I love you, too, but if the man of my dreams comes along, I will live anywhere and you'll just have to visit. And you've always disliked the stress of a high-end salon. What you've really enjoyed about cutting hair is interacting with the people. And you sound as if you love the cabin."

"It's all a moot point."

"You don't know that for sure. I just want to point out that this has the potential to work if you give it a chance."

"No . . . seriously we've both been watching too many holiday movies. Listen, thanks for letting me bend your ear. Please let Mom and Dad know I'm stuck here. Tell them I have bad cell reception. I don't have the energy to talk to them right now and I know I'll start crying and then Mom will start crying and Dad will have a mess on his hands."

"I'll take care of it, sweetie. Call me if anything changes, okay?"

"I will, and thanks again. I love you."

"Me, too."

Claire ended up taking a long, hot, steamy bath after all. When she was toweling dry, she noticed several pink abrasions on her skin from Jesse's stubble. She closed her eyes and felt a hot shiver at the memory but then pushed it aside and slipped beneath the covers. She felt a bit hungry but heard movement downstairs as if he was moving things around . . . probably packing, and so she opted to stay upstairs and after a few moments fell fast asleep.

Chapter Eleven

*O*h, it just wasn't fair. Claire had dreamed about Jesse off and on all night long, and this one was so realistic that she could actually feel his smooth skin and the cozy warmth of his body. In fact, she could even smell his woodsy, spicy scent. . . .

Oh boy . . .

No way . . .

Claire's heart hammered in her chest, and sure enough, when she opened her eyes a mere slit, she encountered wide shoulders and dark wavy hair. She had managed to hook one leg across his hips and one arm over his waist. She frowned while trying to figure out just how Jesse had ended up asleep next to her. She peeked beneath the covers. She was wearing his flannel shirt, and he was shirtless but in his sweatpants, and since there wasn't any eggnog involved, she would surely remember. . . .

Oh God. He shifted and her hand slipped lower, but she didn't want to move and wake him until she remembered how in the world he ended up in her bed! The last thing she recalled was talking to Chloe. Frowning, Claire eased up just a tiny bit to sneak a peek over his shoulder at the digital clock on the nightstand. It was ten o'clock! What about the train? Should she shake him awake?

Claire inhaled a deep breath and blinked in confusion when she smelled cinnamon, coffee . . . and *pine*? Oh . . . she caught her bottom lip between her teeth when she spotted several pine needles caught in Jesse's hair. Nothing was adding up, and when curiosity got the best of her, she whispered, "Jesse?"

He mumbled something and rolled to his back, causing the cover to slide. Her hand rested just beneath his belly button and she got an eyeful of his bare chest. Sexy dark stubble shaded his jaw, and damn if she didn't have the urge to lean in and kiss him.

"Jesse?" she repeated a little bit louder.

"Mm?"

"What time is the train leaving?"

"Eight," he mumbled.

"Um, it's after ten o'clock."

Claire fully expected him to open his eyes and sit up straight in alarm. But he turned *toward her* and slipped one arm around her waist, drawing her closer. "'So-kay," he mumbled again. "Go back to sleep."

"But I smell coffee. Who made coffee?"

"Elves."

"Jesse . . ."

"Anybody ever tell you that you talk too much?" He kissed her shoulder.

"Yeah, all the time. But—"

"You're not gonna let me sleep, are you?"

She shifted so she could look at him. "What's going on?"

He opened his eyes. "Come with me." He rolled from beneath the covers and held out his hand.

Claire sat up and slipped her hand into his. She was full of questions but didn't know where to begin, so she simply followed him out of the bedroom to the stairs. "Oh . . . *my*." She put her hand over her mouth while she gazed at a magnificent Christmas tree decorated from top to bottom. Fingers of sunshine sliced through the window and glinted off the ornaments. "Jesse . . ." She tore her gaze from the tree and looked at him. "It's breathtaking. You . . . you did this?"

He grinned. "I already told you. Elves. Little guys made all kinds of noise and kept me up all night."

Claire pressed her lips together and swallowed hard. "Oh, Jesse . . ." When she tried to blink back tears but failed, he cupped her cheeks in his hands and swiped the moisture away with the pads of his thumbs.

He looked at her and said, "Last night when I was clearing the road with my Bobcat, the thought of escaping to the beach suddenly held no appeal. For the first time since the loss of my parents, I suddenly wanted to celebrate Christmas." He paused to swallow and then said, "And I wanted to celebrate it with you." He leaned in and kissed her softly. "Claire, you've brought joy and laughter back into my life. I have no idea how we're going to make this work, but if you're willing, I want to give it a shot. What do you say?"

"Yes," she managed to answer, and smiled through the tears.

Jesse grinned. "Good, because the train has already departed, so you're stuck anyway."

"And you made sure of that?"

"Kinda."

She arched one eyebrow.

"Okay . . . yes." When Claire laughed, he tugged on her hand like an excited kid. "Come on. I have something for you." Claire followed him over to the tree. There was a package wrapped with her name on it. She put a hand to her chest when he handed it to her. "Open it."

With trembling fingers she fumbled with red ribbon tied around newspaper.

"Sorry, I didn't have any wrapping paper."

"Oh . . . ," she breathed when she revealed an exquisitely carved angel. "Jesse, she is absolutely beautiful."

He smiled and then shook his head. "I found her on my workbench when I went out to get the Bobcat. It's funny, because I thought I had sold all of them, and yet there she was. Her face haunted me while I started plowing the road, and before I knew it, I was chopping down a tree."

Claire was so overwhelmed with emotion that she couldn't speak.

"I remembered that you collected angels and I wanted you to have her."

"She is a treasure. Thank you." Claire carefully set the angel down and then gave Jesse a hug but then pulled back and said, "Ohmigosh. It's your birthday and Christmas Eve! And I don't have anything for you!"

Jesse picked up the discarded red ribbon and tied it around her neck. "I couldn't ask for anything more."

Hot for the Holidays

Susanna Carr

Chapter One

The silver tinsel looked as if it had been ravaged. One spot was crushed, another part stripped bare. A long stretch of the decorative string was twisted, the silver strips fanning out wildly. It was beyond repair.

Maybe no one would notice. Rachel grabbed for a tack from her desk. Once she pinned it back up, she could hide the damage with a few well-placed Christmas cards.

"Whoa, Rachel." She recognized her friend Nikki's voice at the doorway. "What happened to your cubicle?"

Shoot. So much for no one noticing. Rachel felt the unfamiliar heat sting her cheeks. Was she blushing? Terrific. She used to think she was physiologically incapable of showing embarrassment. The inability had come in handy many times over the years.

"It was a wild party last night," Rachel said, keeping her head low and her attention on the denuded tinsel so Nikki couldn't see her blush.

"The *office* Christmas party?" Nikki asked in disbelief. Rachel heard her friend step into her work space. "Were we at the same party?"

"Pretty sure," she muttered as she drove the thumbtack into the wall with more force than necessary.

"Really? Because the highlight of my night was getting stuck in the corner with the drunk copy machine guy."

"He's cute." Rachel took a step back and surveyed the repair job. "Did you get very far with him?"

"He talked nonstop about the best way to get copy toner out of clothes. His cuteness factor took a big hit," Nikki said. "Now, if he had plans of rolling around with me in copy toner, that would have been a different story."

"Agreed." Rachel stabbed a strategically placed Christmas card over the worst spot of tinsel.

"Why didn't you get me away? I looked for you."

Rachel turned around and faced her friend. Nikki was a short, voluptuous woman who loved to show off her curves in low-cut shirts and tight jeans. She made up for her lack of height with stiletto heels and by piling her long red hair on top of her head.

"Sorry about that. I got . . . distracted." *Well, that's one word for it*, she thought.

Nikki didn't say anything as her attention was drawn to Rachel's desk. "What happened to your chair?"

"Uh . . . nothing." She wanted to wince at the lame answer.

"It's totally destroyed." Nikki gave the wheels a kick and watched the lopsided piece of furniture sag. "It looks like there was an orgy in here. . . ."

All of Rachel's muscles locked. She knew there was no getting out of this. She watched Nikki's face with dread. She saw her friend's eyes flicker over the cubicle, indexing every damning piece of evidence.

Nikki's jaw dropped as her shoulders hunched. "Oh, my God!" she screeched excitedly. "Did you—?"

"Look around, Nikki." Rachel raised her hands as if she could stop her friend's thoughts. "This cubicle isn't big enough for an orgy."

"Rachel Bartlett, what were you doing last night?" Her voice dropped low as delight shone in her eyes. "More important, *who* were you doing it with?"

Rachel raised an eyebrow, trying to appear indifferent. She needed to deflect Nikki's probing questions. "You have an active imagination."

"Apparently it needs to be broadened." Nikki grabbed Rachel's arm and drew her close. "Come on, Rachel, don't hold back," she whispered. "You obviously didn't last night."

Rachel looked around, hoping no one could hear the conversation. Most of the work spaces were empty, as her coworkers were seemingly having difficulty dragging themselves to work after the late night. They obviously didn't have as much practice as she and Nikki did.

The closest person around was Chuck. She didn't have to worry about him. His gaze was focused on the computer screen, and his earbuds couldn't contain the marching band music blasting through his MP3 player.

Nikki's sharp inhale echoed as she followed Rachel's gaze. "You had sex with *Chuck*?"

"Oh, hell no." How could her friend think such a thing?

Then again, she was trying to date a different kind of guy. But that didn't necessarily mean she was going for odd or weird. She wanted a sweet and stable guy. Now, if only the nice guys weren't so afraid of her.

Nikki's shoulders slumped with relief. "Then who?"

Rachel carefully avoided eye contact. "Nikki, seriously. This is me you're talking to. I've given up my wild ways." *Give or take a relapse. Like the one last night.*

"Still?" Nikki looked like she wanted to shake some sense into her. "I was hoping that was a phase."

Rachel removed her arm from Nikki's grasp. "I like the new and improved me."

"We could debate on the improved," Nikki muttered, frowning at Rachel's tight ponytail, button-down shirt, baggy jeans, and chunky shoes. "You know, there's nothing wrong with a little cleavage, especially with the size of your—"

"Thanks, but I'm comfortable with what I'm wearing." Rachel wasn't going to apologize for the uninspired outfit. When Rachel first met Nikki in high school, everything they wore was skintight and barely there. She had fun testing the boundaries with her hemlines and necklines, but those days were over. Rachel had tossed out all her party clothes when Nikki encouraged her to apply for this job. The move was a chance to stop hitting rock bottom, and Rachel wanted to dress for success. Her wardrobe suited her new life in a quiet mountain town, and her new job as a graphic artist. She was getting used to the buttoned-up look, but Nikki still missed the old Rachel. "I need to get back to work."

"Yeah, fine." Nikki looked around the cubicle one last time. "So you didn't get lucky?"

She didn't want to lie to her friend, but she wasn't ready to reveal how badly she'd relapsed. Nikki would encourage it, and she needed to be stricter with herself more than ever. Rachel settled for a partial truth. "I came into work and found my cubicle looking like this."

"Bummer." Nikki tsked. "Why would they use your work space?"

Good question. "Geographic bad luck?"

"Hmm, that's possible." She tilted her head as she studied the bald patches on the tinsel. "Who do you think it was?"

Rachel shrugged. She wasn't going to make this worse by pointing any fingers. "It could be anyone."

"I bet it was Leah." Nikki looked over at the nearby empty cubicle. "She was all over Ben last night."

Rachel was about to disagree when she caught the faint sound of footsteps coming down the corridor. She knew that purposeful, confident stride anywhere.

"But then that new guy . . ."

Nikki's voice faded to nothing as Rachel's heart started to pound. The last time her heart pounded against her rib cage like this was two years ago. It was right before she got caught by the cops for skinny-dipping in a park fountain. Sadly, that event was not the most stupid moment of her life, but the fiasco, with a heavy fine, was a turning point and helped her get on the straight and narrow.

She recognized the pulse-tripping, heart-pounding, nerve-racking feelings. Caused by the one guy who could make her go wilder than she had imagined.

Her pulse gave a violent skip as Justin O'Rourke came into view. His head was tucked down as he stripped off his worn olive green jacket, revealing a navy blue merino wool sweater.

She hungrily stared at him, noticing everything from his short brown hair that looked like he had run his hands through it a few times this morning to the dark stubble covering his angular jaw. Her gaze skimmed the hard planes of his chest to his lean hips to the way his soft, faded jeans clung to his strong legs.

Justin pushed the sweater sleeves up, exposing an intricate dragon tattoo that curled along his right forearm. The colors were dark and muted, the fierce lines emphasizing the dragon's savagery, but Rachel always saw the beauty and power of the mythical beast.

Realizing that she was staring, Rachel made herself look away. Her gaze collided with Justin's. His light blue eyes were playful. Mischievous. This guy was a charmer. He could talk his way into bed and out of trouble.

"Hello, Rachel." His low and rough voice sent a tingling flutter down her spine. Only two words from him and her self-control was ready to splinter.

Rachel gritted her teeth. "Good morning, Justin." If he noticed how forced her greeting was, he didn't show it.

"Hey, Justin." Nikki motioned for him to come forward. "Get a load of Rachel's office."

Rachel winced. That was the last thing she wanted, but before she could come up with a reasonable excuse, Justin stepped inside the cubicle. She was immediately aware of the tight fit.

She stood next to him, so close that she felt his body heat. His scent distracted her. It was clean, masculine, and irresistible. She wanted to move closer. So close until they were pressing against each other.

"Wow," Justin said.

Rachel's head jerked up. She momentarily forgot about the state of her work space. She had to keep Justin from saying anything. "Nikki is under the impression someone had a wild night in my cubicle," she said in a rush.

Justin looked over at her with a lazy grin. "I'd say."

Rachel felt the blush zooming up her neck and flooding across her face. She glared at him. "She's trying to figure out who."

"Oh." Justin looked at Nikki. "That's easy."

Rachel went completely still. Her muscles froze with such intensity that she was surprised she didn't fall over. Her breath caught in her throat as her stomach gave a twist.

"Who is it?" Nikki asked excitedly. The woman always enjoyed a good gossip session.

"You see where that tinsel is worn off?" He pointed at the portion that Rachel had just tacked back up. "That could only happen from friction. Hot and sweaty friction."

Rachel blinked several times, but it didn't work. She couldn't get rid of the memory of when Justin took her against the wall. They had been naked, their skin flushed and damp, their lips clinging together as they gasped for their next breath. Her arms and legs were wrapped tightly around Justin as he drove into her, the cubicle wall shaking with each thrust.

"You're making that up," Nikki declared as she smacked him on the arm with her palm.

"I'm simply offering my expert opinion," Justin said. "You need to find someone who has rug burn on their back."

Rachel squirmed as her shoulder blades began to sting. She stopped the moment she saw Justin smile at her telltale move.

"And they probably have bruises on their legs from giving a lap dance on that." Justin pointed at the broken chair.

Rachel squeezed her sore legs together as heat flashed through her body. She had felt sexy and powerful as she mesmerized Justin with her moves. Christmas songs had pulsated from the party a floor below them, but she and Justin had found a sensual rhythm that kept them going long after the chair broke.

"I'm gonna have to disagree with you there," Nikki said. "It could have been *Cosmo*'s sex position of the day. Yesterday's was called the Joystick Joyride and—"

"So all you have to do is look for someone with rug burn and bruises," Rachel interrupted before Nikki gave a thorough description. "That's going to be difficult, since it's the dead of winter and everyone's covered up."

"That's true," Nikki said with great disappointment.

Justin suddenly crouched down and reached under her desk, his hand grazing Rachel's leg. She flinched and backed up.

"And"—Justin retrieved something small and pearly white—"the guilty party is missing this button."

Damn, she'd missed that. Rachel curled her hands into fists. She wasn't going to snatch it away. No matter how much she wanted to.

Justin stood to his full height as he tossed the button in his hand. Rachel's head bobbed up and down as she focused on the pearl. "Probably happened while they were ripping each other's clothes off."

Rachel tugged at her shirt collar as she remembered brazenly tearing off her ivory lace blouse and offering herself to Justin. But her wanton behavior had hit a new level when she clawed off Justin's clothes.

Nikki studied the pearl button in Justin's hand. "Wow, you're good."

"So I've been told." Justin gave a sidelong look in Rachel's direction. "Repeatedly."

Rachel closed her eyes and prayed for patience. She knew it was probably dangerous to close her eyes whenever Justin was around, but she didn't think she could handle much more.

The phone rang, and Rachel yelped. Her eyes shot open and she wildly reached for the phone. "Sorry, I have to take this."

"No problem," Nikki said as she hooked her arm with Justin's. "So, Justin, I didn't see you at the Christmas party."

Rachel's hand stopped midway as she reached for the phone.

"How could you see me?" Justin asked. "You always had a group of guys surrounding you."

"True," Nikki said with a laugh.

Rachel exhaled with relief. Justin wasn't going to slip. He knew how to dance around the truth. That would usually worry her, but right now it was an asset.

No one would find out about her mistake through Justin, Rachel decided as she grabbed the phone. He would be discreet, and she would keep this dirty little secret to herself. She was confident of this until she saw Justin pocketing the pearl button.

She wanted to get that souvenir of her relapse back. Throw it away, give Justin the usual it-was-a-mistake-never-to-be-repeated speech, and then she could act like it never happened. She needed to retrieve the button. Today.

Justin wondered how long it would take Rachel to approach him. Their cubicles were across from each other, but she seemed unusually busy today, flitting from one meeting to another. She didn't stay at her desk for more than a minute. He kept his distance, knowing Rachel had to come to him.

Justin bet himself that Rachel would show up under the guise of a work project at the end of business today when no one was around. He knew she wanted to say something this morning. She was almost vibrating with suppressed nervousness.

But if there was one thing he'd learned about Rachel since she started working at the studio almost a year ago, it was that she was private. He suspected she had a wild past, based on the amazing time they had together, but there were no rumors about her. In fact, no one had anything to say about her. Nikki probably could, but she was uncharacteristically silent on the matter.

Of course, one had to work very hard to be scandalous in this quiet town. The only reason a sexy woman such as Rachel would pick a remote town like this was that it offered little temptation. If Rachel indeed was as wild as he expected, why would she move here? Why not to some big, bad city? It was this drastic measure and her obvious self-discipline that intrigued Justin even more.

It was a surprise when Rachel dropped by after three o'clock. He looked up when he heard a soft, hesitant knock against the wall of his cubicle.

"Rachel, it's a pleasure to see you." Justin leaned back in his chair and laced his fingers together. "Always."

And it was. Rachel Bartlett was a striking beauty. Her long black hair was contained in a tight ponytail. He preferred it falling in waves around her face like it had the night before, but this style allowed him to see every nuance of her expressive face.

As far as he could tell, she wore no makeup. Her lips were pale, pink, and pouty, and there was a sprinkle of freckles over her high cheekbones. She was trying to look proper and innocent, but nothing could hide Rachel Bartlett's wild nature.

Justin decided it was probably because of her large, dark blue eyes. She used them to great effect with a sultry side glance or a bold stare. And when she looked up from beneath the long, dark lashes, the mix of vulnerability and vixen made his head spin and his body temperature rise.

"I wanted to thank you," she said quietly. Her arms were crossed tightly against her chest and she looked around to see if they had an audience.

"I should be thanking you."

Rachel pressed her lips together with impatience. "I meant for not telling Nikki."

His eyes narrowed. "Did you think I would?"

She paused as if she was weighing her words. "You aren't easy to predict."

He took that as a compliment. "I don't kiss and tell. But I'm happy to discuss what I really do after I kiss. Or I could just show you." He rose from his seat. "Let's say dinner tonight."

"Dinner?" She couldn't hide her surprise. Or her panic.

"Despite all evidence, I'm not a barbarian." He took a step toward her and saw how she backed up against the wall. "I like to date a woman. Take her somewhere nice. Definitely out to dinner. It helps with the stamina for later."

Rachel didn't crack a smile. "Listen, Justin. About last night."

He hesitated as he heard that tone in her voice. Yep. He'd played it all wrong. It was time to try a new tactic.

"I don't know what got into me," she said. "I'm not like that."

He took another step until he was standing in front of her, almost touching. "Yes, you are."

She did a double take. "What?"

"I don't know who you think you're fooling with your shirts buttoned up to your neck"—he flicked his fingertip against the starched collar—"and your hair pulled back tight." He wrapped his finger along the curl of her soft hair. "You're trying to act like a lady, but you're—"

"Okay, that's enough." She tried to look away, but he held her in place with a sharp tug of her ponytail. Annoyance flared in her eyes, and he was tempted to give another pull. "And you don't know what you're talking about."

"I'm surprised I didn't find a tattoo on you last night. You seem the type." He smiled when she gave a guilty start. Hmm . . . interesting. Either she had considered getting a tattoo or she'd had one removed.

She unwound her hair from his finger and tucked it behind her back so he couldn't reach it. "It sounds like you don't know me very well."

He flattened his hand on the wall by her head and leaned in closer. "I'm working on it," he confessed in a whisper.

Rachel seemed to take his promise as a threat. She thrust her chin out and squared her shoulders back. "As I was saying, I apologize for last night and I promise I'll keep my hands to myself from now on."

"If you insist," he said, focusing on her pink lips. "What about your mouth? I enjoyed—"

Rachel put her hands up. "Okay, let me be blunt. Having sex with you was a mistake."

He knew she was leading up to that, but it still hurt. He refused to show it, though. "Aw, come on, Rachel. I was going to go with 'a surprise.' Maybe even 'an enlightening experience.' But not 'a mistake.'"

She looked down at the floor. "I apologize for my behavior," she said stiffly, "and I can guarantee that it will never happen again."

He didn't want to hear that. He had visions of how they would spend the next few weeks together. It had a lot to do with her hands and mouth and his bed.

But he knew when to retreat. If he kept on pushing, she'd

run a mile in the other direction. "Okay," he said as he took a step back. "If that's what you want."

"It is." She looked at him from underneath her lashes. He got the feeling she was a little suspicious of his immediate retreat. "I also want my button."

Justin tilted his head. Did he hear that right? "Your button?"

She held her hand out. "The one you took from my cubicle. I want it back."

He frowned. "Okay." He retrieved the pearl button from his jeans pocket and dropped it in her palm. She pulled her hand back before he could grab it. The woman could predict his moves. He needed to remember that. "Anything else?"

"Yes. I would really appreciate it if you forgot about the whole incident."

"Sure. Consider it done." He could tell that his easy acceptance surprised her. Good. Why should he be the only one off balance?

She turned to leave. "But just one more thing," he said, stopping her. "What caused all this?"

She kept her gaze on the exit. "I don't know."

"You can't blame it on the champagne." He knew from the taste of her mouth that she hadn't drunk any alcohol.

"It doesn't matter."

It doesn't matter? How could she say that? "Yeah, it does. Otherwise how do you know it won't happen again?"

She glanced over her shoulder, her eyes bright with determination. "Because I won't let it."

Justin watched her walk away, her movements tight and

her arms protectively close to her body. He exhaled slowly and rubbed his hands through his hair. She wouldn't let it happen again? Huh. That might be a problem because he was going to do everything in his power to make it happen again . . . and again.

Chapter Two

Six more days until Christmas, Rachel reminded herself as she stood in the break room on Monday morning, staring out the window. She had so much to do, but instead she was studying the dark green fir trees, heavy with snow, standing tall against the gusts of wind. Rachel wrapped her hands around the hot coffee mug and hunched deeper into her sweater as she watched the big snowflakes drifting down and coating the cars in the parking lot.

"You're hugging that coffee mug a little tight," Leah said as she walked into the break room.

Rachel gave a little start. She hadn't heard Leah clomping down the hall in her heavy boots. Rachel felt like she was in a fog and nothing she did would lift it.

It'd been that way since the office Christmas party. She'd thought that being away from the office would give her some breathing room, some perspective. Quite the opposite. She felt the pull to be with Justin even stronger.

Rachel also found herself staring off into space at the most inconvenient times. But the nights were the worst. She tossed and turned in her bed, aching for Justin's touch.

"Are you feeling all right?" Leah asked.

"Not much sleep," Rachel said hoarsely, her lips against the rim of her mug as she took a bracing sip of coffee. She needed to snap out of this. She had done so well for the past two years. No chaos, no drama. It should be second nature to slip back into her structured life, but she didn't know how. Worse, she didn't know if she wanted to.

That worried her. No, Rachel thought as a shiver ran down her spine, it scared the hell out of her.

"I know," Leah said as she poured herself a cup of coffee. "There's so much to do before Christmas. I'm so glad this company closes for the last week of the year. It makes my life easier. Don't you agree, Justin?"

Rachel's body went into full alert at the sound of his name. She turned her head sharply just in time to see Justin walking to the coffee machine.

Her pulse skipped a beat as she stared at his face. She couldn't get enough of the sharp angles and harsh features. His stubble had rasped against her soft skin and she flushed from the memory. Rachel's gaze skimmed his black hoodie and dark jeans, and she remembered the lean, muscular body underneath.

"What's that?" Justin asked as he poured coffee in his mug.

"Justin isn't much into celebrating holidays," Rachel explained to Leah.

The other woman gave Justin a strange look. "Is that true?"

"How did you know that, Rachel?" Justin hid his surprise with a comical raise of his eyebrows. "You've been keeping an eye on me. I'm touched."

Rachel wrinkled her nose at his teasing. She wished she had kept quiet about her observation. "I thought it was obvious. You weren't at the Christmas party even though it's mandatory participation." That would divert Leah's attention to Justin and away from her conspicuous slip.

"I had some work to do," Justin explained as he walked to her. "You didn't stay at the Christmas party. Why was that?"

Rachel glared at him.

Nikki walked in, carrying a decorative plate overloaded with gingerbread cookies. "Another gift from one of those hot-shot computer companies we work with," Nikki announced. "Eat up."

The scent of ginger and cinnamon wafted over Rachel. She froze, her heart lurching, as the memories collided. She stared at Justin's throat, remembering the spicy tang of his aftershave when she had licked his warm skin. The hit of cinnamon made her mouth go dry. She had inhaled that scent when she gasped for her next ragged breath as Justin bit and teased her nipples.

"Rachel?" Justin tilted his head to one side.

Her nipples tightened and stung at the sound of his rough voice. Heat washed over her and she leaned closer to him.

"She says she hasn't had much sleep."

She blinked at the sound of Leah's voice. Her memories spiraled and fragmented, crashing her back into the present.

Justin reached out and placed his hand on her forearm. His hand was big and warm. But his touch accelerated her disturbing response. She stared at Justin's mouth, swiping the tip of her tongue along her bottom lip before biting down.

Justin's look of concern morphed into one of knowing. The corner of his mouth tilted up as he slowly rubbed his thumb along the pulse point at her wrist. His smile deepened as he felt the erratic beat under his touch.

"Rachel?" Nikki's voice shattered the warm, sensuous cocoon. Rachel jumped and broke away from Justin, almost dropping her coffee mug.

"I'm sorry. What?" Her skin tingled and her breasts ached. Her clothes felt way too hot and tight.

"You want a cookie?" Nikki held up a gingerbread man. "The sugar might help."

She took another step back, clasping her mug as if it were the only thing keeping her grounded. "No, thank you. I don't want anything right now."

That wasn't true. She wanted Justin again. The sweet and spicy scent inspired so many fantasies. Right now she imagined pouring some sugar on Justin's naked body and licking her way down to . . .

"In fact, I think I'm off sugar totally," she declared, looking straight at Justin. "I'm never going to have it again."

Justin didn't look troubled by her rash statement. In fact, he looked amused. "Never say never."

Rachel whirled around, ignoring the quiet buzz of conversation in the break room, and marched off to the relative safety of her cubicle. Her body longed to be closer to Justin, but she didn't trust herself. The next few days were going to be tough, but she had to remain strong. If she stayed focused on her goal to follow her carefully organized life, these inconvenient longings would fade way. They had to.

Justin frowned as he watched Rachel sitting in her cubicle, speaking on the phone. Today she was trying to look prim with a pin-striped button-down shirt, a long straight black skirt, and black ballet slippers. Her attempt was backfiring, because he didn't want to keep his hands off. In fact, he wanted to strip the confining clothes from her body and reveal the luscious and sensual woman underneath.

Her outfit was a big sign of what he already knew. She was avoiding him again. He should have followed up on their run-in yesterday in the kitchen. He wouldn't make that mistake again.

No, if he was going to regret anything, it should be his behavior the night of the office party. He shouldn't have let loose to fulfill a few of his fantasies. He knew better.

He had wanted Rachel since the moment he saw her, but all his instincts told him to hold back and wait. It went against his nature, but Justin knew it was the only way he would get Rachel in his bed.

And he'd screwed up the first time Rachel came on to him. Worse, he'd gotten it into his head that he had been granted a gift for being such a good little boy this year. For the first time in a very long time, he had actually looked forward to the Christmas holidays. He had images of Rachel and him enjoying long, leisurely mornings and dark, cozy nights.

He should have known better than to dream. Justin leaned back in his chair and rubbed his hands over his face. Usually he hated the holidays—every one of them—from Valentine's Day to Fourth of July to Thanksgiving. His mother lived for the special occasions, spending and celebrating as if there were no tomorrow. His father would inevitably find the brand-new decorations and the bills. Holidays were a freaking minefield, and the aftermath lingered long after the decorations were put away.

It was easier to ignore the holidays. He didn't have any fond Christmas memories he wanted to continue. Sometimes he felt like an outsider, but he didn't mind being alone. Or so he thought.

He shouldn't have hoped for something wonderful this holiday season. Or thought this time it would be special. He had been better off viewing it as just another day. He made the mistake of believing he would get exactly what he wanted for Christmas: Rachel Bartlett.

Now the upcoming Christmas break stretched before him like a never-ending black hole. Justin rose from his seat, determined to fight off this dark, bitter feeling. He rushed out of his cubicle, immediately colliding into Rachel.

The impact had him staggering back as Rachel's papers flew out of her hand like snowfall. He reached out to steady her, but his arm curled around her waist. Suddenly her body was flush against his. So much for his attempt at chivalry, he thought. She had to lean into him if she didn't want to fall on her face.

Rachel stretched her hand out to steady herself. Her palm

flattened against his chocolate brown shirt. "Sorry," she said breathlessly.

But Rachel didn't move back immediately. Her stunned gaze went from his face to where her hand lay. Her pupils dilated as her thick black lashes fluttered. He watched, fascinated, as her cheeks turned pink and her lips parted.

Justin felt Rachel soften against him. Victory roared through his veins at her silent surrender. His heart began to thump heavily. He was intensely aware of the heat swirling around them, insulating them from the rest of the world.

Rachel seemed mesmerized by the rise and fall of his chest. She bunched her hand against his shirt, wrinkling it under her tense fingers. Her eyes drifted shut and he suddenly realized what she was thinking.

He was wearing the shirt he wore the night of the office party. She was remembering how she had torn it off him with an urgency that made him rock hard thinking about it. From the flush of her cheeks, he suspected she was reliving every wicked, delicious moment they'd shared.

Just when he was about to slide his hand down the curve of her ass and clasp her tightly against him, Rachel took a reluctant step back.

He felt a sense of loss immediately. Damn, he needed to move faster.

"Sorry," she repeated as she crouched down and frantically scooped the papers off the floor. She held them out at arm's length, not daring to move any closer. "These are for you."

He automatically took them, but she made sure he had no

opportunity to touch her. She wasn't taking any chances of setting off a chain of sensations that would draw them closer.

"Uh, Rachel?" But Rachel didn't look at him. The moment he took the papers, she hurried down the corridor as fast as her feet could take her.

He learned his lesson yesterday and he wasn't going to let her get away from him this time.

She had to get out of here. Rachel brushed a shaky hand against her hair. So what if the offices didn't close for another hour? This was an emergency. If anyone asked, she'd come up with a good lie about why she cut out early.

Rachel hurried to the bank of elevators and pushed the down button several times. She had to put as much distance as possible between herself and Justin. Her control was slipping, and it wouldn't take much more to throw caution to the wind and do something reckless.

She crossed her arms and looked around. There were colorful and festive decorations everywhere. Multicolor stars dangled from the ceiling, and a Christmas tree stood in the corner next to the bank of elevators. Everywhere she turned, there were wreaths and ornaments. Rachel focused all her attention on the black elevator doors, willing one of them to open.

At least she had hidden her disturbing reaction from Justin, Rachel thought as she impatiently tapped her toe. If he had an inkling of the lust coursing through her veins, of the wrenching longing, of how close she was to mounting him for a rough ride, she would be in big trouble.

But he would never know. She kept her head down these days, and she didn't attract attention. Not anymore. The more invisible she became, the safer she was. If only she were invisible to Justin. It was like the man had radar. No matter how quiet she tried to be, or how often she tried to blend into a group, Justin O'Rourke always knew where she was and what she was doing.

Rachel went still when she heard the familiar footsteps. She lifted her head like an animal sensing danger. As much as she wanted to look over her shoulder, she remained still. She knew Justin was walking to the elevators.

Maybe if she didn't move, he wouldn't notice her. . . . No, he would notice her. Maybe this time he'd leave her alone.

Justin stood right behind her, although there was plenty of space in front of the elevator. Rachel pressed her lips together as her muscles quivered. She would not give in to temptation. She was stronger than this need for him.

She inhaled the faint spice of his aftershave. He smelled so good. Rachel wavered, leaning toward Justin. She just wanted one taste.

She kept her tongue cleaved to the roof of her mouth. No tasting, no licking, no laving. Hadn't she learned her lesson the last time? Her tongue was going to remain firmly in her mouth at all times.

She closed her eyes and tried to gather the last of her self-control. Rachel tried not to inhale his scent or remember the taste of his skin. She wasn't going to look at him and imagine him naked. She refused to think about how powerful she had felt, how his muscles had flexed under her touch.

Wow, they really needed to turn down the thermostat in this building. No, wait, it was just her. And Justin. The heat rippled between them.

She didn't know if she should make a run for it or brave it out. If she ran, he would follow. If she stayed, he would touch her. Whatever she did, there would be only one outcome.

His gaze felt like a caress. There was something different about the way he looked at her. This time he was pursuing her. This time he wasn't going to hold back.

She sensed Justin's tension, and she felt him shift. Rachel knew he was going to pounce. Her skin tingled and her breath caught in her throat.

"Rachel." His voice was raw.

She turned and grabbed him by his shirt, creasing the fine cotton. She flattened her body against his, hip to hip, chest to chest.

She tilted her head to grind her mouth against his. She paused when she saw his face. No longer was he playing the charming flirt. The severe lines in his face were uncompromising. His eyes were the darkest blue. This wasn't just a game to him. He was serious in his pursuit, and he was determined to catch her. The unconcealed longing in his eyes matched what she felt.

The elevator bell chimed.

It took her a moment to understand the significance of the sound. *No, no, no.* Frustration pulsed through her. She wasn't going to pull away. She couldn't hold back anymore.

Rachel took a few quick backward steps and dragged Justin toward the Christmas tree. She heard the elevator doors open just as she felt the prickly branches against her back. She yanked Justin behind the tree and noticed he didn't resist.

Justin didn't question or make any remark. He held his arm up, protecting her face from the sparkly ornaments and pointy lights.

The fir branches scraped at her clothes and skin. Her hair caught on one of the ornaments. There was hardly any room between the tree and the corner, but Rachel didn't care. They were hidden. That was all that mattered.

She leaned against the wall and pulled Justin closer. His strength excited her, but it was his unexpected gentleness that made her shiver. He sank into her, cradling her face with his big hands and kissing her with a passion and intensity that made her ache.

She opened his shirt, pulling and tugging, but her fingers couldn't move fast enough. Tearing at the buttons, she slid her hands against his hard chest. Touching him was addictive. She sighed against his mouth and rubbed her hands along his compact muscles and warm skin.

Justin tilted his forehead against hers and looked deep into her eyes. "You don't know what you do to me," he said in a low, husky voice.

"Show me." She grabbed at his belt and unbuckled it with fumbling fingers.

He grabbed her hands. "Not here."

"Yes, here." She had held back for so many days, and she didn't think she could wait much longer. The desire inside her was so greedy. All-consuming. She wanted his cock filling and stretching her. She wanted Justin rutting against her until she screamed.

His chest rose and fell. His breathing was harsh and unsteady as he tried to hold back. She knew he wanted her in his bed, where they could explore each other's bodies for as long as they wanted. But she could tell that her urgency was an aphrodisiac to him. She wanted him so much she couldn't think straight, so much that nothing else around them mattered.

"I'll make it worth the wait," he promised.

"No, Justin." She grabbed the hem of her blouse. "Take me now." She pulled it over her head and tossed it on the ground. She arched her spine, offering herself to him. Her breasts felt full and heavy. Her nipples tightened and poked against the delicate lace. She was shamelessly aroused. She felt powerful and beautiful, knowing that Justin would not reject her offer.

He stared at her breasts, which threatened to spill from her thin lacy bra. The muscles in his cheek bunched as a ruddy color stained his high cheekbones. He slid the straps off her shoulders and peeled the bra from her curves.

Justin palmed one of her breasts. He didn't look down but kept eye contact with her. She wanted to look away, but couldn't. As he splayed his fingers and grazed her sensitive nipple with his palm, he watched everything she felt through her eyes.

He fondled her breasts, knowing exactly what she wanted without saying a word. He pinched her nipple just right, squeezing hard, knowing she wanted the bite of pain with the pleasure. She leaned her head back and gasped as she felt the sting go straight to her clit.

Suddenly his hands were under her skirt, his big hands skimming her bare thighs. He snagged her panties and discarded them with one simple move. Then he grabbed her waist and slid her up the wall to rest on his hips. The wall was smooth against her bare spine, but the feeling of being caught between a strong, muscular man and the unyielding corner heightened her senses. She was trapped and she didn't want to break free. She wanted Justin to overpower her. Overwhelm her.

Shoving her skirt up past her hips, he wedged himself intimately between her legs.

Rachel wrapped her legs tight around his waist, and the Christmas tree wobbled. The colored lights behind Justin were a blur to her. The bell ornaments jingled wildly as the fir needles poked against her knee.

Her naked breasts were almost level with Justin's mouth. He dipped his head and captured one tight nipple with his teeth. Rachel gasped as he drew her in his mouth. She bit her lip when she heard the elevator chime again. She heard footsteps nearby and knew she should stop this madness.

But she didn't. She couldn't. Not until she had Justin inside her and every inch of her was pulsating with satisfaction.

Justin slid his hand under her skirt again, seeking her clit. When his fingertips brushed against the swollen bud, slick with desire, he discovered she was already wet and ready for him. She should be ashamed at how willing she was, how fast she became aroused. Justin grunted his pleasure against her breast, and she almost felt proud of her body's quick response.

He glided his hand along the folds of her sex, and Rachel bucked against his hand. The tree shook. Justin dipped his finger in, and her flesh gripped him. He began to pump, teasing her with shallow thrusts. He licked and nibbled her breasts. He whispered against her hot skin, but she only caught fragments of his words. His tone was dark and reverent as if he was under her spell.

He curled his finger, and Rachel moaned as the pleasure sparkled and fizzed. She tilted her head back just as Justin covered her mouth with his. He gave another sexy curl of his finger and silenced Rachel's series of broken sighs and hitched gasps. The tree teetered as she climaxed against his hand.

Her body pulsed and jerked as the pleasure screamed through her. She heard the bells jingling and the rustle of denim as Justin unbuttoned his jeans and shoved them down. She gripped his shoulders and her legs clenched around his hips as he guided his cock against her moist sex. Justin surged into her with a shuddering sigh.

Rachel thought her heart stopped when he filled her to the hilt. Heat and pleasure flashed through Rachel as her body accommodated him. She struggled to breathe as Justin withdrew and plunged into her again.

The tree rocked with each deep thrust. The bells were pealing, the ornaments swaying, as Justin drove into her again and again. Rachel held on tight, burrowing her head against his neck, as he rode her relentlessly. She moved her hips to match his primitive rhythm as another climax took her by surprise. It flowed white-hot from her pelvis before flashing through her body, stealing her breath.

Her core squeezed Justin's cock. His rhythm faltered and he slammed into her with a ferocious strength, grunting in her ear until he found his release.

Rachel felt Justin head's loll against her shoulder, his body shaking from the vicious release. The bells slowly swayed to a standstill. She felt lethargic but satisfied. Out of breath, but vibrant.

"Has anyone seen Justin?"

She tensed when she heard the voice near the elevator bank. Who was that? How long had they been standing there?

Justin sighed against her shoulder, the warm air buffeting against her skin. "Maybe we should have gone somewhere else."

"Ssh."

"My place is more private," Justin whispered as he trailed soft kisses along her neck. "And comfortable."

"I can't find Justin." The female voice was right next to the tree. "I need him to sign off on this before I go on my vacation."

Rachel's breath caught in her throat as fear seized her chest. She couldn't place the voice. And whom was she talking to?

Justin arched his back and his cock withdrew slightly. Rachel dug her hand in his shoulder when she heard the jingle of a bell ornament. "Ssh," she said as softly as she could against his ear.

The elevator bell chimed, and Justin bucked against her. Rachel gasped as the pleasure sparked and fizzed just under her skin. She glared at him in silent warning, and his eyes twinkled back at her.

Rachel's pulse thudded in her ears as she waited to hear the people walk into the elevator. She was afraid to move even after the doors closed.

Justin thrust again. She swallowed back a groan and gripped

him hard with her legs. "We need to wait at least to the count of thirty before we move. Otherwise someone might hear us."

"Sounds like you've been in this situation before."

"Hush." She had found herself in one predicament after another in the past. Though never in a compromising situation behind a Christmas tree. That was new for her.

"If we get caught, we can always tell them the Christmas lights weren't working and we were looking for the plug," Justin suggested before he playfully nipped her ear.

Rachel clenched her teeth but didn't move away from his teasing touch. Every time she thought she was rebuilding her life, her reckless streak knocked it down in one fell swoop.

She had to stop doing this. And she would. Right after she climbed off Justin and got her clothes back on.

Justin thrust deeply inside her.

Rachel closed her eyes as she countered his thrust with the rock of her hips. *Any minute now . . .*

Rachel hurried out of the office building. It was already dark at five o'clock, but today she didn't care about the lack of sunlight. She just wanted to get far, far away from the office.

She ran down the salt-coated steps, hoping and praying that she didn't bump into Justin. She couldn't face him right now. Her breath frosted in the air and she shivered in her oversized coat while frantically looking for Nikki's car in the poorly lit parking lot.

The bright red hatchback was on the far end. Of course it was when she needed a quick getaway. Rachel marched for it, her feet skidding on patches of ice. She saw the plumes of exhaust and knew Nikki was already in the car, waiting for her.

Rachel got into the bitterly cold car and dumped her purse next to her seat. "I'm sorry I'm late," she said as she hunted for the seat belt.

Nikki didn't say anything. Rachel glanced at her friend. "Are you okay?"

Nikki cocked her head to one side and stared at Rachel. "There's tinsel in your hair."

Rachel froze and hurriedly smoothed her gloved hands along her ponytail. Sure enough, the prickly metal was caught in the rubber band.

"Strange. I don't know how that got there," she murmured. *I don't know how I missed it!*

Nikki shrugged and put the car in reverse. "Probably happened when you and Justin were fooling around."

Rachel's hands dropped into her lap and she stared openmouthed at her friend. "Okay, how did you know that?" A horrible thought occurred to her. She dipped her chin down and braced herself for the possibility. "Did you see us behind the Christmas tree?"

Nikki stepped on the brakes. "Behind the Christmas tree?" Her smile was wide and proud. "Tell me more. Which one? Is it still standing?"

Rachel pressed her fingertips against her forehead. She felt a headache coming on. "Forget I said anything. How did you know? I was so careful."

"Too careful," Nikki informed her as she left the parking space and shoved the car into drive. "I could tell by the way you guys *weren't* looking at each other. Don't worry. I haven't heard any rumors. Your secret is safe with me."

Rachel relaxed. "Thanks."

Nikki was silent for a moment and then slapped Rachel on the arm. "But why didn't you tell me? I gave you every opportunity."

Rachel covered her face with her hands. "Because I'm embarrassed." She had no willpower around the man.

"Why? You and Justin are a good thing. It's a reason to celebrate." Nikki thumped the steering wheel to punctuate her point. "What are you getting him for Christmas? I vote for handcuffs."

"Whoa. Whoa. Whoa." Rachel waved her hands to stop her friend's naughty Christmas list. "No celebrating. No presents. And definitely no handcuffs."

"Why not?" Nikki whined.

"Don't you get it? I slipped up. I had a major relapse. For two years I have walked the straight and narrow. No wild nights, no boyfriend drama, and no policemen knowing me on a first-name basis. I've kept a job, an apartment, and food in my refrigerator."

"Even more reason to celebrate."

"No. Because I feel like it could all fall apart any minute. When I'm with Justin—just looking at him, thinking about him—I forget everything." She weakly closed her eyes and rested her head on her seat. "All I want is him, and nothing else matters. If I keep this up, I'm going to be right back where I was. Staggering into work from an all-nighter, hooking up with one loser after another, and living on your couch again."

"I don't know what you're worried about," Nikki said as she concentrated on driving on the icy road. "Justin is nothing like the men in your past."

"That's true. He's worse." She didn't get this hot this fast for any guy.

"No way." Nikki gave her a quick look. "Worse than the guy who kept stealing from you?"

She gave that a thought and nodded her head. "Yep, Justin is worse than Vincent."

"Wow," Nikki said with a touch of concern. "I didn't think anyone could top him."

Rachel wiggled in her seat, uncomfortable with the notion that Justin was rock bottom on her list of men. "Vincent was a jerk, but he wasn't dangerous. Justin is different. I feel weak." She struggled to describe it. "I feel . . . crazy. I feel . . ."

"Alive?" Nikki suggested.

"Alive," Rachel repeated. She bit her bottom lip as she re-membered the warm, thick heat that flooded her body when Justin . . . Rachel abruptly sat up. "*No*, not alive. I feel out of control. It's like he's my kryptonite."

Nikki stopped at the red light and looked over at her. "Then you're in trouble, Superman, because Justin is here to stay. And you can't afford to quit your job when you haven't been there for a full year."

Her fun-loving friend made a practical point she should have thought of days ago. It was an indication of how far gone she was. "So what do I do?" Rachel asked. "I swear if I see him again, I'll rip his shirt off."

"You were doing just fine until the Christmas party," Nikki said as she watched the stoplight, waiting for it to turn green. "What happened?"

"I don't know." Rachel had been wondering the same thing. Where had it all gone wrong? "I was walking toward my cubicle to get my purse and he was putting a file on my desk. He said something, I shot him down, and the next thing you know, we're all over each other and tangled in the tinsel."

"Hmm, that doesn't give me much to go on," Nikki said as she continued to drive. "Who made the first move?"

Rachel cringed. "Me."

"Really?" Nikki drew the word out and wagged her eyebrows suggestively. "What happened right before you pounced?"

"I don't know. He was his usual flirty self. I don't know what made it different."

"Well, you better figure out before it happens again."

Rachel was surprised by Nikki's warning. "I thought you'd be ecstatic about these new developments."

"I am," she insisted, tucking her tongue in the corner of her mouth as she made a tricky turn. "But if the boss catches you having sex in the office, you're out of a job."

"Oh, right. I know that." She realized she hadn't given their tryst behind the tree much thought. "Ugh! See what Justin does to me?"

"And then you'll be back to square one."

She shuddered at the idea. She didn't want to go back to that stage again. It was ugly, painful, and scary.

"Here's my advice," Nikki said. "All you have to do is figure out what's triggering these sex cravings so you can control them and jump Justin after hours."

Rachel leaned back in her seat and sighed. "How about if I just don't jump Justin?"

"Well, that's one option." Nikki flashed a naughty smile and waggled her eyebrows again. "But what's the fun in that?"

Chapter Three

*R*achel hurried out of the store, her shopping bags banging against the doorframe and her legs. She was running behind on her Christmas to-do list and was taking the opportunity to find a few more presents during her lunch break.

In fact, she was trying to come up with a list of excuses to get out of the office. She'd do just about anything to steer clear of the building. Away from temptation. Away from Justin.

It really was bad luck that her cubicle was right across the corridor from Justin's. She was hyperaware of everything he did. Every hour she became more distracted. If this kept up, she was going to miss her project's deadline.

She walked across the courtyard of the open-air mall. Rachel was sure the setup was supposed to make her think of a quaint outdoor marketplace, but the climate in the mountains didn't always make shopping convenient. It snowed six months of the year, and rained the other six months. Most of those days she'd prefer to be inside instead of wrestling with the elements.

But having the open-air mall outdoors at Christmas kind of made it worth it. A light snow drifted on the brick sidewalks, and made the evergreen and red ribbons so much brighter. In the middle of the courtyard there was a gigantic fir tree decorated with gold ornaments and colorful lights, which reminded her of the magic and wonder of Christmas.

And what she did with Justin.

Rachel abruptly looked away. *Stop thinking about Christmas trees. Move away from the fir tree and don't look back. . . .*

She dipped her head and hurried out of the courtyard. She needed to get back to the office. She'd had plenty of time to get some fresh air and clear her head.

Rachel strode to the street corner, hearing the rhythmic bell chime. She looked up just in time to see Justin at the corner pouring a handful of change into a bright red charity bucket. Rachel rocked back on her heels. Justin hadn't seen her as he was talking to the bell chimer. She was very tempted to turn back and find a different route to the office.

Justin glanced up just when she was about to turn around. Great. This was what she got for hesitating. She braced herself and walked to him.

"Hi, Justin. Getting some last-minute shopping done?" she asked breezily. Or what she hoped was breezily. It was difficult to pull off when her pulse skittered.

"No way. You can't get me in the stores the week of Christmas."

Rachel pressed the button for the walk sign, unable to concentrate in Justin's proximity. The bell ringer wasn't helping much either. *Jingle . . . jingle . . . jingle . . .* There was no deviation from the monotonous rhythm.

"I love shopping the week of Christmas," Rachel told Justin. "It's all about the hunt. The challenge."

"Sounds like hell to me," Justin said as he stood beside her, his arm almost touching hers. "Which is why I do everything online."

Jingle . . . jingle . . . jingle . . . Rachel frowned. Why did that sound so familiar? Was it a song she'd heard before? "You don't know what you're missing."

"Believe me, I do. I spent most of my childhood in malls."

Jingle . . . jingle . . . jingle . . . Wow, that bell was really getting annoying. "Were you a store clerk?"

"My mother is a shopaholic. Christmastime was the worst."

"Ah." That could explain why he wasn't much into celebrating. He had seen the dark side of the season. *Jingle . . . jingle . . . jingle . . .* "But you got lots of presents, right?"

"More like a new Christmas theme each year. The worst was probably the pink Christmas." He shuddered from the memory. "Pink wreath and pink Christmas tree. Lots of Barbie and flamingo ornaments. Pink stockings and pink candy. I can't stand the taste of peppermint thanks to that Christmas."

Jingle . . . jingle . . . jingle . . . Rachel stiffened as she suddenly remembered where she'd heard the bell. It wasn't a song! It was the sound she heard when she was behind the Christmas tree with Justin!

"Uh, yeah." She squeezed her eyes shut as she tried to forget the shaking bell ornaments on the office Christmas tree. "I really can't picture an all-pink Christmas."

"Don't try, it will give you nightmares."

Jingle . . . jingle . . . jingle . . . Rachel lurched for the signal button and smacked it with her open palm. "What is wrong with this crosswalk?"

"It's always slow."

Jingle . . . jingle . . . jingle . . . The memories crashed and mingled in front of her eyes like a kaleidoscope. The scent of fresh evergreen and the salty taste of Justin's skin. The flash of red ribbon and the lust glazing in Justin's blue eyes. The shaking of the bell at every thrust, and Justin whispering hot, sexy words as he buried himself deep inside her.

Sweat trickled down her spine as she took a deep breath of cold air. *Bad move.* The scent of the evergreen decorations was powerful. She tried to take small, shallow breaths. *Oh, even worse.*

Jingle . . . jingle . . . jingle . . . Her breasts started to ache, her nipples tightening as she remembered Justin's big, rough fingers. Her hips twitched as the heat billowed inside her.

Jingle . . . jingle . . . jingle . . . She remembered exactly how Justin slammed his cock into her. At first it had been deep and measured. Until he lost control. And then he drove into her, fast and furious.

Rachel whimpered when her core clenched with need. She dropped her shopping bags as her knees buckled. But she didn't fall down. Justin had caught her by the arm.

"Rachel? What's wrong?"

Jingle . . . jingle . . . jingle . . .

Justin gathered her close. His face was right above her, his mouth a kiss away. His body wrapped around hers, his heat, his scent driving her over the edge. She clasped her hands on both sides of his face and slammed her mouth against his.

She pressed her fingertips against the stubble on his cheeks as she kissed him greedily. He tasted exactly as she remembered. Hot, masculine, and forbidden. She couldn't get enough, dipping her tongue past his lips.

Justin held her tightly against him. He drew her tongue deep into his mouth and sucked hard. Rachel gasped as she felt the pull straight to her sex. She rubbed her aching breasts against his chest, hating the barrier between them.

A car horn pierced through her sensual fog. Rachel jerked back and stared at Justin's face. His face was ruddy, his features taut, and his blue eyes clouded with desire.

Rachel swallowed hard and dropped her hands from his face. "I am so sorry." She wasn't sure what to say. Or how to explain what came over her. "I didn't mean to do that."

"I don't mind." He sounded composed, but he looked ruffled and undone. Slightly baffled and pleasantly surprised.

She took a step back and felt the resistance in Justin's arms before he reluctantly let go of her. Rachel bent down and grabbed her bags. "I'm really sorry."

"I'm not," he assured her.

She looked wildly at the street and saw the blinking red light for pedestrians. Rachel sprinted across the crosswalk and hoped Justin wouldn't follow.

So much for getting a clear head, she thought as she ran the rest of the way to the office. If anything, the shopping expedi-

tion made it worse. The bells, the evergreen trees, the decorations . . . everything Christmas.

Christmas. Rachel shuffled to a stop, huffing big puffs of
air. *It's all about Christmas!* Every time she slipped up, something
about the holidays triggered her relapse. *No . . . that can't be
right.* That was crazy. Or was it?

"Nikki?" Rachel whispered urgently an hour later as she
stepped into her friend's work space. "Nikki!"

Justin paused as he heard Rachel's confidential tone. He
sat alone in a nearby cubicle, going over Leah's work for their
project. Leah had left early for the day to start her vacation.
Now that he thought about it, this floor was so quiet it felt
abandoned. Rachel and Nikki probably thought they were
alone. He should let his presence be known.

"Nikki, guess what," she whispered. "I figured out why I
keep having sex with Justin!"

Or not. He was tempted to lean back into the chair, but he
didn't want to make a move or a sound. He discovered he was
holding his breath as he remained very, very still.

"Well?" Nikki asked. "What is it?"

"It's the holiday stuff!"

There was a pause after her dramatic announcement. Justin
frowned. Holiday stuff? What holiday stuff? Could she be a
little more specific so he could use it to his advantage?

"Uh"—Nikki dragged out the word—"repeat that again."

"Everything about the holidays is making me hot for
Justin."

Justin pressed his lips together hard and tried not to laugh.

Was she serious? It wasn't him? It was the freaking holiday? She was so wrong.

"That can't be."

"Think about it," Rachel said. "I jump him during the office party. I have my wicked way with him behind a Christmas tree."

That didn't have anything to do with the holidays, Justin decided. If they had been next to a closet, she would have dragged him in there.

"Coincidence," Nikki said. "You guys are coworkers and this place is crawling with decorations."

"All right, well how about this? I take a whiff of gingerbread and want to take him right then and there."

Justin smiled as he remembered that coffee break. The way she had looked at him made him feel irresistible. If only there hadn't been anyone else in that room.

"Okay, that is a little weird," Nikki said. "Gingerbread isn't usually considered an aphrodisiac."

"And then when I heard the jingling bells . . ." Rachel gave a deep sigh. "Well, let's not get into it."

"Jingling bells? You're hearing bells?" Nikki asked. "And you're conditioned to have sex when you hear bells?"

Justin shook his head. She thought that was why she kissed him? Not because she believed he was sexy, but because of the jingle bells? *Note to self: Wear a bell at all times.*

"No, the bells are Christmasy," Rachel explained, her voice thick with frustration. "Don't you get it?"

"What's the correlation between sex and Christmas?" Nikki asked. "And why Justin? Why not Chuck?"

Justin jerked his head up and glared at the wall. Hey, he was way better than Chuck! At least he'd like to think so.

"Okay, obviously I don't have all the answers," Rachel admitted. "But at least I've identified the problem, right?"

"Uh, right."

Uh, wrong. Christmas had nothing to do with it. It was more like she was flailing for excuses. She was scared at how much power her feelings for him had over her, Justin thought with a wicked smile.

"So the solution is easy," Rachel said, her voice high with relief. "All I need to do is make sure I'm always in a Christmas-free zone until the season is over."

Justin swallowed back a laugh and almost choked. Rachel Bartlett was in for a shock after the New Year. This sexual attraction wasn't going to fade that easily. He wouldn't let it.

"Good luck with that, Scrooge."

"I'm doing it for survival."

Justin frowned. He was forgetting one very important fact. It didn't matter how long this awareness, this need, lasted. Rachel didn't want this sexual attraction between them. Ouch.

Nikki scoffed. "And you can't survive wrapped naked around Justin?"

He always had liked Nikki.

"No, I can't," Rachel said. "Not if I want some peace of mind."

"So what are you going to do about it?"

"As of now," Rachel said in such a haughty tone Justin imagined her thrusting her chin up, "I'm going to go take down the decorations in my cubicle."

"Oh, yeah, that's going to make all the difference," Nikki muttered as he heard Rachel walking away. Nikki paused for a moment before calling out to her friend, "And peace of mind is overrated!"

Justin sat quietly, staring in the direction of Nikki's cubicle. Rachel didn't want to desire him. Real flattering.

He knew that Rachel was wrong. This fire between them had been building for almost a year. She jumped him at the office party not because it was the holidays but because she was relaxed and having a good time. She had let her guard down because she was tired of holding it up all the time.

She couldn't keep her hands off him then, and she still couldn't. She'd had one taste of how good they were together and wanted more. So much more that she couldn't think straight. He couldn't blame her for that.

But blaming it on the holidays? That was just crazy. But she seemed to believe it. Or she was grasping for the easiest, quickest solution. She wanted to believe that this was temporary insanity. That she could get it out of her system by tearing down a few decorations.

Justin leaned back in the chair and rolled the problem around in his mind. It didn't matter what was true or what was correct. Rachel believed the holidays were seducing her to have sex with him. Fine. If that was what it took to disarm Rachel, he'd use it. He'd take all the help he could get, even if it meant making the Christmas decorations a permanent fixture of the decor.

And if it meant he had to embrace the holidays, then he'd do it. Now that he knew what turned Rachel on, he would put aside the plans for roses, champagne, and candlelit dinner. All he had to do was sing a few carols, spread a little holiday cheer, and wear those Christmas sweaters his mother insisted on sending every year.

But what would he do once Christmas was over? He didn't want this to end once December 26 arrived. Justin closed his eyes and sighed. He would have to come up with something, but for now he would make this office the North Pole if it meant getting Rachel back into his arms, where she belonged.

Justin was lying in wait for her the next day. He didn't pounce the moment Rachel stepped into the office. She would be with Nikki, who always gave her a ride to work. He needed Rachel to be alone with as few exits as possible.

He waited in the break room when she usually took her coffee break. She was running late, and he was almost going to give up. Standing by the windows and drinking a rapidly cooling cup of coffee, looking out over the snow-laden trees, he heard her walking toward the break room.

Anticipation flooded his bloodstream. He always felt like this when he knew he was going to see Rachel. She was fun, challenging, and sexy as hell. Rachel managed to fascinate and frustrate him like no other woman.

He turned just as she stepped into the room. She looked simply gorgeous wearing a gray turtleneck sweater, jeans, and black knee-high boots. Today she didn't hide her slender curves underneath layers or bulky clothes.

Rachel was startled to see him and her eyes zeroed in on his chest. She came to an abrupt stop, her hands up, almost in a gesture of surrender, as she stared at him. Her mouth opened and closed, and nothing but a squeak came out of her mouth.

"Morning, Rachel," he said as he casually took another sip of coffee.

"Oh, dear God," she finally said, clapping her hand over her mouth. "What are you wearing?"

He frowned as if he hadn't expected the question. "A sweater?"

She stared at him. Justin couldn't blame her. The blinding red holiday sweater was a gaudy eyesore. "Are those . . . ?"

"Flying reindeer," he answered for her. He suspected they were flying, but he could be wrong. The sweater looked like it had been knit by drunken elves.

Rachel dropped her hand, and he saw her fingers curl up into a fist. She took a step closer to him. He felt the aggression shimmering off her, but it wasn't the kind he was hoping for.

"What?"

"Interesting choice." Rachel eyed him suspiciously.

"It is the season, you know." He hid his smile as he took a hurried sip of his coffee.

"You don't do the holidays." She gave another quick glance at the sweater and then glared at him. "Where'd you get it?"

"My mom buys me one every year." Sad, but true.

"Does she live nearby?" she asked, trying her best not to look at the reindeer. "Is she coming over for lunch?"

"God, I hope not."

Rachel's jaw shifted to one side as she visibly controlled her temper. "Then why, of all days, are you wearing this?"

He shrugged and tried for an innocent expression.

Rachel gasped and took a step back. She pointed a finger straight at his chest. "You know!"

He was never good at being innocent, but it didn't stop him from trying. "Know what?"

She wagged her finger under his nose. "Don't try that with me, Justin. How did you find out?"

He decided to drop the innocent act and go for clueless. He was better at that. "You're speaking in code."

Rachel put her hands on her hips. "Take off the sweater."

"Are you coming on to me?" he asked as he set down his coffee mug.

"I'm serious, Justin." She motioned for him to whip off the offending clothing. "Take it off now."

"The sweater is that sexy to you?" He sang the drumroll for a stripper and grabbed the hem of his sweater. As he bunched it up and revealed his bare abdomen, Rachel's eyes widened. He slowly pulled it up farther, showing off the defined muscles of his chest that she couldn't get enough of the night of the office party.

Rachel blinked as if she were pulling herself out of a trance. "No, forget what I said." She held her hands out. "Put it back on, put it back on."

"Are you sure?"

She nodded frantically.

"All right." He continued humming the stripper song as he slowly smoothed the sweater back in place, all the while watching her response.

Rachel wasn't as upset as she appeared. She was trying to

hide her arousal, but it wasn't going to work. Her face was too expressive. He saw how her eyes dilated when she saw his naked chest. She was also breathing unevenly. Her cheeks were flushed and that thin turtleneck couldn't conceal her tight nipples.

As if Rachel could sense his gaze, she crossed her arms over her chest. "I'm surprised you didn't go all out. Put on reindeer antlers! Wear Rudolph's blinking red nose!"

"I think the sweater is all that I need." He patted the neon red monstrosity, pleased that he hadn't donated it to charity yet.

She leaned forward and her glare deepened. "You are shameless."

"True," he said as he retrieved his coffee mug. "But that can be a good thing."

She shook her head and tossed her hands in the air as if she couldn't deal with him. "I have to get out of here." She turned on her heel and started to walk away.

Justin started whistling "Jingle Bells."

Rachel's body went still with tension. Or was it indecision? Was she going to turn around and jump him? He hit a high, piercing note as anticipation squeezed his chest.

She squared her shoulders back and marched away.

Justin continued to whistle the song as she disappeared from his view. She was going to crack, he decided as he left the break room and followed her down the corridor to his cubicle. She started to walk faster. Once she got to her desk, she grabbed her headphones and slammed them onto her ears.

Very, very soon. Justin strolled into his cubicle and sat down with a sense of impending victory. All he had to do was keep this up and Rachel Bartlett would be in his bed by Christmas morning.

There was only one more workday before the Christmas break, but she wasn't going to last, Rachel decided as she hunted for Nikki through the maze of cubicles. If she just looked at Justin, she would drag him to the nearest bed—no, the nearest horizontal surface—and have her way with him.

Rachel saw Nikki step out of the women's restroom and ran after her. "Nikki, I need a favor."

"Name it."

Rachel grabbed her friend by the wrist and dragged her back into the bathroom. The movement took Nikki by surprise and she skidded on the tile floors with her stiletto heels.

"What's the rush?" Nikki asked as she pulled away from Rachel and regained her balance.

"Wait." Rachel gave a cursory look under the stalls to see if anyone was around.

"I'm sure Justin isn't here," Nikki said, placing her hands on her hips.

"I know that." Although she wouldn't put it past him. "I'm just checking to see if we're alone."

"Really?" Nikki leaned against the wall. "How very odd. What's the favor?"

"I need a ride to the airport."

"Now?" Nikki checked her watch.

"Tomorrow. I have to get out of this place," she explained in a low voice. "It's time for a full detox."

"Honey, I'm sorry. I can't make it. I'm going out of town to spend Christmas with my parents."

Right. She forgot about that. Rachel puffed her cheeks and gave an exasperated sigh. "Know anyone who could give me a lift?"

"I'll ask Danny," she suggested, her on-again, mostly off-again boyfriend. "He'll do it."

"Thanks." Rachel was already feeling her tense muscles relaxing. This was all going to work out.

"What brought this on?"

Rachel wasn't sure how to say it without sounding insane. How did one explain that she needed to leave town because of a sweater? "Have you seen Justin today?"

"No." Nikki frowned. "Why?"

"He's wearing a Christmas sweater and whistling carols," she answered as calmly as she could.

Nikki's mouth fell open and her eyes widened with alarm. "He knows!" she whispered fiercely.

Rachel was glad Nikki said that. It was good to know she wasn't completely paranoid. "He acts like he doesn't, but there's no other explanation."

Nikki ran her fingers through her hair and looked at the bathroom door. "How did he find out?"

"That doesn't matter." Rachel waved her hands in the air, dismissing the question. "What matters is that I need a complete Christmas detox. I'm going somewhere hot for the holidays. Somewhere that doesn't look like a Thomas Kinkade painting. Somewhere that doesn't have snow or Christmas sweaters or smell like gingerbread." Or that included Justin.

"Where is that? Hawaii? Florida? Las Vegas?"

"I don't have a plane ticket yet," Rachel admitted. It wasn't like the new and improved her to do something impulsive, but this was an emergency. "I'll just go to the airport and get the first plane out of here."

"Oh, that sounds like the Rachel Bartlett I used to know." Nikki clasped her by the shoulders and peered into her eyes. "I knew the old you was in there somewhere."

Rachel shrugged her off. "Don't say that."

"Fine." Nikki sighed. "What if going away doesn't work?"

"It worked the last time I did a detox." She had gone cold turkey and went from a wild party girl to a woman with a good future ahead of her. Sure, there had been a few withdrawal symptoms in the beginning, but she made it through.

"It worked because you didn't go back to your old lifestyle," Nikki argued. "Once you return from your Christmas vacation—"

"Christmas detox."

"—you're still going to see Justin."

"Yes, but I will have broken the addiction by then," Rachel explained. "I'll be stronger, and it won't be Christmas."

Nikki rolled her eyes and groaned. "There are so many holes in your theory, I don't even know where to start."

"You can start by calling Danny." She guided Nikki out of the bathroom with a confident spring in her step. By this time tomorrow she would be far, far away from Christmas and Justin. "Don't worry, this is all going to work. I can feel it."

Chapter Four

$\mathcal{R}$achel checked the stove again and turned off all the lights. Danny should be here any minute to take her to the airport. She hated not having a car and depending on friends and friends of friends. One day she'd have her own car, Rachel vowed, but first she had to get her life back on track.

She walked into the sitting area and felt a pinch of disappointment. Her apartment was small with very little furniture, but the miniature Christmas tree and deep red poinsettias had made the place bright and cheerful. She had taken down the decorations last night and packed them away. For some reason it made her place look smaller.

It was probably because of the curtains, she decided. They were drawn tight to keep the neighborhood Christmas lights out of sight. That was why her apartment looked dark and uninviting.

Don't think about it, Rachel warned herself as she started to pace. One more hour and she'd be somewhere hot, sunny, and exotic. A place where there was no snow and no Justin. This was a major detox. She was using all her savings, but it was necessary. Once she got Justin out of her system, she could get back to her quiet, safe life.

She heard a car pull up to her apartment complex, the tires crunching in the snow. That had to be Danny. Grabbing her weekend bag of bikinis, shorts, and tank tops, Rachel stepped out of her apartment, locked the door, and headed outside.

The cold air stung as the snowflakes swirled around her. She squinted as the bright white blanket of snow reflected the sun. Rachel frowned when she saw the silver sports sedan parked at the curb. The car teased Rachel's memory. She'd seen one just like that in the office parking lot. It looked a lot like . . .

Rachel stopped to a halt as Justin stepped out of the driver's side. *Yep, a lot like Justin's car.*

He was wearing his olive green coat, a charcoal gray ribbed sweater, battered jeans, and boots, so there was nothing Christmasy about him. She should be thankful, but she was too busy fighting off the need to walk up to Justin and greet him with a deep kiss. Why did she long to curl up against his warmth and slide her hands under his sweater when he wasn't wearing anything remotely festive?

It was a sign that she was getting out of town in the nick of time. It was weird that he showed up right when she was leaving. *This is simply a coincidence*, Rachel thought as she took a deep breath to combat the excitement building up inside her. Justin was here for another tenant. Or . . . her mind couldn't come up with another reason. She just knew he wasn't here for her. He better not be.

"Hey, Justin," she greeted him cautiously. Dread started to twist her stomach as she watched him go to the passenger-side door. "What are you doing here?"

"Danny can't make it," he said as he held the door open, "so he asked if I could drop you off at the airport."

Rachel wasn't aware that Justin knew Danny. It was a small town, but not *that* small. What were the odds? "You don't have to. I can ask—"

"Get in the car, Rachel," Justin said firmly. He saw how she bristled at his tone. She still didn't move.

Maybe this was a mistake, Justin thought as he studied her. She was smart not to go anywhere near him. Not after the sweater stunt.

Rachel was still hesitating and actually glanced back at the safety of her apartment. That didn't bode well for him. He tried to decode her body language, but she was bundled up in a bright red woolen hat and striped scarf. Her hands were stuffed into red mittens and her black coat was about a size too big. Rachel's baggy jeans and thick boots hid the rest of her body.

The only things he could see were her eyes and nose. The nose was pink from the cold, and her eyes were glittery with anger.

Yeah, it probably wasn't his best idea to take the job over from Danny. All this time Justin thought it had been pure luck that he had gone to the corner bar and heard Danny complain about driving Rachel to the airport. Justin hadn't even known Rachel was making a run for it. He called off work and wanted to talk Rachel into making other plans for Christmas. The kind that included him.

"What happened to Danny?"

"Too much eggnog." That was the story he and Danny decided on. Justin wanted to make the drive, and Danny didn't want Nikki to know he bailed. "The guy had a major hangover and he is in no state to drive."

"Oh." She stared at his car. He knew his presence unsettled her. He needed to keep her moving before she tossed up any more obstacles.

"It's getting cold," Justin prompted Rachel. She walked to the car with great reluctance. As she sat down in the passenger seat, he could practically feel her mind whirling, looking for an excuse to get another ride.

Yeah. Terrific idea. Justin closed the door and walked around the hood of the car. It was time to retreat. He wouldn't make a move or say a word. His instincts told him to play it safe and play it honest. He'd never tried that before. It'd probably kill him before it did him any good.

Once they got on the freeway, Rachel risked a glance in Justin's direction. The guy was unusually quiet, focusing on driving through the harsh winter conditions. The roads were slick and the snow was coming down harder, but that shouldn't take all of Justin's concentration.

"Thanks for doing this," Rachel said, breaking the awkward silence. She should have thanked him and was ashamed of her lack of manners. Justin might be the burr in her side lately, but he was going out of his way to take her to the airport.

Justin didn't take his eyes off the road. "It's the least I could do since I made this past week uncomfortable for you."

Rachel raised her eyebrows. *And he decides the best way is to share a small space together for at least a half an hour?* "Don't worry about it."

"So, where are you going for the holidays?" he asked.

"The first plane out to somewhere warm and tropical." It sounded perfect, especially as the cold air whipped the snow around them.

"And where's that?"

She shrugged. "Haven't decided yet."

That got his attention. He looked at her with surprise. "You don't know where you're going?"

"As long as it's not here, I'm good." She grimaced when she realized how that sounded. "There's nothing wrong with here. But it can get a little claustrophobic."

"Especially when I'm around," he muttered.

Rachel drew her arms closer to her body and looked out the window. "I didn't say that."

"You didn't have to," Justin said. "I know you're leaving because of me."

She didn't want him to know that. She didn't want Justin to know how much power he had over her. "No, I'm taking a vacation," she lied. "People do it all the time. And what about you? What are you going to do this Christmas vacation?"

"Same as always," he said as he slowed down the car to accommodate the amount of snow on the road. "Sleep in, hang out."

She turned to him. "That's it?" She knew Justin didn't really do holidays, but what about a small tradition? Didn't he do anything that made him connected with his family and friends?

"That's all I need."

"It sounds . . . relaxing." But it also sounded like a regular day off. Not special at all.

He glanced at her and flashed a smile. "You know, you could always join me."

A week of sleeping in, hanging out with Justin would not be relaxing. Mind-blowing and life-changing, but far from peaceful. "That's very tempting, but I can't."

His smile grew wry. "I'm that scary, huh?"

"Excuse me?"

"I'm why you're running away."

"I'm not running away." Okay, maybe she was. It was what she used to do best. Whenever she had made a mess of things, it was an indication to leave and make a fresh start elsewhere. The idea that she was falling back into an old habit didn't sit well with her, but at least this running away was temporary. "I'll be back in a week."

"You're running away from Christmas, and I know why." Justin locked gazes with her. "Because everything about Christmas reminds you of us."

"Don't flatter yourself." How did he figure this all out? Was she that easy to read? The thought was horrifying.

"I know, Rachel," Justin said emphatically. He hesitated before he said, "I overhead you talking to Nikki. Why else would I wear that horrible sweater?"

Her infuriated gasp rang in the small car. "I knew it!" She wanted to move, to leave, to get out of this car. He knew! He knew how she felt about him. He'd always known and used that knowledge!

Rachel slapped her gloved hands on her seat, but it didn't do a thing for the anger and embarrassment rolling through her. "Well, don't think you can have your way with me by singing 'Rudolph the Red-Nosed Reindeer'!"

Justin laughed. "That wouldn't do the trick. 'Santa Claus Is Coming to Town,' on the other hand, would. . . ."

"Not funny." She fidgeted in her seat and searched for a sign to see how much longer she had to stay in this car with Justin O'Rourke. It didn't matter how many miles were left; she already knew it was too many.

"Or how about 'All I Want for Christmas Is You'?"

"Shut up." She made a show of looking out the window.

"'Santa Baby'?" Justin asked, laughter wobbling his voice.

She turned quickly, her seat belt tightening around her from the sudden move. "I'm going to bury you in the snow if you don't stop making fun of this situation."

His smile grew impossibly wider. The creases fringing his mouth and eyes deepened. She couldn't tear her gaze away and her heartbeat skittered to a stop. The embarrassment she felt started to seep away, replaced with something warm and tingly.

"You have to admit that you're being"—he paused to choose his words carefully—"irrational. You didn't have sex with me because it's Christmas."

Her heart started to pump harder than ever. She wasn't sure what just happened, but she didn't need her emotions going all over the place. She needed to be calm, cool, and collected. "I wouldn't have had sex with you any other time of the year."

"Don't bet on it." Justin's smile faded. All the teasing was gone. "I've been on my best behavior all year."

Somehow she believed that. "That's as good as it gets?"

"I kept my hands off you because it was obvious you were trying to be some sort of good girl. That all changed at the office party."

"What? Did I have a 'Do not open until Christmas' sticker on me somewhere that I'm not aware of?"

"No." His expression softened as he remembered that night. "It's because this time you came on to me."

"I flirted back." With the subtlety of exploding dynamite, she admitted to herself. She was trying not to think about that. It had been impulsive and it'd felt natural. She had wanted Justin and went after him with reckless abandon.

"You were feeling good and relaxed," Justin said as he cranked up the heat to defrost the windows. "You were feeling like your old self."

"You are not qualified to say that," Rachel said as she pulled her coat tighter around her. "You didn't know me until this year."

"You were wild before I knew you," he said with supreme confidence. "You still are."

"No, I am not." Why didn't anyone believe her?

"I can tell it by the way you walk. It's a strut." Justin's voice dipped low. "You also can't tame your laugh, and when you yawn, you put your whole body in it. It's a very erotic sight."

"There's nothing wrong with the way I walk. Or—"

"Never said there was," Justin said, his eyes twinkling with pleasure. "I also can tell a lot about you by how much you restrain yourself. That much self-control over the littlest things tells me how wild you really are."

"Okay, Justin. Maybe you don't know that you are on dangerous ground. I prefer my quiet little world, and if you mess with it, I will fight hard and dirty."

Justin gave a nod as if he understood. "You feel safe in your quiet little world, but you still miss your wild days."

"No, I don't," she argued. She didn't miss feeling like a loser, never making ends meet, and never finding her place in the world. She didn't miss her impulsive, destructive behavior.

"Your wild ways show in your work," Justin explained. "The only time you go all out is in your art. Well, also in sex. But your artwork reveals every one of your bad-girl fantasies."

She didn't want to hear this anymore. "I'm warning you. . . ."

"I can make every one of them come true."

Yeah, that was what she was worried about. Justin's husky promise tempted her, and she shifted in her seat, warding off the delicious heat that billowed inside her. "I don't need your help in tapping my inner vixen."

"Don't be too sure about that. I'm the only guy in your quiet little world who can give you what you want."

"What is it you think I want?" Rachel rolled her eyes. She was used to guys offering to rock her world, but they had been too interested in their own fantasies to care about her own. "Multiple orgasms? A dominant lover? A long weekend with multiple partners?"

"No," Justin said as he concentrated on the road, "you want something you haven't had before."

She gritted her teeth and pressed her lips together tightly. What had Justin heard about her? And who told? "And what do you think that is?"

"A guy who is still there once you wake up."

She whipped her head around and stared at him. Whoa. She knew Justin was smart, but she didn't think he was this insightful.

"You want someone who is strong enough to hold you back when you're feeling reckless," he said, catching her gaze. The sincerity in his eyes took her breath away. "But you also want someone you can be wild with in bed."

How did he know? What did she say that gave herself away? And would he use that secret wish against her? She scooted closer to the door. "And you think you're that guy?" she asked, hoping she sounded cool.

"Oh, I know I am. I'm waiting for you to know it, too."

"Don't hold your breath," she mumbled.

"It'll be sooner than you think."

His confidence was really beginning to bug her. "Shut up and drive."

He squinted as he looked through the windshield. "That might be a problem."

Rachel sighed. "Why is that?" The man was a charmer and knew when to talk and when to be quiet. How hard could it be to leave her alone?

"This snow is getting worse."

Rachel looked out the window and saw that what he said was true. She had been aware that the snow was coming down fast and heavy, but they were now thick in a snowstorm. Cars were struggling through the piling snow, and visibility was low. "Maybe we should pull off somewhere and wait it out," she suggested.

"Or I could take you back home."

She had a feeling he meant *his* home. It was a tantalizing offer, but she had to be strong. She had to get him out of her system. "No, that's not an option."

"Okay. Your wish is my command." Justin slowly changed lanes and carefully got onto the next exit. "Can you read that sign?"

Rachel peered through the window. "Not really. The snow is covering most of the words."

Once they got off the freeway, Rachel noticed how much worse the streets were. It didn't look like a snowplow had been by. Justin maneuvered his car down the street, inching along one block, and then another and another, only to discover that there was no place to stop and warm up. No gas station, no restaurants. Nothing.

"I'm sure there's something around here," Rachel insisted as they continued down the treacherous road that was lined with huge evergreen trees. "Wait, there's a sign up ahead. I can't read it just yet."

The car slowed down as the tires struggled through the snow. "We might be delayed here for a while," Justin warned.

"It's okay. I'm not on a strict timetable." A small delay was not a big deal. She jerked forward as the car suddenly stopped.

"What makes you think the planes aren't grounded?" Justin asked as he pressed his foot down on the gas, but the tires churned in the snow.

"Don't talk like that." She had to get out of here. Today. Rachel squinted as she tried to make out the wood-carved sign mottled with snow. " 'Welcome to Sleigh Bell Summit.' "

"Never heard of it." He shoved the car into another gear and pumped the gas pedal. The car didn't budge.

Sleigh Bell Summit . . . Why does that sound so familiar? "Oh crap!" Her eyes bulged. "We're in Sleigh Bell Summit! Turn the car around! Right now!"

Justin did the opposite. He shoved the car into park and leaned back on the seat, one arm draped on the steering wheel. "I can't. We're stuck."

"What?" She started to panic. Her breaths turned into short, choppy huffs. "Are you serious?"

"Are you okay, Rachel? We're just stuck. Nothing to worry about."

It suddenly dawned on her. "Oh, I get it. You did this on purpose!"

The humor and warmth from Justin's blue eyes disappeared. "What are you talking about?"

"Sleigh Bell Summit? I knew you were devious, but this?" She shook her head and flopped back in her seat. "This is just plain mean."

"What are you accusing me of? And what the hell is Sleigh Bell Summit?" He gestured at the sign. "Is it cursed or something?"

It was for her. "You never heard of Sleigh Bell Summit?"

She highly doubted that. The panic started to rise, suffocating her. She took a big, wheezy breath. "It's famous."

"For what?"

"For Christmas," Rachel said in a monotone. She closed her eyes in surrender, knowing she was doomed. "It's Christmastime at Sleigh Bell Summit every day of the year."

Chapter Five

"*I* can't believe you did this to me," Rachel said with a grumble as she stomped her way along the snowy lane. Giant fir trees flanked the road, weighed down with snow and thousands of strands of colored lights.

It would have been picturesque, but at the moment she didn't care. The wind was whipping through her layers of clothes, and the snow found its way underneath her coat. She was cold, wet, and spitting mad.

Justin's sigh was loud and long. "For the last time, I didn't plan this."

"Of course you planned this," she accused. "I should have known you were up to no good when you decided to drive me to the airport. You were really going to trick me into Santa's love nest."

Justin shuffled to a stop. "What?"

Rachel tossed her hands up. "Well, congratulations. You succeeded."

He shook his head slowly. "Next you're going to blame me for getting stuck in the snow."

Rachel tilted her head, raised her eyebrows, and looked at him, waiting for him to confess.

Justin's mouth dropped open. "Are you kidding? Did I secretly decide to start a snowstorm, too?"

"I should have known when you wore that sweater the other day," she declared as she adjusted the strap of her weekend bag on her shoulder. "You will stop at nothing to seduce me."

"Rachel, take my word." He held up a hand as if he were taking a solemn oath. "Seduction is the last thing on my mind at this moment."

"Only because you're waiting for the right moment to make your move," she said as they started walking again. "Probably while I'm surrounded by Christmas clutter."

Even if they stayed only an hour at Sleigh Bell Summit, she was still in danger of pouncing on Justin at every Christmasy location. She would have the most uncontrollable urges and would probably take him in full view of everyone. She'd be banned from town in record time and gain a reputation. She'd be known as Santa's Slut. The Fa La La Floozy. She could see it all now.

"You're the one who heard of this place," Justin said, bending his head as the wind howled around them. "You're the one who guided us here."

Oh, so now it was her fault? This was unbelievable! She whirled around and almost lost her balance, but Justin grabbed her elbow and held her up. "I couldn't read the sign," she reminded him.

"But you knew about this place," Justin insisted, his eyes twinkling with amusement. "Maybe it was your subconscious."

She scoffed at the idea and pulled away from him. "I don't want to be here."

"Yes, you made that crystal clear," he said. "If it weren't for your constant complaining, your frantic attempt at shoveling the car out of the snow with your fingers was a big clue."

The lane made a slight turn and she saw the brick wall that circled the town. The wall was about a story high and evergreen boughs were draped on the edge. It didn't look any more festive than the outdoor mall.

"You know, maybe Sleigh Bell Summit isn't all that Christmasy," she said hopefully as they walked through the entrance. "It could be all hype and . . ." Rachel's voice trailed off as a bright red sleigh went by them, pulled by eight white horses.

Her gaze followed the sleigh, which carried an overwhelming number of squealing children. The sleigh went past a row of shops that looked like gingerbread houses, complete with thick snow dripping from their pointed roofs.

Rachel dragged her gaze away, past the carolers, past the shoppers carrying towering piles of gift-wrapped boxes, and to the center of town where the biggest, fattest Christmas tree stood. The tree was so festive, so beautiful, that it almost hurt to look at it.

Justin turned to her. "You were saying?"

"I feel like I just walked into a Christmas card." It was her worst nightmare come to life.

"Let's hope they have a snowplow," he said as he placed his hand on the small of her back and guided her into the Christmas village. "And a hotel."

Panic flashed through her body and she went still. "A hotel?"

"We're stuck here until the snow stops and the snowplow comes through," Justin predicted. "That's going to take more than a couple of hours."

She looked back at the road they just walked. It was blustery and dark. Their footprints had already disappeared under a fresh layer of snow.

Her shoulders slumped in surrender. "Fine, we'll ask about a hotel. But so help me, if they make one crack about no room in the inn, I'm walking to the airport."

"Only one room left?" Rachel muttered as they waited in the lobby for the elevator. "Seriously?"

"It's their busiest season. We were lucky we got it. There was a cancellation because of the weather."

She had to share a room with Justin. Rachel shook her head, wondering what she did to deserve this kind of luck. The elevator doors slid open and she stepped in. She valiantly ignored the candy-cane motif in the elevator car and tried to block out the Christmas music.

How will I survive a few hours in this place? she wondered as the elevator took them up. She had to take this one minute at a time.

"What's our room number?" she asked.

Justin looked at the envelope the key cards came in. "We're on the Frankincense floor, suite three."

Rachel slowly turned and gave him a look of disbelief. "Frankincense?"

"Weren't you listening to the woman?" Justin asked as the doors opened. "There's the lobby, then the next floor is Gold, then Frankincense, and—"

"Don't tell me, let me guess. Myrrh?" she asked as she stepped out of the elevator. "As long as the whole floor doesn't smell like frankincense, I'm not going to say a word."

"Somehow I doubt that," Justin said as he trailed behind her.

She found their suite and slid the key card in the door. Once she heard the click, she opened the door and stepped over the threshold. Rachel stared at the room in horror. She took a step back, closing the door as she moved, and collided into Justin.

"What's the matter?" he asked, putting his hand on her shoulder.

She stared at the closed door. "It looked like Christmas threw up in there."

"It can't be that bad." He opened the door with his key card and stepped inside. He slowly looked around but didn't move.

"What do you think?" she asked.

"You weren't exaggerating."

She cautiously stepped back into the room. There were elves everywhere. On the green wallpaper, stenciled on the wood furniture, and embroidered on the chair pillows. Freaky, dancing, mischievous elves.

"We probably won't even need to use the room," Rachel said brightly. "The snow will stop, and we'll get out of here before you know it."

"You really weren't listening to the woman at the registration desk," Justin said as he stared at the mural of Santa's workshop on the ceiling. "There's now a snow advisory and avalanche warnings."

In other words, they were well and truly stuck. "We'll make the best of it." She had no doubt Justin would. Everywhere she turned, it was Christmas. All he had to do was sit and wait, and she'd jump him. He wouldn't even have to wait that long.

"Okay, here are the ground rules," Rachel announced.

Justin dragged his gaze away from the acrobatic elf pattern on the curtains. "Ground rules?"

"We'll flip for the bed." While elves pranced around the room, they were absent on the bed. The gorgeous, decadent, and seductive bed.

The dark wood of the sleigh bed gleamed in the daylight, and the thick, luxurious blankets promised to be soft and sensual. There was a cascade of pillows in satin cases of every jewel color. It made her think of gift boxes piled high in Santa's sleigh. She would love to take a tumble in that with Justin.

"And where is the loser going to sleep? On the floor?" He looked at the bright red rug that had elves frolicking around the border. "It's too cold."

She crossed her arms. "I am not sharing a bed with you." Definitely not that bed. If she got in there with Justin, she wasn't going to come back out until New Year's Day.

"I promise I'll keep my hands off you." Justin's eyes lit up when she didn't say anything. "Oh, I get it," he said as he strolled closer to her. "That's not worrying you. You're afraid you won't keep your hands off me."

She didn't deny it. "I'm surrounded by Christmas."

"So?" He slid his hands in his coat pockets. "You can make that excuse all you want, but you're wrong."

She pursed her lips. "What's your theory?"

He leaned down until their eyes were level. "You had a taste of how good it is between us and can't resist."

There was some truth in that, but she had been tempted before and never reacted this strongly. There had to be more to it. "Think that if it makes you feel better."

"I will." He turned and walked toward the window. "And I can wait for you to come around, too."

"What are you talking about?"

"I'm not going to take advantage of you while we're here," he promised as he looked out the window.

"That's very . . ." Noble? Suspicious? "Why?"

He looked over his shoulder and held her gaze. His blue eyes gleamed with desire. "Don't get me wrong. I still want you. More than ever."

He was confusing her. "Then . . ."

"When you took me at the office party, you wanted me as much as I wanted you."

She flushed as she remembered how aggressive, wild, and hungry she had been that night. "So?"

"Nothing to be ashamed about. That was the hottest night of my life."

His confession flustered her. "I . . . it's . . ."

"You were kind of aggressive behind the Christmas tree, too," he said with a smile.

"I'm not a sexually aggressive person," she declared. Or

at least she was trying not to be, but Justin blew all her good intentions to smithereens.

"Yeah, you are. And I like you that way, but I'm not going to take whatever I can get. I'm going to wait until you want me to the point that nothing else matters."

He was going to have to wait a long, long time, Rachel decided. She wouldn't let that happen again.

"And that's not going to happen while we're here," he said with a resigned shrug.

"Bull. Look at this place." She gestured at the room. "It's more seductive to me than Paris and Venice rolled together."

"No, you won't be seduced because you're going to be on guard. You'll spend too much time worrying that your self-control is going to snap. You won't go wild here."

"You think so?" She wasn't so sure. She kept sneaking looks at the bed, imagining how Justin would look naked and waiting for her on the satin sheets.

"Look at you right now," he said as he walked toward her. He motioned at how her back was at the wall, her arms crossed in front of her. "You're on the defense. I prefer my lover to be a little more relaxed and adventurous."

"Guess I don't meet your requirements," she said, and snapped her fingers. "Shucks. Darn."

"Come on." He reached out and wrapped his hand around her wrist.

"Where are we going?"

"We're going to walk around town," Justin replied as he tugged her gently. "Maybe even hit a few shops."

She gave a sharp nod at the window. "There's a snowstorm."

"It's not snowing as hard anymore," he pointed out. "And it's better than staying in here together."

She wasn't sure about that. She'd seen a glimpse of a store that sold only nutcrackers, and another that sold blown-glass ornaments. That could send her over the edge.

"I tell you what. If you try to seduce me, I'll throw you in the largest snowbank to cool off," he promised.

She glared at him, but she was considering her options. Walking around Sleigh Bell Summit was less dangerous than staying in the hotel room. Outside they would have several layers of clothes, lots of space, and people around them. That was better than being here, alone, near that big, inviting bed.

"Okay. I'm trusting you, even though every bone in my body says I shouldn't."

"It's okay, Rachel," he said softly as he draped his arm around her shoulders and guided her to the door. "You won't do anything you'll regret. I promise."

She narrowed her eyes, trying to find any hidden message in his statement, but he whisked her out the door before she could protest.

He couldn't believe he was Christmas shopping. In a winter wonderland. Two days before Christmas. Only Rachel could get him to do that.

Justin looked around the candy store as the other shoppers jostled around him. The stench of the peppermint was beginning to get to him. He lost Rachel somewhere between the holiday bark and the fudge.

All this time he thought she would have problems, but he was the jumpy one. He had fun looking at the trinkets in the stocking-stuffer store, and found himself humming along with the carolers. He relaxed in the café and drank hot buttered rum while quietly looking at the big Christmas tree.

He was enjoying this holiday, but he didn't want to get his hopes up high. Rachel was stuck with him and trying to make the best out of a bad situation. He wasn't going to read anything into it.

"Justin?" He jumped and saw Rachel at his side. "Are you doing okay?" she asked, her eyes darkening with concern. "The crowds aren't getting to you?"

"No, I'm good."

"How can you say that? The smell of peppermint is overwhelming. Let's get you out of here." She grabbed his gloved hand and pulled him out of the store.

Justin hid his smile. As much as he loved Rachel's wicked and wild side, he didn't mind how protective she got with him. It was kind of sweet. It made him feel as if he was important to her.

When they stepped out of the cozy store and into the freezing cold, Justin noticed Rachel didn't have any packages. "Didn't find anything you want?"

"No, I'm just browsing," she said as she huddled closer to him in hopes of warding off the cold.

Browsing for hours in Christmas stores and not once was she overcome with lust. Too bad. But her behavior was blowing her theory clear out of the water, he thought smugly. Either she had superhuman control, or the holidays had nothing to do with her libido. It was all him.

"Huh," she said as she gave him a sidelong glance. "I know that smile."

He looked down at her face and noticed she didn't seem too threatened by it. She was responding to it. "Do you?" he murmured.

She didn't look away. He didn't move. There was something about the moment. The scent wafting from the candy store intensified. The color of Rachel's eyes brightened.

He'd have her. Not tonight, but soon. He was going to get closer, get to know her, and unwrap her like a present.

He understood the thrill of anticipation. The sounds got louder; the air became crisper. He wasn't an outsider, but part of the excitement.

A snowflake fell on Rachel's cheek. He slowly reached out and brushed it off her skin. She tilted her head up. She was just a kiss away.

He wanted this kiss more than anything. Justin swallowed roughly. Just one brush of lip against lip would tide him over.

He lowered his head and paused. He'd made a promise that he wouldn't seduce her. He had to prove that he was strong enough to resist.

Justin turned his head, but he didn't pull away. The need was just too much. As if he couldn't control it, he turned back.

Rachel hadn't moved. She was waiting, her eyes sparkling with expectancy. Her lips parted. She was hoping for a kiss.

A squeal of childish delight splintered through the air. Justin took a sharp step back as a few children ran past them and toward the roasted chestnut vendor.

He didn't look away from Rachel. He couldn't.

That was a close call. His chest rose and fell as if he had been running hard. One strong impulse and he nearly blew it. Not the best way to build her trust in him.

Justin took another step back. "The stores are going to close soon," he said gruffly. "Do you need anything before we go back to the hotel?"

She cleared her throat and looked away. "Yes, one more thing." She pointed at the store and he squinted through the drifting snowflakes.

Vixen's Lingerie. Panic gripped his insides as the words rolled in his brain. *Vixen's. Lingerie.* The gold silhouette of a reindeer in the sign didn't make him feel any better.

"Seriously?" he asked gruffly.

"We need something warm to sleep in."

We. His gut gave a good, vicious twist. He had a vision of the two of them underneath the quilts in the sleigh bed, and they weren't wearing anything at all. "Uh, I'm good."

"You have no luggage," she reminded him.

"I need to get a toothbrush and . . . stuff." He jerked his thumb over toward the drugstore.

"Fine," Rachel said with a touch of exasperation. "I'll get you something, too. I'll meet you at the hotel."

"You don't have to." But she obviously didn't hear his words as she hurried toward the store.

This could be bad, he thought as he watched her leave. She might buy herself something sexy and wild, just to mess with his mind. He wouldn't put it past Rachel.

No, she didn't want anything to happen between them. She'd probably buy a shapeless granny nightgown. Something that would hide every inch of her and make him all the more curious.

Either way, he was in trouble.

Justin made his way to the drugstore, not sure if he should buy a pack of condoms. If he didn't buy them, he might regret it. If he did buy them, he might regret it.

He grimaced as his gut gave another ferocious twist. Yep, everywhere he turned, he was headed for trouble.

Chapter Six

*J*ustin leaned against the window frame, his arms crossed, one ankle resting over the other, and stared out into the town center in the direction of the Christmas tree. It was close to midnight and only a few brave souls were walking around outside. The snow had stopped, but there had been no sign of a snowplow. Sleigh Bell Summit was blanketed in white, the ice glistening underneath the colorful Christmas lights.

He tensed when he heard the bathroom door click open. Steam billowed into the room along with a hint of citrus. It was the scent he associated with Rachel.

Justin stared out the window as if his life depended on it. He didn't want to look at Rachel while she was damp and rosy from a hot shower. He focused on the giant twinkling light on the tree. He was going to keep looking at it until Rachel was safely tucked into bed.

"Justin?" Her voice was soft and uncertain.

"Yeah?" he asked, not moving. She didn't respond. That meant he had to turn around. Damn.

He could do this. He could look at Rachel and not touch. He did just fine when they shared a very quiet and unexpectedly romantic candlelit dinner. He did better than fine.

Which was going to make this night even more difficult. Justin had felt the awareness that shimmered between them across the dinner table. He had sensed every glance and every move that Rachel made. He had seen the interest in her eyes and how she kept touching her mouth, her hair, and, most of all, him. The tension had almost been unbearable.

Justin braced himself before slowly, reluctantly turning around. He had been fully prepared for an onslaught of senses. But this one left him speechless.

Standing on the other side of the room, Rachel looked effortlessly sexy. Her hair fell into thick waves over her shoulders. She looked young and innocent, her face bare. She wore a red flannel pajama shirt.

And nothing else.

Justin swallowed hard. "Uh, you're . . ." He gestured to her legs. Her long, bare legs that he knew were warm and soft to his touch. Not to mention flexible.

Justin closed his eyes briefly. He hoped she hadn't saved any hot water for him. His shower needed to be icy cold if he was going to get through this night.

"They didn't have that much to choose from for adults," Rachel informed him. "So I bought the last pajama set. I get the top, you get the bottom."

She gets the top. . . . Justin imagined lying underneath Rachel as she straddled his hips. She was riding him hard and fast as she peeled the shirt off her body.

Justin shook his head, clearing the image from his mind, and ignoring how his cock twitched. He had to stay focused on his goal. There wasn't going to be any sex tonight.

"Here, let me get them for you," she offered.

He kept his gaze rigidly above her shoulders as she walked to the desk, but he still noticed how the hem of her shirt barely covered her ass. Heat washed over his skin and he found it a struggle to breathe.

Did she know what she was doing to him? Was this some sort of test? It had to be. But no matter what she threw at him—even if it was herself, naked and willing—he wasn't going to fail.

"Catch."

His reflexes were slow, especially since her toss caused the pajama shirt to hitch up just a little. His arms went up just as the red flannel threatened to hit him in the face. Justin gripped tightly on to the pajama bottoms. He looked down at them, refusing to watch Rachel as she walked to the bed.

It was only then he saw the printed fabric. "What is on these?" he asked, looking up at her. The big bed was between them, but that didn't make the gnawing lust inside him go away.

"They're supposed to be reindeer," she said, "but they look more like puppies with antlers."

"Sexy." He regretted the word the moment it sprang from his mouth. "You're going to be okay with it? You went a little wild with my sweater."

"It's going to be dark," she assured him.

Like that was going to be the answer to all their problems,

Justin thought as he strode to the bathroom. They were alone together. All night. In one bed. But it was going to be okay because it was dark.

Riiight.

Rachel waited until Justin closed the bathroom door behind him before she gave a ragged sigh. She could do this. She wasn't going to go sex-mad in this winter wonderland. It wasn't the detox she had hoped for, but she was handling it.

All afternoon she managed to keep her hands off Justin. There were moments when she contemplated the best strategy of getting him under the mistletoe, or sliding just so on the ice so she could fall in his arms. Fortunately she didn't do any of those things. If she had, she might not have pulled herself together in time. She would have gotten swept away with the wild sensations churning inside her, and she would have taken Justin on one crazy ride.

As the day had gone on, she realized her surroundings weren't encouraging her erotic thoughts. It was being near Justin and having his attention lavished on her. Whether they had been laughing over a novelty item or bickering over who would pay for the hot toddies, she couldn't get enough of him.

That realization had crystallized when she enjoyed the quiet and elegant dinner with Justin. The restaurant hadn't been overtly festive, but it might as well have been. Red-hot desire had streaked through her veins, flooding every pore until it pooled low in her hips. She had wanted Justin more than ever.

Her stay at Sleigh Bell Summit had been inconvenient and uncomfortable, but it proved Justin's theory. It wasn't the Christmas season that made her hot and bothered. It was all him.

Which made her predicament worse. Rachel groaned. This was a disaster. It meant she wanted him like this every season. Every day. Every hour.

But it didn't feel like a disaster. It felt like a whole new world was opening up to her. A promise of something better. All she had to do was take the first step. Rachel bit her lip and thought about it. The idea was scary, but exciting, too.

She shouldn't be scared. Justin wasn't anything like the men in her past. Maybe that's why she was nervous. She couldn't figure him out. He was a bad boy made good. He was a rascal, smart enough to cause trouble but never get caught. Justin wasn't the most honorable guy, and he didn't have the traits to be a gentleman, but he was trying. Every tender touch, every time he reluctantly held back, her heart would give a slow flip. There was something irresistibly sweet about his struggle to be on his best behavior.

She had to stop daydreaming about him. It was only going to make the night longer. Rachel briskly rubbed her face and ruffled her hair before she launched into action. She double-locked the door, turned off the lights, and closed the curtains, plunging the room into darkness. The curtains weren't as thick as she had hoped, and the Christmas lights outside cast a romantic glow in the room.

She felt a whisper of a chill and hurried for the bed. Burrowing under the warm blankets and satin sheets, she hoped the layers would keep her from reaching for Justin.

Of course they would. She curled up into a tight ball on the edge of the bed. It was time for some positive thinking. The Christmas surroundings weren't going to make her go crazy.

She was an intelligent and rational woman who wasn't driven to indulge her base desires.

Everything was going to be fine, she told herself as she plumped up her pillow. Especially since Justin made it clear that he would wait until after the holidays to go after her.

And if she made it through the night, she could work with Justin without tearing off his clothes. She could do her best at her job and stay on track with her structured life. She could totally do this.

The bathroom door opened and the light shut off. The Christmas decorations outside offered a stream of colored light as she watched Justin step into the room. Her breath snagged in her throat as her gaze ran over his defined chest and muscular arms. The dragon tattoo on his forearm looked almost pagan.

Her gaze dropped to the pajama bottoms riding low on his lean hips. The red flannel skimmed the impressive bulge of his cock. The mutant-reindeer pajamas didn't look so ridiculous anymore.

Justin silently walked to the bed and got under the covers with an economy of motion that she envied. Rachel was impressed that he managed to settle into bed without touching her. That took some maneuvering.

"Good night," she said softly.

"Good night, Rachel."

The husky timbre of his voice did something to her. She lay on her back and bunched her fists next to her sides. Rachel stared up at the ceiling and studied the cartoon mural. She didn't feel sleepy at all. She felt energized.

Rachel tried every sleeping trick. Counting from one hundred to one. Counting sheep. Singing "Twelve Days of Christmas" in her head. Nothing worked.

Dasher . . . Dancer . . . Prancer . . . Vixen . . .

Okay, that wasn't going to work. She gave an exasperated sigh. Not when her mind was picturing the reindeer covering Justin's lean hips and muscular thighs.

Her body hummed with awareness. Pure need flooded her body. She felt Justin's heat coming off in waves. Rachel shifted and turned toward him.

"Go to sleep, Rachel." He said it quietly, but there was a hint of steel in his tone.

"I'm trying," she whispered. But it wasn't going to happen. Not when every nerve ending crackled. "Why aren't you asleep?"

"I'm working on it." He punched his pillow with a little more force than necessary.

She was looking directly at Justin. The pillow was balled under his head. His eyes were closed, his hands tucked under his pillow. The blankets had already fallen off his shoulders and revealed that amazing chest.

She could stare at him for hours.

Okay, she could stare at him for hours if she were also allowed to touch and kiss him.

Rachel bit her lip. She wasn't going to touch him. Her fingertips stung as she fought the urge. She could get through this night.

Justin's eyes suddenly opened, his gaze snagging hers. "Forget it."

She blinked. Had she said all that out loud? No, he would have said something sooner. "Forget what?"

"We are not having sex tonight." He was emphatic.

"I wasn't asking."

"Hmm." He closed his eyes again.

"I wasn't!" She hadn't said a word. Her body, on the other hand, was screaming for his touch.

"You're constantly moving," he complained.

"I'm a restless sleeper," she informed him. "Nothing you can do about it unless you tie me to the bed."

Justin became dangerously still. "Stop putting thoughts in my head." His voice was a rasp. "I'm not accepting your invitation."

"You think *that* was an invitation?" She had been teasing him, but it boomeranged. The thought of being tied up and helpless underneath him was a powerful suggestion. She was feeling a little bit reckless and she didn't think she could hold back anymore.

He opened his eyes again. "I know it was."

"Justin, you need to get out more," she purred. "That was no invitation."

Caution flared in his eyes. "You are up to no good."

"You're right," Rachel said with a naughty smile. She rolled closer until her breasts were pressed against his bare chest. Hooking her thigh over his hip, she set her pelvis flush against his. She rubbed her feet along his leg while brushing her hand over his arm. "Now, this is an invitation."

"No, this is playing with fire." Justin grasped her wrist. His hold was firm, but she felt the tremor in his fingers. He was much more aroused than he let on. "I gave my word to you. I will not let you do anything you're going to regret in the morning."

"I won't regret it. I promise." She arched her spine, rubbing her breasts against his chest. "You want me, too."

He didn't deny it. "And I'll have you," he said hoarsely, closing his eyes as if he was harnessing the last of his self-control. "But not tonight."

"This might be your only chance." It wasn't, but he didn't need to know that. When it came to seducing this man, she could be shameless.

She saw his throat clench as he swallowed hard. "I'll risk it."

"Why?" She rolled her hips, grinding against his hard length. Rachel bit her lip as she imagined his cock deep inside her. "You can have me all night, any way you want."

He gave a cynical chuckle. "This place really is getting to you, huh?"

"No, you were right," she said as she pressed her mouth against his throat and licked her way up. "The Christmas decorations have nothing to do with it."

"Wow, you will stop at nothing."

"I'm serious." She kissed the line of his jaw, his stubble tickling her skin. "It wasn't about Christmas, but the memory of our first time together."

"Good answer."

She paused with her mouth against his chin. Rachel raised her head and locked eyes with him. "What can I do to prove it to you?"

A muscle bunched in his cheek. "Don't try to have sex with me until after December twenty-fifth."

She propped herself up on her elbow and stared at him in shock. How could he say that? When she was desperate for him now? When it was obvious that he wanted her just as much? "But it's the twenty-third!"

He rolled her onto her back and gently pushed her leg off him. "And to be on the safe side, we should probably wait until January first."

"What?" Her voice echoed loudly in the room. She wasn't going to wait that long. No way. Not going to happen.

"January sixth, now that I think about it."

Her mouth fell open. Did she hear that correctly? "January *sixth*?"

"That's Epiphany," he reminded her. "You know, the three wise men."

"Justin, please." She couldn't wait that long. She reached for him, but he blocked her, holding her forearms.

"The anticipation makes it sweeter," he promised.

"You're crazy." There was nothing sweet about how she ached for him. The need coiled low in her pelvis, twisting tighter and tighter. It was torment.

"I'm crazy? I'm not the one who gets hot over snowmen."

"I don't get crazy over snowmen," she insisted as she tried to wriggle closer. "I get crazy over you."

He released her and stared in her eyes for a long moment. "Wow. You really mean that."

"Of course I do." She inched closer, almost touching him.

"Took you long enough to figure that one out."

"Now figure out how much more I can take of this no-sex rule." She grabbed the back of his head and shoved her fingers in his hair before she planted a rough kiss on his mouth.

Justin rolled over on top of her. She gasped as his chest crushed her breasts. Her hips cradled his, and his cock pressed hard against her sex. Rachel immediately softened, welcoming his warm, strong body closer.

He grabbed her wrists and forcibly held them above her head. She was caught and surrounded by him. Excitement flared low in her pelvis. Her nipples tightened until they stung.

"You really don't want to do this," he said against her mouth.

"You need a lesson in body language." Rachel wrapped her legs around his hips and linked her ankles behind him. She arched into him. She felt his groan vibrate in his chest as his fingers tightened around her wrists.

Justin broke away from her kiss. "You're going to regret it."

"I won't. I promise." She captured his mouth with hers. Her lips were swollen, and her skin chafed from the stubble on his jaw, but she couldn't get enough of his mouth. She couldn't get close enough. She wanted to feel his hot skin on hers. "Take off your pants."

"Not a chance."

"Please," she whispered. "I need you."

She could tell that her plea enticed him. His cock swelled against her and his body tightened. She felt his restraint waver and smiled against his mouth. She only needed to push him a little more and he would yield.

"Don't roll your hips," he warned her.

She rocked them deliberately against Justin so he could feel the wet heat of her sex.

He squeezed his eyes shut as a growl tore from his throat. "Rachel . . ."

She'd tried to be good. She asked nicely, and she made promises. She would get down on her knees and beg if he'd let her.

To hell with that. It was time to take matters into her hands. "Ow!" she cried out as if she were in acute pain. She hissed, allowing the tension to lock her muscles. "Oh, that hurts."

"What's wrong?" Justin immediately let go of her wrists and rested against his forearms, lifting his weight from her body. He searched her face as she took a deep breath. "What happened?"

Rachel took advantage of his distraction, pressing her hands against his shoulders and rolling over with all her might. He now lay beneath her as she straddled his hips. Justin looked a little disoriented and pissed off as she hovered above him, her hands pressing his shoulders against the mattress.

"Now I got you," she announced, and started to lick her way down his chest. "I can't believe you fell for that."

"You don't play fair," he complained, and flinched when she gave his flat nipple a playful bite.

"Did you think I would?" She reached for the elastic of his pajama bottoms.

"I could toss you onto the floor," Justin pointed out. But he didn't make a move.

"You could," she agreed as she lifted her hips and pushed his pants down his legs, revealing his thick cock. "But you won't."

"You are—" His gasp came out rough and jagged as his hips vaulted from the bed when Rachel wrapped her hands around his cock.

"I'm sorry," she said sweetly, holding him in a clench, "I didn't catch that. You were saying you were going to throw me off the bed?"

He closed his eyes in defeat and his hands bunched the satin sheets beneath him. "Rachel . . ."

"Yes?" she asked as she slowly pumped his cock with her hand.

"I can't refuse you anymore."

"Good to know." She had already figured he surrendered. Her first clue might have been the encouraging rock of his hips, or the way he lay spread-eagled on the bed beneath her. Justin wasn't going to fight her off.

Rachel pumped his cock faster, enjoying the friction from the slick heat. His panting was harsh as he hardened and swelled under her touch. She loved watching Justin twist and writhe, and his face contort with an intoxicating mix of pleasure and pain.

She couldn't wait any longer. Rachel rose onto her knees and brushed the tip of his cock against her slit. She gradually sank down on him, her descent slow enough to drive Justin mad. It teased and tormented her, too. Rachel moaned with pleasure as Justin's cock stretched and filled her.

Justin's hands were suddenly on her hips, under her flannel shirt. His fingertips dug into her skin as he held her with a fierce grip. He thrust up as he slammed her hips down. Rachel cried out as the sensations whipped through her body.

"Ride me," he ordered in a rasp as he tugged at her hips. "Hard and fast."

She rocked against him, each move sending a hot shower of pleasure through her veins. Rachel picked up the pace, her hair falling in her face, as the bed squeaked.

Justin's gaze was rapt on her fingers as she unbuttoned her

shirt. One button revealed cleavage. . . . Another showed the underside of her breasts. . . . Her fingers hovered above the second-to-last button and she pulled away to scrape back her hair.

"Take off your shirt," Justin demanded.

The dark edge in his voice thrilled her. She wondered how close he was to losing all control. Rachel didn't break eye contact with Justin as she reached down between them and quietly unbuttoned her shirt. When the last button slid free, she shrugged the red flannel off her shoulders.

"Now touch yourself." His voice was thick and gravelly.

He really wanted her to show how hot she was for him. "I want you to touch me."

"I will," he promised with a wicked smile. "But ladies first."

Rachel grinned at that. He knew she was no lady. It was time to remind him of that. She reached up and tousled her hair before dragging her hands down the sides of her face and neck. As she rode his cock, Rachel caressed her chest.

She cupped and fondled her heavy breasts before playing with her tight nipples. Rachel pinched them and moaned, rocking her hips, as the fire stormed through her. She tossed back her head, her hair cascading down her back, as she chased the wild sensations.

"Keep going," Justin urged, bucking against her.

With one hand on her breast, she trailed the other hand down her stomach, past her hips, and to the strip of dark hair. She slid a finger along the wet folds and rubbed her fingertip along her swollen clitoris.

Her hips jerked and twitched, grinding against Justin. Her touch wasn't enough. She needed more. "Justin," she said with a whimper. "Please."

Justin sat up and drove her hips down on him. She leaned back and offered her breast to his mouth. He moved desperately for her nipple, sucking it deep into his mouth. Rachel grabbed the back of his head and pressed his face in her breast.

She dimly heard a roar and her world shifted. Rachel blinked and felt the satin sheet under her spine. She saw a glimpse of Justin just before he devoured her with a kiss and surged into her. Rachel clung to him, her fingers scratching his sweat-dampened back. Justin's thrusts grew ferocious and the last of his iron control disintegrated. He shuddered and climaxed as the white-hot pleasure inside her burst.

Rachel stilled, the blaze scorching through her, tearing through her mind. It broke free, splintering. She felt like she was shattering into a million little pieces and the only thing that held her together was Justin's strong arms.

Justin slumped against her, his breathing harsh and choppy as he gulped for air. Rachel went limp, satisfied. Her body throbbed, her skin hot and sweaty. She closed her eyes and cradled him against her, her arms wrapped around his back.

"Justin?"

He stiffened. "Yeah?"

"I'm not feeling one bit of regret."

She felt his chuckle against her neck. "Rachel, the night isn't over."

Chapter Seven

*J*ustin lay in bed and held Rachel close. She slept soundly, her legs intertwined with his, her heartbeat matching his. Streams of light filtered through the curtain as the sun began to rise. Justin looked down at Rachel, brushing her long black hair from her face.

Last night was hot. Wild. Perfect. Momentous.

And it was all one big mistake.

Justin looked away from Rachel, ashamed at his unrestrained response throughout the night. He should have stayed strong. He should have held Rachel off with a candy cane.

He should have slept on the floor.

But he was weak when it came to her. Always had been, and always would be. Her insatiable need for him drove him over the edge. How could he reject the one thing he wanted most?

He wanted to live the dream that she was hot for him. That her need rivaled his need for her. Justin wished it could continue, but in the light of day, he had to admit the truth: She said she was crazy for him to get what she wanted.

And he accepted the answer because he wanted to believe. He saw the look in her eyes and it had felt right. But the way he was struggling to keep his hands off her, she could have told him Santa landed on the roof and he'd believe it.

And now she was heading to the airport to get him out of her system. It'd probably work like a charm. And when she returned, every day at the office was going to be torture. He would still want her, and she would want him out of her sight.

Unless he could trap her here for the rest of her Christmas vacation. He could lie about the weather reports or claim there was a massive airline strike. Tie her up with a red ribbon . . .

No. Justin sat up in bed and drew away from her. He didn't deserve Rachel. He said he could handle her wild ways, but he only made it worse. He needed to admit defeat, even though he wanted to stay with her. He could trick her only so far, but it wouldn't keep her at his side.

He sighed and looked at the alarm clock. No time like the present to test his resolve. Justin cupped his hand on Rachel's shoulder. He paused, enjoying the feel of her skin before he gave her shoulder a gentle shake. "Rachel, it's time to get up."

"Five more minutes," she mumbled sleepily.

"No, we need to leave now." His tone was sharper than he intended, but it was either that or lie back down and kiss Rachel thoroughly awake. "Checkout is before noon."

Justin was in a bad mood, Rachel realized as she swallowed the remaining bite of her breakfast. She thought he would be sated and satisfied, but that might have been arrogance on her part. Was he impatient because he'd gotten what he'd wanted all along? Her mood took a dip at the thought. Now that he had her total surrender, was it time to move on?

"Are you okay?" she asked before she gulped down her coffee.

"Never better." He didn't meet her gaze as he grabbed for the check.

He was capable of lying better, that was for certain. Rachel made a face as she rose from the table and followed him to the cash register. She waited until they stepped out of the hotel restaurant before she tried again. "You want to talk about it?"

"Nothing to talk about." He shrugged. "Come on, I had my car brought out front."

Oh, yeah. Now he sounded like the men from her past. She hurried to catch up with him. His strides were eating up the ground, and they were already halfway across the lobby.

"Did I do anything to upset you last night?"

He looked straight ahead. "You mean besides making me wear reindeer pajamas, tackling me in bed, and having your way with me?"

"Most guys would take that as a compliment."

He shrugged again. "Most guys would have lasted longer."

Longer? Seriously? The guy had her screaming for mercy long before he climaxed. "Your self-control was admirable."

"My self-control was nonexistent," he said in disgust.

"Is that what is bothering you?" Men were all the same. They talked the talk, but deep down they weren't confident about their performance. Justin had nothing to worry about. "I thought you had amazing staying power."

He frowned as they stepped outside the hotel. "No, I didn't."

"You mean you could have held out for longer?" Her skin felt tight and prickly. "What's your record?"

Justin finally stopped and looked at her. "Huh?"

"You could go on and on," she said a little breathlessly as she remembered. "I'm the one who couldn't take it anymore."

He tilted his head to one side and narrowed his eyes. "Are we talking about the same thing?"

"Your amazing stamina?" Rachel unbuttoned the top of her coat. She was a little flushed.

"No!" He paused. "Well, yeah, my stamina is good, and I could have held back for . . . Wait, that's not my point."

"Well, what are you talking about?"

He looked around and noticed they were attracting attention. Justin placed his hand on her back and guided her to his car. "I promised I wouldn't have sex with you. It was my full intention to keep that promise."

"I'm not holding it against you."

"That's not the point," he said. "I wanted to prove that it wasn't just this Christmas crap that made you hot for me."

"You did," she insisted. "I'm not arguing with you on that anymore."

"I was determined to prove that I'm just what you need. And not just in bed."

She stopped in front of his car, stunned by the misery in his voice. "Justin."

"But all I managed to prove is that I can't say no to you." He raked his hand through his hair. "I failed you."

"Wow." She blinked. "I didn't know that's how you felt."

Anger flashed in his eyes. "How did you think I'd feel after last night?"

"Satisfied," she suggested with a smile. "Sore?"

He glared at her, obviously not in the mood to be teased. "Try defeated. I could have held out for something much more, but I grabbed for just one night."

"Who said it was just for one night?" She took a step closer to him and reached out, but he was already turning away.

"We should get you to the airport."

She suddenly had a better idea. Rachel nervously licked her lips. For a reckless impulse, this was the craziest, and probably most dangerous. "I decided not to go to the airport."

He whirled around. "Say what?"

"There's no point, is there?" She hated how her voice trembled. She wanted to sound confident, as if there was no way Justin could reject her.

"Oh, I get it." His mouth drew into a straight line, his eyes dulled with disappointment. "It's because you already made the mistake you were trying to avoid?"

"No, because I want to spend Christmas here." She reached out for him again, grasping his coat and tugging him forward. "With you."

He resisted. "No, you don't."

"Yeah, I do." She took another step until her boot touched his. Their coats brushed, and she hated the barrier their clothes put between them. "Justin, you make me feel things I haven't felt for years. In fact, you make me feel things I've never experienced."

He looked at her suspiciously, as if waiting for the zinger. "But . . . ?"

She bit down on her bottom lip, knowing she had to tell him exactly how she felt. She hated revealing her mistakes when she wanted his admiration and adoration.

"Okay, here's the thing. It's taken me two years to get my life back on track, and I'm still dealing with the consequences from when I went off the rails. I was scared that this wildness I felt would make me go back to square one."

"I wouldn't let that happen."

She knew he wouldn't. She heard the sincere promise in his voice. "I appreciate that, but this was something I wanted to do on my own. I needed to trust my instincts and my choices. Especially in men."

Rachel felt Justin bracing himself for what came next. "And?"

"And I really thought you were bad for me."

He took a step back as if he had been punched in the gut. Justin exhaled slowly. "Thanks a lot."

"Until we came here," she quickly added.

A muscle twitched in his cheek, and she saw the pain shimmer in his eyes. "I'm taking you to the airport and I'm not taking no for an answer."

"Are you listening to me? That's what I thought until I came here. I could blame it on the Christmas craziness. I could blame it on you, but we both know the truth. I'm wild about you because you are everything I want."

"You don't want me." He unlocked the door with his remote key chain. "You don't want wild. You said so yourself."

"I don't want to fall back into my old habits," she corrected him. "Or my old life. That's not going to happen with you."

He opened the passenger door. "How do you know?"

"Well, for one thing, I'm done running away." Every stupid thing she had done in her past was an escape or a distraction. It had been easier to walk away than make it right. It had taken her until now to see that. With Justin, she wanted to dig her feet in and make this work.

Justin leaned against the door. "As of three minutes ago?"

She winced. It sounded harsh, but it was true. She had been ready to run away up until a few minutes ago. It wasn't Justin's fault that he called her on it.

"Fair enough. You don't have to believe me if you don't want to. That's fine." She was tempted to walk away, but that would totally defeat her statement.

Justin dipped his head in regret. "I'm sorry. I didn't mean to hurt you."

"Listen," she said as he tossed her weekend bag in the backseat. "I'm not the easiest person to be around, and you still haven't seen me at my worst."

He lifted his head and held her gaze. "I'm not worried."

She could see that. Either he liked a challenge or he was delusional. Or possibly both. "I'm still figuring things out," she confessed. "I make mistakes more than I get things right, and I have the uncanny knack of letting a great thing pass me by."

"You know you're not the only one, right?"

"I'm not asking for a lifetime or asking you to move in," she explained, "but I'm asking for Christmas vacation."

He stepped around the car door. "To start."

Rachel felt a sparkle of hope. "You may want to rethink that once New Year's comes around." She felt obligated to give him an out. She knew she was no prize.

"I don't need to, Rachel. I already had to rethink my life the day I met you."

"Really?" She remembered that day vividly. The moment she met him, she had turned into a rambling, befuddled mess. "That was a really bad first impression."

"Then you still haven't figured out how much you affect me," he said with a lopsided smile. "Get in the car, Rachel. I'm taking you home."

This time she knew without a doubt he meant his home. Rachel put one foot in the car and stopped. She looked up at Justin. "By the way, there's one more thing you should know about me."

"What's that?" he asked indulgently.

"I do have a tattoo."

"No, you . . ." His voice trailed off as his chin dropped in surprise. She saw the devilish look in his eyes as the curiosity got the better of him. "Where?"

"You just haven't looked hard enough," she said as she sat down and pulled at the seat belt.

"I will make it my mission to find it," he promised in a husky, low voice. She felt Justin's hot gaze linger on her, as if he was considering the possibilities.

"Come on, Justin," she urged him, and patted the driver's seat. "Our Christmas vacation has officially started. I don't want to waste a second of it."

Hot Arctic Nights

Janice Maynard

*For Bob and Sally, dear friends from high school days
who invited us for a wonderful visit at Fort Wainwright
and helped us fall in love with Alaska.*

*Sally, you were our hostess extraordinaire, and Bob—
we'll never forget our long day trip to the Arctic Circle
and back in your poor, abused car!*

Good memories and old friends are the best. . . .

Chapter One

*W*here was the snow? Hallie Prentiss huddled inside the warmth of her newly purchased fleece-lined coat and frowned. She was standing on the sidewalk outside the Fairbanks International Airport, and there was no snow—well, correction: no snow *falling*. There was plenty of packed-down grayish white stuff underfoot. But no soft, quiet flakes tumbling in movie-worthy fashion from the leaden sky.

She felt cheated. If she was going to have to spend two interminable weeks in the frozen tundra, at the very least she expected some ambience, some picturesque postcard scene.

Not that the piped-in Christmas carols inside the terminal had been a positive. Each chirpy note and syrupy lyric grated on her frayed nerves. Her stomach churned despite the antacids she popped like candy, and she hadn't slept worth a damn since the morning her boss apologetically handed her a pink slip. *Terminated*.

Hallie shoved the nasty memory aside and turned to speak

to a baggage handler, who was bundled up from head to toe in some serious outdoor gear. She waved a hand in his direction. "This is Alaska. What happened to the snow?"

The older man shrugged and grinned. "We've been having a really warm and dry December. But don't worry. The snow will come. You can count on it."

Hallie gaped. *Warm?* Was he kidding? The large weather station hanging on the wall over his head registered a temperature of minus eight degrees Celsius. And although it had been a long time since Hallie had been asked to do the required conversions, she was pretty sure that meant it was somewhere in the neighborhood of fifteen degrees. Her frozen nose verified the calculations.

She slung her carry-on over her shoulder and grabbed the handle of her large rolling suitcase. The sooner she made it to her destination, the sooner she could wallow in a tub of wonderful, scalding-hot water and finally feel her toes again.

Picking up the rental car was painless. The agent handed her a map marked in yellow highlighter, and in no time she was on the Mitchell Expressway. Thank God it was only an eighteen-mile trip. Her eyes were gritty with fatigue, and she didn't want to fall asleep at the wheel. She had imagined having to navigate treacherous roads, but though there were piles of snow on the shoulders, the thick, dry snowpack on the roads was not particularly hazardous.

The sun hung low and sullen in the sky as if it didn't have the energy to make it all the way overhead. Hallie could sympathize. Her usually high-powered personality was in idle mode. She'd had the breath knocked out of her, metaphorically speaking, and inside, she was floundering.

To the rest of the world, she had managed to keep up a facade of practical calm. But her confidence was cowering in front of what at the moment could be described only as a hazy future.

She found the turn for the Richardson Highway with no trouble, but when she saw the sign for her final exit, she snorted. The ramp was marked SANTA CLAUS LANE. Good grief. She felt like she was starring in a Charlie Brown Christmas special . . . especially when she passed the sign that said, WELCOME TO NORTH POLE, ALASKA.

A few minutes later, amidst a plethora of cutesy street names like Kris Kringle Drive and Snowman Lane—where the streetlights were candy canes and even gas stations were decorated in the spirit of the holiday season—Hallie pulled to a stop in front of her destination and sighed. She'd come more than two thousand miles and one time zone from Seattle, and she was operating in a mental fog.

The modest-sized building in front of her fit right in with the explosion of holiday mania. It was made of cedar and stone, and Christmas lights outlined every available nook and cranny. Victorian gingerbread trim edged the gables and roof. On the lawn, Santa sat jauntily in his sleigh, prepared for the eight plastic reindeer to do all the work. Resin elves, arms upraised, loaded the packages.

Hallie had glanced briefly at the town's Web site while preparing for her trip and had rolled her eyes when she realized that the seasonal hoopla was not "seasonal" at all. North Pole, Alaska, was dedicated to Christmas cheer all year-round.

She sighed. She had never felt less like celebrating the holidays. But for the next two weeks, she was sentenced to tinsel and eggnog and Lord knew what else. It boggled the mind.

She left her luggage in the car and trudged up the walk. Before dinner last night, Hallie's best friend, Julie, had brought over a set of keys to the Dancing Elves B&B. Julie's parents owned and operated the lodge, but they were eager to spend the holidays with Julie, so Hallie had agreed to play innkeeper for a little while. Hallie found the key marked "front door" and let herself in. The air was filled with the scents of cinnamon and evergreen. An enormous live fir tree, decked out with enough ornaments to bury old Santa himself, presided over the space in front of the bay window. Everywhere Hallie looked—from the walls to the stairs to the floor beneath her feet—knickknacks and doodads and tchotchkes abounded.

Christmas was everywhere.

But even that unpleasant realization took a backseat to the much bigger surprise. Santa himself stood not three feet away . . . wearing red pants, black boots, and silver suspenders. His rotund belly had been replaced with granite-hard abs, and his shoulders were as wide as Texas.

He was tanned and toned, and the smile on his face made Hallie think that being on *his* naughty list might not be such a bad thing. Her knees actually quivered.

He reached out and engulfed her cold fingers in his warm, hard hand. His grip made Hallie want to cling . . . and she was not at all the clingy type. She shook his hand with a businesslike pump and stepped back from temptation. "Who are you?"

His grin was a wicked slash of white in a tanned face that was all sharp angles and masculine lines. "I'm Daniel Reynolds, your semipermanent resident . . . room two. Hazel and Roy asked me to make sure you got settled in." His brown eyes sparkled with warmth.

Hazel and Roy. Julie's parents. And yes . . . Hallie did have some faint memory about a long-term guest, but she hadn't paid all that much attention. She cleared her throat. "Well, that's kind of you, Daniel. I'm Hallie Prentiss. I guess Hazel and Roy told you I'll be running things for a couple of weeks so they can spend time in Seattle with Julie. I'm supposed to take their room. Can you please point me in the right direction?" *So I can get on with the bath and the nap, please God.*

He ran a hand through his thick, short-cut dark hair, appearing a little frazzled. "Before I do that, I've got a huge favor to ask."

Her heart actually skipped a beat. But she kept her expression calm. "Oh?"

He tapped his stomach, drawing Hallie's eyes once again to that intriguing expanse of subtle muscle and the arrow of fine, silky hair leading southward to the off-limits area below his large, silver, Santa-inspired belt buckle. "I'm due over at the elementary school in twenty minutes. When I tried on the costume a while ago, I realized that I can't fit behind the steering wheel with the potbelly in place. I don't want to chance any little kid seeing me without it, so I was hoping you might drive me over there."

Hallie tasted desperation. She would give her last traveler's check for a warm bath and a soft bed. But when Santa called, what was a woman to do? She closed her eyes and did her best not to inhale the insidious scent of Christmas cheer and warm male. But no matter how hard she tried to ignore it, something about this house and this *man* was turning her usual assertive self into a blob of indecision.

"What about the B and B?" she asked, grasping at any reason not to go back out into the cold.

Daniel grinned. "No guests on the books today. We can lock up and head out immediately."

She was too tired to fight. "No problem," she lied morosely. "I'd be happy to help a Santa in need."

Daniel folded his gut-enhanced body into Hallie's rental car and smiled inwardly. Nothing like an early Christmas present to make a man sit up and take notice. Hallie Prentiss was one long, tall drink of water. Even travel-rumpled and wearing a parka that made her resemble a sky blue Michelin Man, she was stunning.

Her slightly pointed chin saved her beautiful oval face from complete perfection. Her cheekbones were dramatic, and her skin was pale cream. The smudges of exhaustion beneath her cornflower blue eyes gave him a moment of guilt, but he really did need her help.

He pointed to the dash. "You might want to turn your lights on. It will be dark pretty soon."

Hallie slanted an incredulous look in his direction. "It's barely two o'clock."

He chuckled. "Did you look up anything about Alaska before you came? We only have around four hours of daylight right now."

"Four hours . . ." Her voice trailed off, and he could swear she turned white. But it was hard to tell in the fading light.

Her eyes were fixed on the road ahead, so he took the opportunity to study her again. She had tidied her waterfall-straight blond hair before they left. He'd seen it down for only a split second before she bundled it back up into a prim, bun-like thing on the back of her head.

Her delicate earlobes sported small, gold hoop earrings, and her neck, at least the part he could see in the open collar of her coat, was long and graceful. He felt a stirring of lust and shifted restlessly. Hallie was going to be in town for only a couple of weeks. It was the perfect scenario for some hot and heavy, no-strings-attached sex. But hell, he didn't even know if she was in a relationship with some lucky guy.

He had yet to see her hands. They were covered in soft, cream gloves—probably cashmere. From head to toe, Hallie looked like a polished, sophisticated city dweller.

He watched her grimace as she hit a pothole. She drove with a quiet confidence that underscored her air of capability.

He broke the silence. "This is a great thing you're doing for Roy and Hazel . . . running the inn so they can visit their daughter."

She shrugged, still not looking at him. "It's entirely self-serving," she muttered. "I need the money."

A more polite man wouldn't have asked. But Daniel was endlessly fascinated by his new landlady. "Hmmm," he said in a teasing voice. "Down payment for a new house? Hush money for the cops? Gambling debts?"

Finally, she smiled. And he felt like he'd won the lottery. She went from beautiful to knock-your-socks-off gorgeous.

Her grin was wry. "Foreign investors bought the big Seattle hotel where I worked. Ninety percent of us were pink-slipped the Monday after Thanksgiving."

He winced in sympathy. "Ouch. That sucks."

She nodded. "My sentiments exactly. Roy and Hazel's daughter, Julie, is my best friend. She came up with this idea to give her parents a break over the holidays and provide me with some short-term employment. I just hope my experience working at a four-hundred-room hotel translates into running a B and B."

"You'll be fine." Daniel glanced at his watch and put on his hat. They were going to make it. "Turn here," he said.

Hallie parked in a visitor spot. "I'll wait in the car."

He shook his head. "No way. You'll freeze. Come on in. This will be fun."

Hallie followed "Santa" into the building and couldn't help smiling when every kid in sight, ages five to twelve, screeched a greeting. Teachers were equally welcoming.

The principal was an attractive native Alaskan. She ushered them into the auditorium, where small piles of Christmas presents were neatly arranged on the stage. Daniel's job was to hand them out personally. One of the government agencies in town, along with a men's club, had provided the largesse.

For the next half hour, loosely organized pandemonium

reigned. Hallie would have said that she didn't have an ounce of Christmas cheer left in her body. But seeing the enthusiasm and wonder on the face of each child who sat on Daniel's knee to accept a handful of gifts made her misty-eyed. He was amazingly gentle with each of them.

If children were the bellwethers of decency, then Daniel passed with flying colors.

Hallie had been charged with standing at Daniel's elbow and, as each child finished, providing a reusable bag to carry the gifts. She was tired and her legs ached, but she wouldn't have missed the young students' excitement for the world. There was still one more week of school to go before the holidays, and Hallie didn't envy the teachers who had to keep control in the interim.

Finally, it was done. With one last round of waves and ho-ho-ho's, Daniel and Hallie left the building. The sun had indeed gone down, but a pleasant pinkish glow lit up the sky.

Daniel stopped in the parking lot, despite the frigid temperature, and rested his hands momentarily on her shoulders. He squeezed lightly. "Thanks, Hallie. You make a great elf."

She felt his fat belly bump her stomach. "You're very welcome," she said, not bothering to hide her smile. "It was fun."

Something charged the air around them. A scientist might have called it static electricity. Hallie was pretty sure it was anticipation. But though she'd learned a lot about Santa in her twenty-eight years, she knew nothing at all about Daniel Reynolds.

She took the car keys from her pocket and fumbled awkwardly to unlock the door. Romantic moments in Alaska came with a price. Possible hypothermia.

Both she and Daniel were quiet on the short trip back. When they arrived at the B&B, he insisted on carrying in her two bags and showing her the master suite. Hazel and Roy's quarters were comfortable and tidy. And fortunately they must have run out of Christmas decorations before they got to their own room. Except for a holly-appliquéd hand towel in the bathroom and a small ceramic tree with tiny plastic lights on the dresser, the room was pleasantly neutral in decor.

Daniel set Hallie's bags in front of the closet and started unfastening the big black buttons down his front. He did it unself-consciously, tossing aside the pillow and sliding his arms out of the jacket and suspenders. All the while, he was checking things . . . the wall heater, the carafe of water on the nightstand, the latch on the window.

At last, he seemed satisfied. He turned to Hallie and stretched his arms over his head. She saw muscles ripple and flex. "I know you're beat," he said, "but I owe you dinner for today. Why don't you rest for a while and we'll go out around seven?"

"Sounds great." He hadn't really given her a chance to refuse, but did she want to? Even though she was exhausted, starvation ran a close second. She took off her coat and tossed it on the chair. When she turned back around, Daniel's eyes had glazed over, and his face was almost as red as his Santa pants. He dragged his gaze away from her bust. "Well, okay, then."

Was his voice hoarse?

He slid toward the door. "I guess I'd better let you sack out." He seemed reluctant to leave.

"Yeah. I'm dead on my feet."

He nodded slowly, his gaze warm and intimate. "Welcome to Alaska, Hallie," he said in a low voice, and then he was gone.

Daniel stripped and got in the shower to wash off the sweat. Being Santa was damned hard work. And speaking of hard . . . he put his hand on his swollen cock and closed his eyes. Visions of Hallie, a woman he'd known for less than a day, filled his mental screen.

He'd nearly made a fool of himself back there in her bedroom. When she took off her coat and he'd seen her kick-ass body for the first time, he'd known in an instant what his Christmas wish would be. He wanted Hallie Prentiss. Her legs, clad in tight indigo denim jeans, were long and sexy. And her generous breasts beneath that wine silk turtleneck . . . well, a man could write a sonnet about them . . . or at least create a damned good fantasy.

He ran with that last thought as he continued to stroke himself. He squeezed his eyes shut when he came, imagining Hallie smiling at him, riding him.

He let her sleep for two hours. But he knew that getting accustomed to Alaska's twenty hours of darkness would be easier if she stayed on a normal schedule.

He was dressed and ready far too early, so he did a load of laundry and replaced a couple of lightbulbs upstairs. Finally he decided it was okay to wake Hallie. The door to her room wasn't shut all the way, so he eased it open and whispered her name. The lump beneath the covers didn't move. He wondered if she had undressed before climbing in bed, but he didn't see her jeans and top anywhere. Only her coat.

Poor thing. He felt guilty for shanghaiing her into being his chauffeur earlier, but it had been fun to have her along. Clearly, though, the stress of losing her job had given her some sleepless nights.

He inched closer to the bed. "Hallie?" It was almost six thirty, and he figured she probably needed time to get ready. He planned to take her to a nice restaurant in Fairbanks. The city was only a fifteen-minute drive away, and the choices of eating establishments there were more numerous than in the town of North Pole.

He started to get concerned. Surely no one slept *that* deeply. Not during the daytime at least. Even if it was dark outside.

"Hallie?" He touched her shoulder. No response. He shook her gently. "Hallie?"

She yelped and sat straight up in bed. The top of her head made contact with the bottom of his jaw, and he staggered back, reeling as he saw stars. Shit. He nearly bit through his tongue.

As he was trying to catch his breath, the lights came on, and he was finally able to focus on Hallie's indignant face.

She glared at him, pulling the sheet to her chin despite the fact that she was fully clothed. "What in the heck are you doing in my room?"

He flung his arms wide. "I was *trying* to wake you up so you wouldn't miss dinner."

Her eyes narrowed. "What time is it?"

"Six thirty. And I thought you might want to do some woman stuff before we leave."

She threw back the covers and drew her knees to her chest. "Woman stuff?"

He shrugged helplessly. "You know . . . lipstick, primping, whatever . . ."

He trailed off as her eyes shot blue sparks at him.

"I do *not* primp. That is a demeaning word."

Now his own temper boiled over. "It sure the hell is not. I don't even know you, Hallie Prentiss. I was trying to be nice. So shoot me."

"Don't tempt me," she muttered.

"Are you always this cranky when you wake up?"

She wrinkled her nose and rubbed the top of her head. "Your chin hurt me."

He snorted. "Your *head* hurt *me*," he shot back, not willing to be the bad guy.

She yawned hugely. "Maybe I'll skip dinner," she grumbled, falling back against the pillows.

He was far too tempted to join her. So instead, he got tough. "No way. I'll expect you by the front door in twenty-five minutes."

He was honestly surprised when she showed up. He'd known her all of five hours, and already he sensed that she could be as stubborn as he was . . . and that was saying something.

But he was smart enough not to comment on her punctuality.

They were in his car this time, and for Hallie's benefit, he cranked the heater up full blast. She had covered every available inch of her body with winter clothing.

He put the car in gear. "You can take your coat off if you want to. . . . It's plenty warm in here."

Her voice was muffled by the thick scarf she had wrapped

around her neck. It sounded like she said something sarcastic, but he was willing to give her the benefit of the doubt.

As they reached the outskirts of Fairbanks, she finally shed the scarf. But nothing else. He grinned. "You aren't a vegetarian, are you?"

Hallie's stomach growled audibly. "No. But I'm not eating moose meat . . . just so you know."

He chuckled. "We'll stick to beef for the moment."

Over steak dinners, Daniel learned more about her. She was type A. She liked beaches rather than mountains. Her favorite music was country. And, most important, she was unencumbered romantically.

He sipped his wine and leaned back in his seat. "The men in Seattle must be blind and stupid."

Hallie flushed slightly. "I've had plenty of offers. But I was on the fast track to assistant manager. Working sixty- and seventy-hour weeks. I decided that there was plenty of time in the future for relationships. I was determined to establish my career first." She grimaced. "A pitiful cliché, right? And look what it got me. A one-month severance package, and a *Don't let the door hit you on the way out.*"

Daniel studied her face. Her expression was guarded, but her eyes told the story. They were bleak. He set down his glass, leaned back in his chair, and crossed his arms over his chest. "You do realize that what happened to you was in no way a personal failure."

Her eyes narrowed, her chin at a mulish angle. "Feels like it from where I'm sitting," she muttered.

He opted for humor. "Have you ever wondered why getting *laid off* is so much worse than getting *laid*?"

She choked on a sip of burgundy. "Is this your version of a pep talk? Dr. Phil, you are not."

He sighed. "No one ever appreciates good advice."

"What advice? All you've told me is that getting fired wasn't my fault. And like any guy, you managed to bring up sex in the process."

He shrugged. "Sex makes anything better."

She smiled then. A full-blown, sexy curve of her lush lips. "I'm willing to let some naughty talk distract me from my sucky life."

"Just talk?" he asked hopefully. "Or something more hands-on?"

She caught her lower lip between her teeth and studied his face. He wondered what she was thinking. Chances were, nothing nearly as X-rated as the images that were galloping across his brain.

Unfortunately his question went unanswered. She leaned forward, her elbows on the table. "So, tell me about Daniel Reynolds. What do you do when you're not being Santa Claus?"

He abandoned the previous topic reluctantly. "I'm the Department of Defense police captain at Fort Wainwright. We do road patrols, post security. How visitors are processed at the front gate, how deliveries are vetted, stuff like that."

"So you're in the army?"

"No. Actually, it's a civilian position. I *was* in the army after college . . . for six years. When I got out, I started working at Fort Irwin in California. Worked my way up to police lieutenant. This job opened back in the spring. I applied, and moved here six months ago."

"Sounds like interesting work."

"I think so."

"But don't you miss being at home?"

"My dad was in the military, too, so I don't really have a home base, although my parents are retired and live in Florida. I love Alaska, and relocating here for the foreseeable future hasn't been a hardship."

"How do you know Hazel and Roy?"

"We met in town one day. I hate staying in hotels and motels for more than a few nights. And in the beginning, the job at Fort Wainwright was temporary, strictly on a month-by-month basis. So I didn't want to buy a house right off or rent a generic apartment. I threw myself at Hazel and Roy's mercy and they cut me a deal. I did all their yard work during the summer and fall, and they gave me a room at a drastically reduced rate. They're getting older, so they appreciate having someone around to do odd jobs. It's worked out really well."

He lifted a hand and indicated to the waiter that he'd like the check. "I want you to know, Hallie, that I'll help you as much as I can in the next two weeks. At least with getting breakfast on the table before I have to go to work in the mornings."

Her jaw dropped slightly and confusion filled her deep blue eyes. "Breakfast?"

He grinned as he signed the credit card slip. "Yeah, breakfast. You know . . . the second *B* in 'B and B.'"

She waved a nonchalant hand. "How hard can it be? I doubt there will be too many people booking stays at a B and B in Alaska in December. I have a whole packet of stuff to look at this evening . . . meticulous instructions Hazel and Roy mailed

me a week ago. And I'm supposed to call them if I have questions. We had planned to touch base when they got to Seattle,
but their flights were delayed a day and a half, and I was gone
before they arrived. But I'm sure it will be fine. Especially since
we don't have guests tonight. I kept meaning to go through all
the info they gave me before I left, but there was so much to
do getting ready for the trip. . . ."

He got a bad feeling in the pit of his stomach. "Um,
Hallie . . . have you even taken a look at the reservation book?"
Hazel and Roy refused to use computers. The books were kept
the old-fashioned way.

Hallie bit her lip again and shrugged. "Well, not yet. You
whisked me away to the school, and then I took a nap, and then
we left. . . . Is there something you're not telling me?"

He took a deep breath. "You have fifteen guests checking
in tomorrow. And they're staying through Christmas Eve."

Chapter Two

*H*allie had never fainted in her life. Well, except for that one time when she gave blood on an empty stomach, but that didn't count. Her vision went fuzzy, and she took several deep breaths. "Fifteen people?" She'd had some hazy notion of dusting the occasional bookshelf and catching up on her reading for the next two weeks. B&Bs in the middle of nowhere were not the same as high-end hotels. The occupancy rates were minimal, especially outside of tourist season. Right?

Daniel took her cold hands in his and rubbed them gently. "Take a deep breath. You're a pro, remember? You can do this with your eyes closed. You know the hospitality industry inside out."

But that was just it, Hallie lamented inwardly. She didn't, not really. All she knew were the rigorous schedules that kept her big hotel running smoothly. She knew how to deal with an irate guest and a malfunctioning AC unit. She knew how to pacify a wealthy rock star whose suite was still being cleaned and prepared. She knew how to handle squabbles among the housekeeping staff. But she sure as heck didn't know how to entertain fifteen people in a four-thousand-square-foot bed-and-breakfast. Good Lord.

She yanked her hands away from Daniel's comforting grasp, mostly because she wanted so much to cling to his strength. But this B&B was her problem. Not Daniel's.

She cleared her throat self-consciously. "By breakfast, I assume you don't mean tossing a waffle in the toaster."

He winced. "Not quite. Hazel is legendary for her spectacular breakfast spreads. There's a red and green loose-leaf binder on the kitchen counter where she has all her recipes. Muffins, quiches, fruit salads . . . you name it. And I think she even has meal plans that she rotates every five days . . . so guests don't get tired of the same thing."

"Five days . . ." Her throat was dry. "Excellent."

The expression on Daniel's handsome face was troubled. "You do know how to cook, right?"

She waved a hand. "Of course," she said airily, her heart thumping. "Who doesn't?"

Over the next half hour, she waited to get struck by lightning for her bald-faced, unrepentant lie. Hallie Prentiss had been known to ruin strawberry Pop-Tarts, for God's sake. And the inside of her microwave oven saw more action than a Vegas hooker. If it couldn't be nuked, she didn't eat it. Not at home, anyway.

She followed Daniel out to the car, her pulse racing. Fifteen guests. Arriving tomorrow. She was in deep trouble.

The outside air took her breath away . . . literally. Even dashing from one warm spot to the next required bracing against a jolt of subzero air. But on the upside, the infinite night sky was black velvet spangled with a million stars she'd never been able to see back in Seattle.

She had assumed they were going straight home, but Daniel took an unfamiliar turn, and she didn't challenge him. After a few minutes they wound up a small hill. She saw the sign for the University of Alaska, Fairbanks. Sheesh. Who would voluntarily go to school *here*?

Daniel parked in an empty lot and touched her arm. "Hop out."

Her eyes telegraphed incredulity over the edge of her muffler. "No thanks."

He touched her cheek gently. Even without gloves on, his hands were warm. How did he do that? His grin was wry. "Come on, Hallie. Be a sport. You won't be sorry."

She yanked the scarf away and half turned in her seat to face him. "If you think we're going to indulge in some kind of kinky, arctic, *sex-on-the-hood-of-your-car* thing, you're insane."

He laughed out loud. "I appreciate your inventive mind, Hallie, but I think it's a little early for sex."

Since the clock on the dash read ten p.m., she had to assume he was talking about the length of their relationship and not the hour. Reluctantly, she rewrapped her face in its protective coating and climbed out of the car. *It's not cold. It's not cold. It's not cold.* She'd taken plenty of those *power-of-positive-thinking* workshops, but at the moment, the theory didn't seem to be working . . . at all.

Daniel drew her into his embrace, her back to his chest.

With the multitudinous layers of clothing between them, she couldn't actually feel his heartbeat, but hers was going wild.

She did her best to act as if it were no big thing that a large, handsome man was cuddling her in a decidedly romantic fashion, his thick, muscular arms tucked beneath her breasts. He was just doing his duty as a Boy Scout, that's all. Keeping her from "death by freezing."

His cheek brushed hers as he pointed. "Look. Over there. Keep watching."

She turned her gaze in the direction he indicated, and her breath caught in her throat. An arc of shimmering light stretched across half the sky. As she watched, the color deepened and intensified, first emerald green, then shadowy blue, then a mix of both with hints of pink.

She was awed and humbled. "Daniel . . ."

His warm breath teased her ear. "The northern lights. Pretty amazing, aren't they?"

She was mute. Words couldn't convey what she was feeling. She'd read about this phenomenon . . . even knew the scientific explanation. But nothing had prepared her for the reality of the experience.

In some corner of her mind, she was amazed that somehow the cold didn't seem too bad right at this moment. Not with Daniel's arms cradling her and the sky a palette of soft, swirling colors.

She wasn't sure how long they stood there. The show went on and on, each minute different from the last. Hallie lost herself in the incomparable beauty. But finally, Daniel squeezed her waist. "Come on, Hallie. We've got to get you home and warm you up."

. . .

Daniel could think of several titillating activities that involved himself and Hallie frolicking in a hot tub. But aside from the absence of said tub, tomorrow was a big day for his new landlady.

He drove in silence, enjoying her company and completely comfortable with the lack of conversation. Hallie was a very easy woman to be with.

When they returned to the little town of North Pole, the streets were mostly empty. But Christmas lights abounded, brightening the dark and bringing a feeling of cheer. The candy-cane light poles still made him grin. He stifled a yawn. "It's nice, isn't it? Makes it easy to get in the holiday spirit."

He glanced at Hallie as he spoke, but she was staring straight ahead, her expression pensive.

She sighed audibly. "You'll have to excuse me if I'm not really in that frame of mind."

"Because you just lost your job?"

She closed her eyes briefly and then looked at him. "That's part of it. But it's a long story and I'm not in the mood to talk about it right now."

Her words were firm, and he had to respect her boundaries. "Okay. But I'll be around if you change your mind."

She was yawning by the time they pulled into the driveway of the inn. He hustled her to the door, unlocked the house, and scooted her inside, pausing only to turn up the thermostat.

Hallie was the picture of exhaustion. But she projected an air of determination even so. "What time is check-in tomorrow?"

"Three o'clock. And I know that Roy and Hazel had all the rooms completely prepared before they left. But I'll do a quick peek before I head off to bed just to make sure."

"Thank you. I'm going to get that envelope of instructions they sent me and read it page by page before I go to bed. With the time difference, it's too late to call them tonight, but if I run into any questions, I can get in touch with them first thing in the morning. I'll be ready. Don't you worry."

"I never doubted you."

She shrugged out of her coat, and he swallowed hard. He'd known her less than twenty-four hours. Not since his college days had he contemplated bedding a woman on such short acquaintance. He felt like he and Hallie had jumped forward several steps at once.

She pulled pins from her "do" absentmindedly, almost as if she'd forgotten he was there. Her simple movements weren't meant to be provocative, but he felt himself getting hard.

Her hair was lovely, every bit as dazzling as the northern lights. But instead of blues and greens, her silky blond waves were shot through with gold and amber. He badly wanted to bury his face in those soft tresses while he buried his aching cock deep inside Hallie.

She yawned again, and he realized ruefully that while she was clearly ready for bed, she wasn't in any shape for sex. Which was probably a good thing, because if she had shown the slightest bit of interest, he wasn't sure he'd have been able to do the gentlemanly thing and wait.

He turned out the lights in the foyer, leaving the nearby living room lit only by the Christmas tree. It was damned romantic. But Hallie was unmoved. He was pretty sure she didn't even look once in that direction.

Reluctantly, he acknowledged defeat. It would have been really nice to cuddle on the sofa and get to know Hallie a little better. But it wasn't going to happen tonight. The tree lights were on a timer and would go off in a half hour or so . . . with no one curled up on the nearby couch to comment on the lateness of the hour.

He hung his jacket and scarf on the bear-tree coatrack and turned to face her. Was he the only one in the room feeling a wave of sexual tension? Oh, hell. Nothing ventured, nothing gained. . . .

He took her in his arms, sans coat, and covered her mouth with his. He lingered over the kiss a good thirty seconds, long enough to recognize the moment when she actually moved her lips against his. And long enough to feel her soft, warm breasts pressed to his chest. Then he peeled himself away from temptation and skedaddled for his room.

Hallie was shocked to realize she had slept eight hours straight through. When she crawled into bed the night before, bundled in a warm flannel nightgown and thick wool socks, she'd been sure she would lie awake for hours thinking about her new responsibilities . . . and Daniel's amazing kiss.

Instead, she'd been comatose in seconds. And she had awakened feeling rested, refreshed, and optimistic. Getting up in the dark was not unique to Alaska. Hallie often worked odd shifts at the hotel, and she had taught herself to use a warm shower and lots of caffeine to get going in the morning. Today would be no different.

She threw on jeans and a pink angora sweater and headed for the kitchen. She felt a little guilty that it was already past eight, because Daniel was a paying guest and she owed him breakfast.

But he beat her to the punch. He had the coffeepot cranked up and had apparently dashed out to the local grocery store for fresh doughnuts.

She sat down across from him at the table and bit into a delicious circle of cinnamon and sugar. "Oh. My. God," she moaned. "This is incredible. Why can't I just serve these for breakfast?"

Daniel had a funny look on his face, and he seemed to be preoccupied with watching her chew.

She finished the last bite and took a quick sip of coffee. "Don't worry," she said hastily. "I'm just kidding. I'll follow Hazel's recipes to the letter. But you gotta admit, these are fantastic." So much so that she ate a second one. After all, it was winter in Alaska. Who was going to notice if she put on a pound or two?

She carried her empty coffee cup to the sink and then turned on the XM radio that sat on the counter, tuning it to her favorite news channel. War, death, and mayhem as usual.

Daniel put both of their cups in the dishwasher. "Do you mind if I change it to Christmas music?"

What could she say to such a simple request? "Not at all." Wow. She was getting good at this lying business. Dean Martin started singing about his favorite things, and Hallie's eyes filled with tears. Shit. She turned quickly, but Daniel had already noticed her distress.

"Hallie," he said urgently. "What's wrong?"

She tried to think up a plausible story. Ripping open old wounds wasn't going to accomplish anything. But when he rubbed a hand down her arm and gazed at her with clear concern, she lost it.

He folded her close as she blubbered all over his clean shirt. She hadn't cried once in the last few weeks . . . stiff upper lip and all that. But now her misery reached critical mass.

Daniel let her weep. Even a less perceptive person would have realized that this wasn't all about losing a job.

After a few minutes, he grabbed a tissue and wiped her face. "Feel like talking?" he asked softly.

She looked at the clock. "Don't you have to go to work?"

He brushed a strand of damp hair from her cheek. "I'm the boss. Coming in late is one of the perks."

He took her hand and tugged her toward the living room. It was still dark outside, but the tree beamed its multicolored cheer. And oddly, for the first time, Hallie found herself comforted by the sight.

Daniel rested his arm behind her on the sofa. "Do you hate Dean Martin?" he deadpanned. "Is that it?"

She blew her nose in the napkin, embarrassed as hell. "That was my mom's favorite song. She died of a heart attack last January." The words came out calmly, the sadness a little less acute than it had been moments before. "My dad passed away when I was six, and I'm an only child."

Daniel was quick on the uptake. She could see in his face that he grasped at least a portion of what she was feeling. He touched her cheek in a brief caress. "I'm so sorry, Hallie. This first Christmas without her was going to be tough no matter what . . . right?"

She shredded the napkin between trembling fingers. "I thought I was handling things pretty well. But I guess I was pouring even more time than usual into my job."

"So when you were let go, it must have felt like having the rug pulled out from under you."

She nodded slowly. "Yeah . . . it did. I know it sounds crazy, because it was a huge hotel with a really large staff, but we were kind of like a family. The manager had been there for twenty-five years. He was nearing retirement. Everyone thought I was going to step into his shoes. . . ."

"And instead, it all went to hell."

She sucked in a big breath and exhaled slowly. "Not one of my better years, that's for sure."

"Have you thought about what you'll do next?"

It was a valid question . . . and very logical. She fought back the panic that crept in at odd moments. "Well, I guess I'll start sending out résumés. But the economic climate is still tough."

"Surely your credentials are impressive."

"Maybe so, but a major hotel can hire someone straight out of college, and even train them, for a much lower salary than what I was getting paid. It's a very competitive market." And she had busted her ass to make it to the top. Now she wondered why. Her job hadn't filled the holes in her life. But sheer "busyness" had allowed her to pretend.

Daniel stood up and squeezed her shoulder. "I promise not to rub Christmas in your face anymore, Hallie. And I also promise you that there's a great job out there somewhere just waiting for a woman with your talents. The New Year is right around the corner. Time for new beginnings, new adventures."

He shrugged into his coat as he spoke. Hallie took his words at face value, but were his eyes telegraphing an even more personal message? She stood up and wiped her hands on her jeans, feeling awkward and painfully self-conscious. "I guess I'd better make a grocery-store run. Hazel even has lists for that, thank goodness."

He smiled at her. "You'll be fine. And remember, it's only breakfast. You don't have to entertain them twenty-four/seven."

She nodded, fighting the urge to beg him to stay. She was a competent professional. Fifteen guests. That was nothing. She could do this with one hand tied behind her back. . . .

Two hours later, she huffed and puffed as she carried the last of twelve grocery bags into the house. Putting everything away in an unfamiliar kitchen took another half hour. She ate lunch standing up, a banana and a cup of yogurt, as she pored over the recipe book that was to be her lifeline for the next two weeks.

According to Hazel's notes, blueberry apricot muffin batter could be prepared today, kept in the fridge, and simply ladled into muffin cups and baked in the morning. That didn't sound too bad. But the scary thing about such a plan was . . . what if they didn't turn out?

Hallie decided to make a small batch right then and there to be sure she was on the right track. By the time her slightly burnt muffins were out of the oven and cooling on the counter, the kitchen looked like a war zone. She hadn't intentionally made a huge mess, but how could one bake from scratch and be neat?

The oven must be a bit hot, so she made a mental note to adjust the temps on the recipes. Or maybe she had set the temperature wrong to start with and not realized it. Because surely Hazel's recipes were calibrated for her own equipment. Oh, heck . . .

She tried one of the freshly baked muffins. After she pinched off the dark parts, they weren't half bad. She flipped the remaining muffins out of the pan, put them in a plastic container with a lid, and tucked them far back into the refrigerator. You never knew when an emergency stash of muffins might come in handy.

Hallie glanced at the clock and squeaked in alarm. It was already one thirty. Quickly, she filled the sink with soapy water and cleaned the bowls and utensils she had dirtied. In another twenty minutes, the countertops were gleaming once again.

She dashed to her room and put on black slacks and a royal blue sweater. She doubted she would feel the need to dress up every day, but first impressions were important. And she didn't want to let Hazel and Roy down. This B&B was their livelihood.

When everything was in order, she sneaked down the hall to peek into Daniel's room. His and hers were the only ones on the main floor, along with the large, open kitchen/dining room, the small living room, and a modest-sized TV/game room, which must come in handy this time of year.

Upstairs were four bedrooms with accompanying bathrooms. Each room had two double beds. The group checking in today was sleeping four to a room, information that Hallie now possessed because she had finally perused the reservation book.

Daniel's room was neat as a pin. A leather jacket lay over the back of a chair, and a popular crime novel rested open and upside down on the nightstand. Other than that, there were no personal signs of his occupation. She stood immobile for a long moment, picturing him in bed, the sheet tucked decorously at his waist, his broad, muscular chest bare. Did he sleep in the nude? Her thighs tightened, and she recognized the heated pull of sexual arousal for what it was. She'd been living like a nun for months, and suddenly, all she could think about was sex. With Daniel.

He had made his bed already, which left little for her to attend to other than running the vacuum and putting a quick shine on the bathroom surfaces. She resisted the entirely inappropriate inclination to open all the drawers. Her curiosity about Daniel would have to be answered the old-fashioned way . . . with conversation and the passage of time.

She tucked away all her equipment in the hall closet and fought the urge to linger. She was pretty sure she could catch a whiff of Daniel's woodsy aftershave. Too bad he had to go to work. Having him around was comforting. Which made no sense at all, because they had just met. Clearly, she was feeling adrift due to the newness of her situation. Once she settled into her routine, Daniel would seem like any other guest. Ha. Fat chance. Not a man who kissed as he did.

She didn't have loads of sexual experience, but she knew how to recognize when a man was interested. And Daniel had made no secret of his attraction to her. A two-week fling was not her usual style, but perhaps sex was how people in Alaska made the most of the long winter nights.

She still had a smile on her face when the doorbell rang at precisely three o'clock. Showtime . . .

Hallie had her welcome speech all prepared. But the moment she opened the door, she was engulfed in an overload of excited conversation, a blast of cold air, and an enthusiastic hug from a woman who bore a striking resemblance to Paula Deen.

The leader of the pack, the bright-eyed, casually dressed matriarch of the crowd, released Hallie from a bone-crushing embrace and beamed. "I'm Robbie Denman, and we're tickled pink to be here. It's really *Roberta*, but no one calls me that."

As Daniel had warned, there were fifteen in all. Robbie and her husband had one young teenage boy. Robbie's two adult brothers had wives and four elementary-age kids between them, and Robbie's brother-in law and his wife had a pair of eighteen-month-old twin girls.

Bringing in the luggage and getting everyone settled into their assigned rooms was like herding cats. The children weren't bad. . . . In fact, they were remarkably well behaved considering they had just endured a long plane ride. But kids will be kids, and their boisterous energy filled the house with an almost palpable excitement.

Hallie had picked up some packaged gingersnaps and "just add water" hot chocolate mix, so when her guests were busy exploring their rooms and the house, she quickly set out an impromptu snack. It wasn't promised in the B&B brochure, but traveling was exhausting, and she wanted the extended Denman family to feel at home.

They exclaimed over the decorations, declared themselves in love with the town of North Pole, and gobbled up the refreshments in short order. Robbie shooed the kids off to the game room with the men, and she and the other three women settled in the living room with Hallie.

Robbie sighed and leaned back in a recliner. "Lord, I love this family, but getting through airports these days is a real bitch."

Hallie hid a smile and curled into a comfy overstuffed chair. "So, I'm curious, Robbie. What made all of you decide to vacation in Alaska at this time of year?"

Robbie's eyebrows went up. "Didn't Hazel tell you? She sure told me all about you. Losing your job, you poor thing, and your mom. I vote we adopt you as part of our family. What do you say, girls?"

Even before the other three chimed in with assent, Hallie realized that keeping a conversation on track was going to be a challenge. She smiled gamely, touched by a stranger's openness and kindness. "I'd be honored," she said slowly. "But really . . . why Alaska?"

For a moment, Robbie's air of cheerfulness slipped, and she looked ten years older and measurably sad. She sniffed and wiped her eyes. "My boy Timothy is the oldest of all our crew.

He enlisted in the army the day he turned eighteen. . . . That was six months ago. And now he's stationed at Fort Wainwright. There's never been a Christmas when we haven't all been together. And it just didn't seem right, him being so young and so far away from home. He's being deployed overseas after the first of the year, so we all decided to bring Christmas to him."

Hallie's throat was tight. "But how will that work?"

Robbie shrugged. "We're here for two weeks. Whenever he has time off, we'll be here to do things with him. And once he knows his schedule, we'll plan our Christmas celebration. It's not much, but at least he'll know we're close by."

Hallie nodded, wondering what it must be like to grow up as part of such a large, fun-loving, loyal family. "I think that's a wonderful idea. And the inn is yours for whatever you want to plan. I wish we had a bit more room, but we'll make do."

Robbie's grin was fierce. "You bet. And we won't trash the place, I promise. We didn't have much room in the luggage to bring gifts, so we've got to get cracking tomorrow on some serious shopping . . . and, after that, wrapping. This will be one hell of a celebration. . . . You wait and see."

Chapter Three

*D*aniel opened the front door and listened. There were no cars in the driveway other than Hallie's. Had something gone wrong? The silence was absolute. He tossed his briefcase and the other stuff he was carrying on the table in the foyer and peeked into the living room. Hallie was asleep, curled up in a chair with an afghan, her hand tucked beneath her cheek.

He smiled and went to sit on the sofa, content to watch her sleep. Work had been a bear today, but he hadn't been able to stop thinking about Hallie Prentiss. In fact, he might go so far as to say he was obsessed with her. Which was alarming and confusing at the same time.

By the time he'd hit thirty-four the past year, he had long since given up a taste for one-night stands. He'd had two long-term girlfriends in the past five years, and both relationships had ended amicably. He liked women. He respected women. And it hadn't really struck him until this very moment that since being in Alaska he'd been mostly celibate.

Early on there had been a waitress in Fairbanks who'd invited him for a couple of overnights. They had both been lonely, and the sex had been more utilitarian than fireworks. Eventually they had decided friendship was more their speed. Lately there had been no one. Like Hallie, Daniel had let work fill his life.

So was his intense reaction to Hallie the product of a long dry spell? Or was this a case of love at first sight? He snorted inwardly. Lust, maybe. That he could guarantee. Just looking at her made him hard. But he swore to God that it was more. He didn't understand it, couldn't analyze it, but Hallie Prentiss had knocked him for a loop. And he didn't know what he was going to do about it.

She was here for a short run, so Daniel's opportunities were limited. And he wasn't accustomed to giving up, even when a project seemed like a lost cause.

Her sock-clad foot stuck out from under the afghan. He tugged on her big toe. "Wake up, Hallie."

She stirred and murmured. The afghan fell to her knees, and she opened her eyes, blinking sleepily. "Daniel?"

He grinned at her. "Well, it's not Santa—not this time."

She shoved her hair from her face and sat up. "What time is it?"

"A little after seven. Have you eaten dinner?"

She arched her back and stretched. *Holy Mother of God.* Those breasts were spectacular. He forced himself to look at her face, all flushed and rosy-cheeked. He could eat her up with a spoon.

He asked again, since she seemed to be in a sleep-induced fog. "Dinner, Hallie?"

She tucked her hair behind her ears. It was down this evening, and Daniel was glad. The casual hairstyle made her look more approachable, more open to flirting.

She smiled slightly. "I could eat."

He fetched a bag from the foyer. "I picked up burgers on the way home. There's one for you if you want it."

She brightened, throwing off the last of her drowsy haze, and scooting to sit beside him. "You're a wonderful man. I'm starving."

And just that easily, they were eating and chatting like they'd known each other five years instead of five minutes.

He swallowed a bite of burger and wiped his mouth. "So, did everything go smoothly when the big group checked in?"

"Oh, yeah. It was like a zoo." She chuckled. "They're a charming family, but it was kind of overwhelming for a while this afternoon. Did you know they're here because their son is at Fort Wainwright?"

He nodded. "Hazel filled me in. I thought it was a great story. Christmas reunion at the North Pole and all that. I wouldn't be surprised if one of the local networks picked it up."

Hallie stopped cold, a french fry halfway to her mouth. Her face lit up. "That would be wonderful promo for the inn."

"Yeah it would." He couldn't help grinning. Despite her modesty, Hallie had unerring instincts when it came to running a business large or small. She was smart, and she was focused, and he was pretty sure she would make a success out of anything she tackled.

He discovered that she liked pickles, hated mayo. They shared greasy fries. She wiped a blob of ketchup from his chin with her finger. And then he shocked them both by groaning when she did it.

The atmosphere went from lighthearted to intensely erotic in the blink of an eye. He felt himself go red. "Sorry about that," he muttered. "That burp got away from me."

Hallie sat back and studied his face, her eyes wide. "That wasn't a burp," she said slowly. After a moment of dead silence, she leaned forward and found another spot of ketchup she had missed. This time she removed it with the tip of her tongue.

The second groan was what it was.

Hallie laughed softly and whispered against his lips, "I find you incredibly attractive, Daniel Reynolds. I really do."

He rested his forehead against hers. "Well, that's a damned good thing, because I've been a goner pretty much from the first second I laid eyes on you."

His enthusiasm seemed to please her.

She put her hands on his shoulders and ran them down his arms to his wrists. She linked their fingers and sighed. "I don't usually rush this kind of thing, but I have a feeling that with a houseful of guests, any opportunities to be alone are going to be few and far between. So what do you think . . . your room or mine?"

Her humor relaxed him. Hallie wasn't making a big deal about this. She was a sensual woman who wanted him like he wanted her. It was the perfect situation.

His gut warned him that he might be getting in over his head, but he ignored it. Hallie Prentiss was going to be naked and under him in the next few minutes. It was a wonder his brain didn't explode.

. . .

Hallie saw herself and Daniel as if they were actors in a movie scene. She had just initiated sex with a man she met *yesterday*. What in the heck was she thinking?

She stood up, and he took her hand. Before they could take more than a single step in the direction of her bedroom, the front door was flung open with a crash. Bodies and voices filled the foyer along with a swirl of frigid air. One of the children, a freckle-faced girl with braces and pigtails, ran toward Hallie. "Can you believe it, Ms. Prentiss? It's snowing!"

Soon Daniel and Hallie were surrounded by the entire extended Denman family, including a skinny, clean-shaven young man in army fatigues. Robbie had him by the arm and drew him toward Hallie. "This is my boy Timothy, Ms. Prentiss." She beamed with pride.

The still-wet-behind-the-ears soldier looked sheepish. "Nice to meet you, ma'am."

Hallie introduced Daniel, and before long it was like a family reunion that included Daniel and Hallie. At one point, her gaze met Daniel's across the room. They exchanged rueful smiles before he was led away by one of the men to play air hockey. Hallie was soon occupied helping the women e-mail a brand-new photo of Timothy to an elderly grandparent who had not been able to make the trip.

Before you could say "mistletoe," it was almost midnight. The children had been put to bed a few at a time. The adults held out longer, but eventually the long day of travel wore them down. As the last good-nights were spoken, Hallie and Daniel were left standing together in the living room, almost in the same spot they had been when they were interrupted earlier.

Hallie yawned hugely and then was mortified when Daniel laughed out loud. "I get the hint," he chuckled. "Our time will come."

She wanted him, she really did. But she was dead on her feet. He didn't drag it out. Instead, he kissed her briefly and then held her for a long moment. He was hard and ready. His erection pressed against her abdomen. But he didn't ask for anything more.

He kissed her nose. "Tomorrow's your first big morning. You need your rest, Hallie. Don't worry. We'll have plenty of time for us."

But would they? Hallie fretted about the answer as she got ready for bed. Already, her two-week stint was down to twelve days. The Denmans were to fly home on Christmas Day, followed soon after by Hallie. Would she and Daniel be ready to say good-bye to their holiday flirtation?

Grumpy from unappeased desire, she showered quickly and tumbled into bed. She tried to imagine Daniel lying on the mattress beside her, but the image wouldn't come into focus. She was still lamenting their interrupted evening when she fell asleep. . . .

Hallie's alarm went off at six a.m. She slapped at it halfheartedly, pulled the pillow over her head, and dozed off again.

When the shrill beep sounded a second time, it hit her. Breakfast. At eight sharp. For seventeen people. Dear Lord.

She flung the covers back and bounded out of bed, her

heart racing. Teeth brushed, clothes yanked on, and the bare minimum of morning ablutions completed, she took a deep breath and opened her door.

And smelled coffee.

When she entered the kitchen, her heart skipped a beat. A sleep-rumpled Daniel sat at the table, along with a sheepish-looking Robbie Denman.

Robbie spoke up first. "Now, don't be mad, Hallie, honey. I know this is your domain. But I've been an early riser my whole life, and I wouldn't know what to do with myself if I wasn't in the kitchen. You were so organized with the recipes on the counter and all that, I just started a few things going. I hope you don't mind. The muffins went in the oven two minutes ago."

Hallie shoved her hands in the back pockets of her jeans and smiled. "Of course I don't mind. I was a little intimidated by the thought of feeding this crew. I won't look a gift horse in the mouth. Thank you, Robbie. You're a sweetheart."

She reached in the refrigerator, trying to ignore Daniel. He made her breathing go all haywire, and she needed to concentrate on not ruining her debut breakfast. But when he wrapped an arm around her waist and tugged the package of meat from her hand, her knees wobbled.

His smile was lopsided. "Even I can't ruin bacon," he said. "You set the table or whatever else you need to do to prepare."

Even with the three of them working in tandem, it was a challenge to have everything ready by eight. The large kitchen table seated twelve and there were six barstools. Robbie sug-

gested putting platters of food on the counter and letting everyone serve buffet-style.

When the hungry throng descended the stairs, the morning repast was hot, beautifully laid out, and (since Hallie had
not been forced to do it all on her own) delicious. Pounds
of food, everything from scrambled eggs to homemade gra-
nola (thawed from the freezer), were devoured in twenty minutes. Hallie watched in amusement as a six-year-old boy in the
throes of hero worship sat on Daniel's knee and reluctantly
finished a bowl of cinnamon apple oatmeal.

The room was noisy, crowded, and warm. Not only in
temperature, but in sentiment as well. The Denman's were
a *family*. They squabbled, they joked, they repeated oft-told
stories. And the affection and love they all shared were impossible to miss.

Despite Hallie's inclination to linger on the edge of the
action, she found herself drawn inexorably into the layered
conversations. It was hard to keep up. Perhaps it took experience not to get lost in the crisscrossing laughter and the good-
natured, across-the-table gibes . . . the high, childish voices and
the deep masculine chuckles.

Even as she was sucked into the pleasant chaos, she felt a
pang of loneliness. For years it had been only Hallie and her
mom. No siblings, no cousins. Both of her parents had been
only children. Hallie's grandparents had passed away when she
was in junior high.

Holidays in the Prentiss household, even before her father
died, had been quiet. But Hallie's mom had always gone out of
her way to make them special. Hallie had never doubted she

was loved. And she had many friends, none more dear than Julie.

But this Christmas was different. Christmas was a time for family, and Hallie was keenly aware that this year she was on her own.

She shook off the destructive self-pity and silenced the group with a whistle. Robbie, who had already started gathering dishes, looked up with a raised eyebrow.

Hallie grinned. "Robbie, thanks for everything. But this is your vacation. Go out and have some fun. I'm a whiz at cleaning a kitchen and I have all morning to do it. As of now, you're all banished." She looked over at Daniel. "You, too, Daniel. Go to work. I'll be fine."

When everyone cleared out as ordered, except for Daniel, Hallie suddenly found herself feeling shy. He leaned against the doorframe, arms folded across his chest. She had already noticed that his brown eyes changed colors depending on the light and his mood. At the moment, they looked like rich chocolate. Perhaps because of the tiny smile creasing his full, waiting-to-be-kissed lips.

She wiped her hands on a dish towel, avoiding his gaze. "Shouldn't you be going?"

He shrugged. "I've got time. Don't you think we ought to talk about last night?"

She bit her lower lip, struggling against a wave of longing so sharp and insistent that it took her breath. "Last night might have been a tad premature. We were drunk on the northern lights."

"I've seen them a hundred times," he murmured. "And besides, that was two nights ago. I'm pretty sure their effect doesn't last that long." He straightened and came toward her with a look in his eyes that made her stomach clench. "I was drunk on you, Hallie Prentiss."

She didn't even put up a token protest when he pulled her close and settled his mouth over hers. He was big and warm, and her breasts, pressed against his chest, ached to be touched.

He slid his tongue inside her mouth. "You taste like cinnamon," he said hoarsely. "I adore cinnamon."

Her legs weakened, and she was pretty sure she would have slid to the floor in an ungainly heap if he hadn't been supporting her with his muscular arms. Somehow *her* arms found their way around his neck.

He shifted positions and settled her between his thighs, deepening the kiss as he did so. Hallie heard herself whimper and tried to remember why this was not a good idea. A sound from upstairs brought her back from the edge of insanity. She pushed her hands against his shoulders, gaining a couple of inches, but no more.

"We can't do this here," she panted. "Daniel . . ." She said that last word with some urgency as he lowered his head to nibble the side of her neck with sharp teeth and warm breath.

"Daniel!" She was torn, desperate for him to stop and equally desperate for him to drag her down the hall to his bedroom.

His hands fell to his sides and a mighty shudder raked his frame. Their eyes met, hers filled with confusion, his glazed and sheepish. "Lord, Hallie. This is nuts."

She stepped back and bumped into the stove. He ran a hand across the back of his neck. A noticeable erection lifted the front of his slacks. She swallowed hard. "I need to get started on this." She waved a hand at the breakfast debris.

Daniel shook his head as if to clear it. "The Denmans have their own keys, right?"

"Well, of course. Why do you ask?"

"I'd like you to meet me this afternoon," he said urgently. "Do you think you can have everything here in shape in three or four hours?"

"If I work my butt off." She laughed. "Beds made, bathrooms cleaned. It will be a push."

"Good," he said. "I'll show you around the post."

"The post?"

"Fort Wainwright."

"I thought it was an army *base*."

He grinned. "Rookie. The navy has bases. The army has posts. Learn the lingo."

She saluted sharply. "Aye, aye, Captain."

She followed him into the living room. He jotted down directions, along with instructions about where to meet him. Then he grabbed his coat off the sofa and shrugged into it.

Suddenly, awkwardness returned.

He brushed her cheek with a gentle stroke, as if he couldn't keep from touching her. "I'm damned glad you came to Alaska, Hallie."

She turned her face and kissed his palm briefly. "Me, too," she said simply. "And who knows? You may persuade me to get in the Christmas spirit after all."

Her words hung between them, fraught with unspoken meanings. She had tossed them out jokingly, but the awareness that hovered between them told her that he was thinking what she was thinking.

This time, he was the one to flush. His fists clenched, and the cords in his neck stood out in relief. He glanced at his watch and cursed softly. Frustration etched his handsome, rugged features. "Two o'clock," he said, his voice rough. "Don't let me down."

The morning passed with agonizing slowness, despite the piles of work that needed to get done. When the kitchen was pristine, Hallie set out to make beds, empty the trash, and spot clean the rooms that needed it. She didn't linger in Daniel's bedroom this time. She was too on edge as it was. She didn't need any more reminders of the man who was making her act so out of character.

The Denman clan had gone out to do their Christmas shopping. The snow that had fallen the evening before added only a couple of inches to what was already on the ground, and the weak winter sunlight created diamondlike sparkles in the fresh powder.

Hallie paused at the window, marveling at how much she already appreciated the few hours of true sunlight. Perhaps it was human nature to take such things for granted. But being in Alaska in the dead of winter made her realize how little of the world she had experienced outside of Seattle. There had never been much money for extras like travel, and all her work experience had kept her close to home.

Here in Alaska her eyes were being opened to an entirely different environment. And she wasn't just talking about the weather.

At two o'clock on the dot, Hallie parked her car near a familiar chain pizza place. Daniel pulled up beside her moments later.

He kissed her on the nose. "I have a sudden urge to take you somewhere tropical so I can see you in a bikini."

She laughed as he helped her into his car. "I thought you *loved* Alaska," she teased.

He eased out into the traffic. "I'll be the first to admit that it has a few drawbacks. But don't worry, Hallie. I've got a great imagination."

That deliberately suggestive remark, and the naughty grin that accompanied it, set the tone for the afternoon. Daniel didn't miss any opportunity to let her know that he wanted her.

And the attraction between them sizzled at a slow burn.

He stopped at the visitors' center, which was a grand name for a small, cramped building. There she had to surrender her driver's license, and wait until her identity was verified. Apparently being accompanied by the boss didn't circumvent the red tape.

When the formalities were all in order, Daniel drove her through the gate and onto the post proper. Hallie wasn't sure what she had expected, but Fort Wainwright took her by surprise. It was a big area, for one thing. Vast, unoccupied, snow-covered fields gleamed whitely in the deepening dusk. The road wound around and through them until Daniel and Hallie reached clusters of buildings.

He pointed out administrative areas, a shopping center, a post office, the chapel, aircraft hangars, and finally several neighborhoods of neat, well-kept post housing for military personnel. "Fort Wainwright is really like a small town," he said, pointing out a playground, vacant for the winter. "Very self-contained."

He parked in front of one of the office buildings and they got out. Hallie wasted no time in scurrying up the steps. It wasn't windy today, but the air was just as cold. Once inside, Daniel showed her his modest office and they left their coats there. Then he took her arm and steered her down the hall toward a dimly lit stairwell.

"I'm going to show you something I'll bet you've never seen before," he said as he unlocked the metal gate at the base of the steps.

She bumped his hip with hers. "Bragging now, are we?"

He looked at her blankly for a split second before he understood. "You should be so lucky," he shot back, laughter lighting his gorgeous brown eyes and curving his masculine lips.

He relocked the gate behind them and they took a step forward. Hallie scooted to a halt, digging in her heels. "Um, Daniel?"

He stopped and looked back at her. "What is it?"

She wrinkled her nose. "This might be a good time to mention that I'm slightly claustrophobic."

He took her hand and gave her a quick kiss on the lips, enough to make her toes tingle. "No small dark spaces, I swear. I'm taking you into the utilidors."

He might as well have been speaking Greek for all the sense that made to Hallie. "Utilidors?" Her stomach rolled uneasily.

He put his arm around her waist and urged her forward. "They're a series of tunnels that link most of the main buildings on the post. All of the utilities—water, heat, electricity—flow through underground pipes via the utilidors. It's not scary at all, I swear."

Against her better judgment she let him take her into the passageway ahead. And in fact . . . it was pretty amazing. The tunnel was large and well lit, even if the color scheme bordered on "prison beige." And the air was delightfully warm. So much so that she actually had to shed the lightweight fleece jacket she'd worn over her long-sleeved T-shirt.

"So why the tunnels?" she asked as they walked.

"Think about it," he said. "The ground stays frozen for a big chunk of the year, which would present a big headache in terms of pipes breaking. Even being able to dig to do repairs would be difficult, if not impossible. When the post was built, they constructed this system of tunnels, and then put everything in one place. Pretty ingenious. If you'll look when we're back aboveground, you can see exactly where the utilidors run, because they keep the sidewalks directly above them so warm the pavement stays snow free."

All along the way, there were gates similar to the one they had entered through. One even led directly into the post commander's house. Hallie was fascinated.

In a particular section of the tunnel, there were fewer exits and the lights were spaced farther apart. Daniel stopped and leaned back against the wall, his expression difficult to read.

He tugged her hand until she stood in front of him, almost touching nose to nose. "Thanks for coming over today, Hallie," he said quietly. "I gave the Fairbanks chief of police a tour last week, but you're a lot more fun—and way cuter. . . ."

She laughed, leaning into him and laying her head on his shoulder. "I'm honored."

They stood there in the steamy semigloom, and Hallie felt the mood shift once again.

He put a finger beneath her chin and tilted her face toward his. When his lips brushed hers, retreated, and came back with more force, she sighed. They kissed lazily, as if they had hours, days. She ceased wondering if this was wise—ceased caring about how long she'd known him and how soon she would be leaving. For once, she dived right in, content to live in the moment. Throwing caution to the wind had a certain appeal.

His hands moved beneath her shirt, caressing her breasts through her thin, silky bra. Her breath caught. She moaned and pressed her hips to his. His arousal nestled in the notch of her thighs, making her crazy. In the middle of a busy, crowded army installation, Daniel had managed to find the only warm, deserted oasis of privacy.

But not completely private. At least not enough for what they both wanted so badly.

In the distance, they heard muffled voices.

Chapter Four

*D*aniel swore under his breath and started straightening Hallie's clothes. His breathing was harsh and his hands shook.

Hallie didn't feel so steady herself. "Will you get in trouble for bringing me down here?" she whispered.

He kicked a pillar with his boot and sighed. "No. But I guess we'd better go."

They retraced their steps in silence, and never actually crossed paths with anyone. Sounds echoed in the cavernous spaces, so whomever they heard must have retreated in another direction.

Back in Daniel's office, Hallie didn't know what to say.

Daniel was braver than she. He perched on the corner of his desk and watched as she put her coat back on and buttoned it all the way up to her chin. He cocked his head. "Protective armor, Hallie?"

She looked out the window, marveling at the fact that it was dark at four o'clock. But even so, ambient light from the reflective snow cover lent a pretty glow to the scene.

She wasn't sure how to answer his question, but she had
one of her own. Now that Daniel's arms were no longer around
her, she could think straight. The little voice inside her head . . .
the annoying voice of reason spoke up. "Why me?" she asked
bluntly. "Am I convenient? Is that it?"

He burst out laughing, his face alight with humor. "Lord,
Hallie. You're not convenient at all. We're both living in an inn
surrounded by people. Not to mention the fact that the climate
makes outdoor sex lethal. And you're only here for two weeks.
I'd say this is all pretty damned *inconvenient*."

"So why do it?" Was she hoping he could explain this madness to her?

The office door was closed. Daniel sobered. "Come here,
Hallie." He tugged her close. "I'm no callow twenty-year-old
kid who can't keep his pants zipped. I haven't been with a
woman in several months. And until you showed up the day
before yesterday, I was getting along just fine." He paused and
placed her hand over the bulge of his erection. "But now that
I've tasted those cute lips and touched those lush, curvy breasts,
having you in my bed is pretty much all I think about every
minute of the day. How's that for honesty?"

He might have been feeding her a line. She didn't really
know him at all. But somehow, she believed him.

Slowly, she stroked the ridge of his arousal through two
frustrating layers of cloth. He was unmoving beneath her ten-
tative touch, his whole body braced. Her fingers brushed his
zipper. And for half a second, she toyed with the idea of lower-
ing it. But sanity returned. This was a public building. Daniel
had an important job to do. "You'd better take me back to my

car," she said, her knees in danger of giving out. "I promised Robbie I'd help them wrap Christmas presents."

Daniel hobbled to the car, thankful for the long heavy coat that kept him from embarrassing himself. The arctic air slapped him in the face, but did nothing to dampen his urgent need. Every minute he spent with Hallie made him want her that much more.

They drove in silence the short distance to where her car was parked. He got out and waited for her to unlock the rental. Then he tucked her into the driver's seat. Despite the cold, he didn't close the door immediately. He waited while Hallie turned on the engine, his arm stretched across the top of the open doorframe.

When she had adjusted the heat, she turned to face him. "Thanks for the tour."

He studied her face. She had pulled up the hood of her coat, and flyaway strands of her soft hair danced in the light breeze. He leaned in and caught one, wrapping the blond silk around his finger. "A woman needs to be cautious. I get that. Why don't you call Hazel? She'll vouch for my character."

Hallie grinned. "It's not your character I'm worried about. Let's not overthink this, Mr. Reynolds. We're just having some fun, right?"

Something about her careless statement annoyed him, but he didn't react. He had a feeling that she was fighting the same out-of-control attraction that was turning him inside out.

He was a patient man.

He released her and stepped back. "I'll be late getting home tonight. Drive safely, Hallie."

Hallie made it back to the B&B only moments before the Denmans returned. They brought pizza for dinner and insisted that Hallie eat with them. One of the women plugged her iPod into a portable dock, and soon Christmas music filled the kitchen and dining room.

Hallie devoured two slices of ham and pineapple without blinking, realizing suddenly that she had forgotten to eat lunch. And she thought it was definite progress when the music didn't give her indigestion.

Robbie dropped a third slice on Hallie's plate. "Where's Daniel?" she asked. "We brought plenty for him, too."

Hallie grimaced. "He's working late tonight."

Robbie plopped down beside her and smiled inquisitively. "So what's going on with the two of you?"

Hallie choked on a bite of pizza and had to wash it down with Diet Coke. "Going on?"

Robbie nudged her with an elbow and kept right on eating. "Don't be coy, missy. I may have only been here twenty-four hours, but I've got an eye for romance. And Daniel Reynolds is just about the cutest thing I've ever seen . . . except for my Stanley, of course."

Stanley was sixty-four, carried about fifty extra pounds, and was addicted to ESPN. Love truly was blind.

Over the years, Hallie had perfected the art of the pleasant, noncommittal smile. It served her well in hotel management.

"Daniel is a very attractive man," she said. "He's a pleasant guest."

Robbie snorted. "Pleasant? Pull the other leg. You'd better snap him up, Hallie. Living under the same roof gives you a definite advantage. All the women in Alaska can't be slow on the uptake."

Hallie picked at a piece of pepperoni one of the kids had left in the pizza box. "What exactly are you suggesting?"

"Do I have to spell it out?" Robbie shook her head sadly, eyeing Hallie like a slow student. "Sex, honey."

"I thought your generation was more conservative. Daniel and I barely know each other, and I'm only going to be here for a short while."

"You young people these days are so picky. Life doesn't run according to a script. If something amazing falls into your lap, don't waste time wondering if it was really meant for you."

"And if it hurts when I leave?"

"Nobody can predict the future. But don't you deserve to have a wonderful Christmas this year? You lost your mom and the job you loved. I can see in your eyes, darlin', that you've been through hell these last twelve months. But you're here now. Live in the moment. Kick up your heels a bit. What's the worst that could happen?"

"A broken heart?" Hallie was joking, but she began to wonder whether, deep down inside, that's really what was bothering her. Was she afraid her heart couldn't take any more hard knocks?

That evening she allowed herself to be dragged into the game room, where the Denmans embraced her and made no attempt to pander to her because she was not one of them.

They beat her at Uno. They beat her at Scrabble. They even beat her at Wii bowling.

A game of Monopoly was her only success. She managed to get hotels along two whole sides of the board and wiped out her opponents in short order.

Hallie had a lot of fun with the Denmans. And she was abashed to realize how seldom she allowed herself to goof off for an entire evening.

Daniel never showed. She told herself she didn't care. The Denmans were delightful people and they made her feel right at home. Which was ironic since she was supposed to be the one hosting.

Their son Timothy wasn't off today. Robbie talked about him often, enough that Hallie began putting together a picture of a competent, grounded young man. She wondered if he appreciated his loyal, loving family. But he must, because when she met him last night, his expression, though colored with shyness, had been lit up with happiness.

When everyone finally trundled off to bed, Hallie wandered the downstairs, turning off lights, checking door locks, and adjusting the heat. She sank down onto the sofa near the tree and stared hard at the ornaments. She hadn't bothered to examine them before now, but it was obvious this was a collection accumulated over the years with loving care.

Many of the shaped-glass ornaments, decorated with glitter, were obviously antiques. She curled her legs beneath her and leaned her head back, letting her eyes half close. The swirls of color danced against her eyelids. Her mind wandered, imagining Daniel here with her.

Was it wrong to want him so much? Was she using their flirtation to distract her from the horrible year she'd had?

Where was he? Was he with another woman? He was certainly in no way obligated to check in with her. A guest of the B&B could come and go at will.

At midnight she gave up and went to bed.

The next morning Daniel wasn't at breakfast. Hallie's stomach rolled as she mixed up a quiche Lorraine from scratch. The recipe called for homemade crust, but Hallie drew the line there. The ready-to-bake crusts she'd bought from the freezer section at the grocery would have to do. Robbie was at her side, jabbering away, so Hallie was forced to produce an air of cheeriness that was entirely fake.

She wiped away an onion-produced tear and told herself not to imagine the worst. Daniel had a demanding job. He wasn't avoiding her because he had changed his mind about his feelings. Of course he wasn't.

Her second breakfast went fairly well. She forgot to squeeze oranges the night before. There wasn't any time to do it in the midst of cooking quiche and scones, so she was forced to serve bottled apple juice. But no one seemed to mind.

The Denmans were in higher spirits than usual, the kids practically bouncing in their seats. Robbie tried to help with cleanup, but Hallie shooed her away. "Go have fun with your family. Seriously."

Robbie allowed herself to be persuaded. She dried her hands on a dish towel. "We've got something special planned. Timothy was able to get today and tomorrow off. We're all headed down to Anchorage overnight. I'm sure you'll be glad to have a morning to sleep in tomorrow."

"Oh." Hallie was taken aback.

Robbie misunderstood her silence. "Oh, don't worry, hon. We're still paying for our room here, but Timothy wanted us all to see a little bit of the state, even though it's winter. If we're lucky, we'll get a glimpse of Denali on the way down. It's only a couple-hour drive as long as the weather stays dry, and it's supposed to."

Hallie wrapped her arms around her waist. "I wasn't worried about the money, Robbie. I was surprised. That's all. But it sounds like a fun trip. When do you leave?"

Robbie chuckled. "As soon as I get this motley crew corralled."

They were gone in thirty minutes.

Hallie loaded the dishwasher and washed a few of the bigger pots and utensils in the sink. The work occupied her hands, but not her mind. Where was Daniel? Had he even come home last night?

When the kitchen was set to rights, she went upstairs to do the usual daily "maid" service. The Denmans were a neat bunch for the most part, and Hallie was developing her own efficient system for cleaning. Daniel's room should have been next on the agenda, but she couldn't bring herself to walk in there. Instead, she decided to take a shower and wash her hair.

A half hour later, she slipped into matching bra and underwear, and put on her favorite jeans with an old Seattle University sweatshirt. Her clean hair was still a little damp. A new book in her suitcase was waiting to have the spine cracked, and today was the perfect opportunity for a lonely woman to curl up with a good read.

She was only ten pages into the story before she sighed loudly and tossed the book aside. Daniel was a paying guest. She had to take care of his room. Otherwise she would be admitting that he scared her.

The first thing she spotted was the note on his pillow . . . a small folded piece of paper with her name on it. He had known she would be tidying the room, and he must have assumed she would see his communication.

Berating herself for her own cowardice, she picked up the note and unfolded it slowly. . . .

> *Hallie—*
> *It was late when I got in and I had to be*
> *back on duty at six.*
> *Sorry I wasn't there to help with breakfast.*
> *If you can, stick around the house this morning. I*
> *have a surprise for you.*
> *—Daniel*

Her hands trembled slightly, and she tucked the small paper in the back pocket of her jeans. A surprise? What did that mean?

Her mind raced as she went through the motions of freshening the bathroom and making the bed. She had smoothed out the last wrinkle in the comforter when an amused voice behind her startled her so badly she stumbled and had to catch herself on the edge of the mattress.

She sprawled there awkwardly and looked up at Daniel—a laughing-eyed, red-cheeked, blown-in-from-the-cold Daniel.

He put his hands in his pockets and relaxed in the doorway. "When I asked you to stick around, I wasn't expecting to see you in my bed. But damned if I don't like it."

He straightened and approached her.

She scrambled to her feet. "Why aren't you at work?"

He grinned and kept coming. "I have two whole days off," he said, his eyes locked on her face. "It took some juggling, but I'm in the clear . . . barring any disasters, of course."

Hallie backed toward the window a half step. "Why did you do that?"

He stopped, and some of the humor in his face was replaced by a look so serious and determined, it made her heart skip a few beats.

He gazed at her intently. "I wanted us to have some time to get to know each other. And with me working all day, that wasn't going to happen anytime soon. Now I can be all yours for the next forty-eight hours."

She flashed on a vision of Daniel kneeling naked at her feet and had to clear her throat. "That sounds nice." The words came out choked.

He came close enough to brush a quick kiss over her lips. "Grab your winter gear, Prentiss. We're gonna roll."

Daniel was in a great mood. His second-in-command had things under control at work. The sky was clear, and the temperature was still hovering above zero, which was downright balmy. Most important, Hallie was by his side.

He took her to his favorite barbecue restaurant for lunch. Over thick sandwiches dripping in sauce and huge mugs of hot coffee, he fielded more questions about his job.

Hallie wiped sauce from her mouth and wrinkled her brow. "I still don't understand your civilian relationship to the post. I thought the army has always had a strong military police."

"They have and they do, but with current deployments in two wars, Iraq and Afghanistan, manpower is stretched thin. Civilian employees like us, and even private contractors, remove some of that burden. We still have some MPs on our duty rotation. They do shifts for us here and there while they're training for their next assignment. Those guys ship out all the time. Our crew is the constant that keeps things running."

"And why were you at the school the other day? What's the connection there?"

"My department is in charge of the D.A.R.E. program."

"Drug awareness?"

"Yeah. I got to know a lot of the students and teachers while running programs at the schools in the Fairbanks district, so the elementary principal invited me to be Santa."

"But you had to stay in costume or one of the kids might have recognized you."

"Exactly."

Her face got a funny look on it, like she had swallowed bad meat. "So how long will you stay in Alaska?"

He debated his words carefully. Was his answer going to be the death knell for any possible relationship with Hallie? He drummed his fingers on the table and sighed. "I like it here. The job is interesting and challenging, and even though I'm not active military any longer, I feel like I'm serving my country. I came here for a lark, for a change of pace, but I've decided I like Alaska and Fort Wainwright. And this work is a good fit for me. I'm happy."

"I see."

He couldn't tell from her face what she was thinking.

She sipped her coffee delicately and put down the clunky mug. "Is it dangerous?"

"My job? It can be . . . at times . . . but not often."

"This is only your first winter—right? How do you deal with it? The cold and the dark? And knowing you'll have to do it all over again next winter?"

He leaned back in his chair, weighing his answer. "You need to see Alaska in the spring, summer, and fall. There isn't a more beautiful place on earth."

She rolled her eyes. "Yeah. I got that. From the rental-car guy to the grocery-store clerk to one of the Denman men who has traveled in Alaska extensively. They tell me that August and early September are so amazing that I would never want to leave."

"And you don't believe them?"

"I do, I guess. I've seen pictures, after all. But I'm not sure it makes up for a long run of dark days and nights when it can get down to forty below . . . or worse."

"Do you know how to swim?" He chuckled at her immediate look of suspicion. "I'm not talking about here and now."

"I swim," she said reluctantly.

"Do you remember trying to float when you were learning?"

She nodded. "My father told me I had to relax my body and let the water hold me up."

"And could you?"

"Not at first. But finally, I learned."

He leaned forward, elbows on the table. "That's what you've got to do with winter in Alaska. Don't fight it. That makes it worse. But if you go with the flow, embrace the differences and the amazing extremes, you start to love it."

"Sounds like the voice of experience."

"Think about it. I was living in California, land of warm beaches and hot sunshine, before I moved here. I'll admit that the first time the mercury hit fifty below, I had a *what-in-the-hell-am-I-doing* moment. But then I got kind of psyched about it. This is an amazing place. It's not for sissies. It challenges people, makes them strong."

"Or convinces them to leave."

"That, too."

He'd given her a lot to think about, and he was ready to be done with "serious" for the day. "C'mon," he said, standing up and offering his hand to her. "Let's go see what North Pole has to offer."

Hallie was enchanted in spite of herself. Daniel took her to the Santa Claus House for their first stop, where she got to see and feed real reindeer. Daniel waited patiently while she bought postcards to send to her former coworkers at the hotel, as well as a cute toboggan for Julie.

She lingered over the waiting-to-be-personalized letters from Santa. What would it be like to have a big-eyed toddler on Christmas morning? A child ready to jump headfirst into every bit of Christmas merriment. Her chest tightened with yearning, and her eyes stung as she realized anew that her mom and dad wouldn't be around to be doting grandparents.

Hurriedly, before she gave in to self-pity, she paid for her purchases and joined Daniel at the front of the store. He insisted on taking her picture with the enormous fiberglass Santa outside, and then drove her to the North Pole, Alaska, post office, where "Santa's official zip is 99705." And of course, the building was located on Santa Claus Lane.

Hallie dashed off several quick notes on the Christmas-themed cards, purchased stamps, and popped them in the slot.

She climbed back into the car. "Now what?" In spite of everything that had happened before she left Seattle, she was enjoying today. In Alaska. With Daniel.

He shifted into reverse and looked over his shoulder. "I thought we might take a sleigh ride."

She gulped. "Outside?"

He looked at her like she was crazy. "Yes, outside. It's six degrees, Hallie. They do these even when it's fifty degrees colder than this. Don't be such a chicken."

But before they made it to the place where they could pay for the sleigh ride, Daniel stopped off to show her the ice-sculpture contest in the park. There were the usual wreaths and trees and bells, but what really stunned her was the children's playground equipment made entirely of ice and snow.

She watched a kid, maybe eight or nine, clamber over it with glee. His happy yells to his parents made her smile. "Wow," she said slowly. "And who said there was nothing to do in Alaska in the winter?"

Daniel kissed her cheek. "Not me."

They ate hot dogs and veggie soup in a nearby wooden lodge, and then sought out the sleigh rides.

While Daniel paid for their tickets, Hallie tucked the wrists of her gloves into the sleeves of her coat and wrapped her thick wool scarf tightly around her head, tying it in a sturdy knot. Her heavy, knee-length down coat was plenty warm, but if this ride was more than ten minutes, all bets were off.

She made a face when she saw the animals harnessed to the pretty sleigh. "What? No reindeer?" The placid horses were sturdy, but definitely had no antlers.

Daniel chuckled. "It's probably an animal-rights thing. Use your imagination." He helped her up into the padded seat of the sleigh and tucked the heavy velvet and satin blanket around them both.

Immediately Hallie was hyperaware that their bodies were touching from hip to knee. Given the air temperature, she should have been shivering. But Daniel radiated heat, and when he curled an arm around her shoulders and tucked her against his chest, she immediately felt warmer.

The sleigh took off with a bump and a jerk, and soon they were sailing along over the hard-packed snow. The driver wasn't all that far away, but with the muffled noise from the horse's hooves and the jingling of dozens of sleigh bells, Hallie realized that she and Daniel inhabited a little cocoon of privacy.

They veered onto a path that wound through a copse of hardwood trees, the branches bare black skeletons. Up above, the stars winked and sparkled. And at that very moment . . . Hallie fell in love . . . with Alaska. Riding through the snow on a sleigh with Daniel by her side, Hallie felt as if she were starring in her own movie. And she began to wonder how her humdrum workdays in Seattle could even compare with a world that was fraught with so many extremes, such wild weather, so many interesting people. For years she'd made her job her entire focus. But suddenly the world was a bigger, crazier, more fascinating place.

Alaska might technically be one of the fifty states, but to Hallie it was an alternate universe, each day more eye-opening than the last. She *was* an adventurous person, she really was. But she'd let her workaholic ways get in the way of seeing what life had to offer. Maybe Alaska was going to be more than an interim job. Perhaps it was going to show her what she had been missing.

Daniel leaned closer to whisper in her ear. "If you'll take off your glove, I'll hold your hand."

That was a fair offer. But she hoped he couldn't see her blush. Or if he did, that he would attribute the redness of her cheeks to the cold air.

Their hands linked beneath the blanket, his hard and masculine, hers smaller and softer. It was the kind of simple affection appropriate for young teenagers. But to Hallie, it seemed seductive—even erotic.

Daniel's skin was warm, his fingers rough and masculine. Hallie held on tightly, afraid of losing the moment.

Daringly, she moved their linked hands to his thigh. It was rock hard, and she didn't have to hear his sharp intake of breath to know he was affected by her touch.

When the driver executed a turn that would take them back to the beginning of their trip, Hallie sighed. Pleasure, balmy and sweet and simple, warmed her from the inside out.

They were almost in sight of the horse corral when she turned toward him and pulled his head down to hers. After a quick, decorous kiss, she leaned into his embrace and whispered in his ear. "I have a surprise for you, too. The Denmans have gone to Anchorage and won't be back until late tomorrow night."

Chapter Five

*H*allie tossed back the blanket when the horses stopped, and hopped out before Daniel could help her, landing lightly on her feet and smiling up at him with a taunting grin. Daniel stumbled getting out of the sleigh and nearly fell flat on his face. Hallie's giggle made his ears turn red. *Smooth, Reynolds. Real smooth.*

He steered her toward the car, unable to speak. All the blood in his torso had rushed south to produce an erection as hard as any one of those damned ice sculptures. He and Hallie were finally going to be all alone. Tonight.

She took off her scarf and gloves and unbuttoned her coat. "Are we going to stop for coffee? You know . . . to warm up after our ride?"

He shot her a dark glance. "No. I'm pretty damned warm as it is." That made her giggle again. The little tease was enjoying his discomfort.

When they arrived at the B&B, he parked haphazardly and

rushed her up the walk. He unlocked the front door, scooped her into his arms, and carried her inside. That shut her up.

Her eyes got big. "Did I miss something? Are we playing honeymoon?" she asked.

"No. I just thought this would be faster." He strode toward his room, all his concentration focused on getting her naked ASAP.

When he dumped her on the bed with less than his usual finesse, he paused, stricken. Hallie reclined with her hands linked behind her neck, watching him with a look he couldn't decipher.

"Um, Hallie . . ." Maybe he was out of line. Maybe her naughty whisper had been more in the nature of general information than a sexual invitation. He cleared his throat. "Were you . . . I mean . . . are we . . . ?"

She sat up and took off her coat. "Get naked, Daniel. I have plans for you."

Oh, Lord. There went any last shred of rational thought. He started stripping off his clothes, but when she did the same, he gave a hoarse command. "Stop. I want to unwrap you."

The words came out wrong, but he realized he actually meant them. She was the best Christmas present anyone had ever given him. He paused when his chest and feet were bare. His lungs were heaving and his heart rate was through the roof. He had to gain some control or she would be monumentally unimpressed with his staying power.

Carefully, deliberately, he took off the rest of his clothes.

He moved, buck naked, toward the bed and sat down beside her. "I don't know how I got so lucky," he said soberly. "But this has been one of the best days of my life."

She took his hand and raised it to her lips. "And we haven't even gotten started yet," she said quietly.

He tugged her sweatshirt over her head and gulped inwardly at the sight of her peach and cream lace bra. The lace was almost the same color as her skin. He made her stand up in front of him while he unbuttoned her jeans. It took precious seconds to help her kick out of her boots and socks, but soon he was back at her zipper.

He lowered it so slowly that they both sighed. Her concave belly was covered in gooseflesh. "Oh God, I'm sorry," he muttered. "I'll warm you up, I swear."

"I'm not cold," she said simply.

He put his hands inside the denim and eased it down her legs. Her panties matched her bra. Victoria's Secret, be damned. He had his own angel right in front of him.

Her narrow waist and curvy hips made his hands shake with the need to stroke every last inch of her soft skin. He kissed her navel, grazed her belly with his tongue.

Her hands tangled in his hair, and he thought he heard her say something. But he couldn't distinguish anything over the thunder of his own heartbeat in his ears. He cupped her firm ass in his palms and laid his cheek against her stomach. He knew how to pleasure a woman . . . how to manage foreplay to make a lover eager for more.

But he was suddenly undone. Despite the urgency of his body's driving need, he paused, shaken. It disturbed him to realize that even now, in this first, tremulous intimate touch, he was head over heels in love with Hallie Prentiss. She held his life in her hands.

What would happen if he fucked her, and she left Alaska without a backward glance? His buddies would clap him on the back and congratulate him for nailing a "short-timer." He winced inwardly. God, he couldn't bear to think about that.

He took a deep breath and nipped one of her hip bones with his teeth. That wasn't going to happen, damn it. Once a soldier, always a soldier. He was trained never to give up. To get the job done. To acquire the target.

He put a hand between her legs.

This time, her ragged words were clear. "Daniel, please. Don't make me wait."

Whatever the lady wanted. His thumb parted her folds and found her slick and wet and hot. Her clit was swollen. He skated a finger back and forth over the sensitive spot until her incoherent cries told him she was close to the edge.

And then he stopped.

Hallie groaned aloud, so damned near an orgasm that her breath lodged in her throat. She tugged at his hair, hard enough to make him curse. "Don't stop, Daniel. Do something."

"I plan to," he growled.

Before she could catch her breath, Daniel had scooped her into his embrace and was carrying her from the foot of the bed around to the side. She was tall and not exactly lightweight, but he lifted her with ease. This time, he pulled back the covers and set her carefully in the center of his bed.

He loomed over her, his face a mask of determination. "Spread your legs, Hallie. I can't wait another second."

She didn't chastise him for his bossiness. She obeyed because the alternative was unthinkable—his harsh command did something fierce and amazing to the heat building in her core. She considered herself a feminist, and yet at this moment there was something wildly exciting about feeling out of control.

He rolled on a condom and then put one hard, masculine thigh between hers, widening the V of her legs another inch. "Don't close your eyes," he growled. "Look at me."

Now both of his thighs spread hers. He fit the head of his erection to the opening of her passage and paused. He leaned forward and squeezed her breasts, tugging roughly at her nipples. She whimpered.

And then he moved.

He filled her with one wicked thrust. Her hips lifted off the mattress, her body feeling stretched, filled, possessed. His big hands grasped her waist, tugging her until her thighs draped over his. Now he had her at his mercy. He surged forward, filling her completely, making them both groan.

A lock of dark hair fell across his sweat-sheened forehead. He grinned, his expression piratical. "For a workaholic, you're pretty damned good at this. I think I'm jealous."

She ignored his playful comment. He knew more about the female body than he should, but she wasn't about to protest. She closed her eyes, concentrating on the feel of him moving deep inside her. Her inner muscles clenched, trying vainly to hold him, to control the pace. But it was futile.

He was ferocious and tender, desperate and infinitely patient. When she came with a choked cry, he was only seconds behind, and his big body went rigid in release. He collapsed on top of her as they both struggled to regain their breath.

She licked her lips, her chest still rising and falling. "Yum."

"Yum?" He yawned and rolled to his back.

"It's an adjective I reserve for dark chocolate and other indulgences. I stand by my assessment." Particularly since her thighs were still quivering and her legs were the consistency of wet noodles.

Daniel moved slightly. She felt something that was definitely not a limp noodle as he lifted her on top of him with impressive ease. She wriggled with a long sigh of pleasure, aligning her woman parts with his rapidly recovering cock.

She was glad they had left a lamp on. Looking at Daniel made her happy. Her heart pinched sharply as she thought about leaving . . . going home. But she refused to acknowledge the future.

Instead, she rose to one knee, fit his thick erection to her throbbing center, and joined their bodies.

Daniel laughed roughly. "Damn, Hallie. I can't get enough of you."

This time it was hard and fast. Right at the end, he flipped their positions, putting her on her back once again and thrusting into her so hard that the headboard slapped the wall.

She saw an explosion of stars as she caught her breath and whimpered in the grip of a stunning orgasm. "Daniel!"

Her cry was swallowed up in his roar of completion.

Long moments later, he rested his forehead on hers. "Stay," he whispered, his voice barely audible. "Stay in Alaska."

Out of nowhere, tears stung her eyes. "There's nothing for me here. And we've known each other three days. Please don't do this, Daniel. Please. Let's just enjoy the moment, and not think about what comes next."

He was silent. She couldn't tell whether she had offended him, pissed him off, or hurt him. Not the last, surely.

Her throat thickened and she reached for the lamp, plunging the room into darkness.

They slept for several hours, tangled together in a warm cocoon of blankets and arms and legs.

When Daniel's cell phone rang, the sound was intensely shocking.

Hallie sat up and turned on the light while Daniel, gruff-voiced, dealt with the call. She could tell from his face that it was serious.

He hung up and started dressing immediately. Her stomach clenched. "What is it?"

He ran a hand over his face. "Coal dust sparked a fire at the heating plant. I've got to go. We'll have all kinds of emergency personnel on-site, and maintaining security is a priority." He paused and grimaced. "I'm sorry, Hallie. I didn't want our night to end like this."

She swallowed and summoned a smile. "I understand. Don't worry about me. Go do what you have to do."

He sat on the bed long enough to lean over and kiss her. "This isn't over. Not by a long shot."

Before she could make sense of his words, he was gone.

Daniel didn't make it home for three days. He grabbed sleep in brief snatches on the sofa in his office. There were injuries from the fire. The explosion had decimated heat production. Steam heat from Fairbanks had to be brought in via the utilidors until they could get the boilers back up and running. Men were doing two or three jobs amidst the chaos.

Daniel shouldn't have had a moment to think, but his mind still wandered to thoughts of her. Hallie. In his gut he knew he needed to seal the deal before she had a chance to put up her defenses. It was a lousy time for him to be gone.

But what choice did he have?

When he finally pulled into the driveway of the B&B several days later, the place was ablaze with lights. He opened the front door and was bombarded with Christmas music, the amazing aroma of home cooking, and excited chatter.

The children were running up and down the stairs. Hallie was hunched over a computer looking at digital photos from the Denmans' Alaska excursion. And in every corner, the guests argued and laughed and filled the air with holiday excitement.

Daniel would have enjoyed it more if he hadn't been bone tired.

Hallie spotted him first. Her face lit up in welcome, but seconds later, she tempered her response. He sighed inwardly. Prickly Hallie was in full armor.

She tilted her head toward the kitchen. "Hungry?" She mouthed the word.

He nodded. He was ravenous, in fact.

They made their way via opposite routes to the kitchen. He took her in his arms and kissed her nose, not caring if anyone spotted them. "I missed you."

She gave him a quick hug, but her body was stiff in his em-

brace. She stepped away quickly and turned to the fridge to retrieve roast beef and mustard. "Is everything okay at the post now?"

He shrugged out of his heavy jacket. "Getting there. I'm off
for twenty-four hours."

She turned around as he said it, and their eyes met—hers
hesitant, his frustrated. She smiled weakly. "That's nice."

He watched in silence as she smeared mustard on two slices
of Hazel's homemade bread and piled meat on the bottom half.
Her hands were graceful and quick, and he shifted uncomfort-
ably. Hell, this was the fist time he'd ever gotten a hard-on
watching a woman make a sandwich.

She sat across from him at the table while he ate. With the
kitchen door closed, the roar from the other room was muted.

As he swallowed the last bite and finished off his beer, a
huge yawn took him by surprise. Lord, he was tired. But not
too tired to have sex on the brain. He reached across the table
and took her hand. "I'm sorry we were interrupted the other
night. I can't get you out of my head. I love having you here,
Hallie."

She squeezed his fingers, her expression guarded. "I missed
you while you were gone. Even with all the Denmans around
for company."

"I missed you, too," he said, pleased that she felt comfortable enough with him to admit that. "How have things been
going? It seems like you're a natural at this B&B thing. The
Denmans all look like they're having a great time."

"They're wonderful. I've enjoyed getting to know them all."

"Did you pursue contacting a news station to feature their
story?"

She grimaced. "I didn't even broach the subject with Robbie. After I saw how they are with each other . . . how much they love Timothy . . . how worried they are about his deployment . . . I couldn't bring myself to capitalize on that. It seemed wrong."

He nodded and then cocked his head. "Have you thought about what you're going to do when this gig is up?"

The long pause seemed to last forever. His gut clenched when Hallie didn't answer. He was pushing too hard. He knew it. But the urgency he felt couldn't be denied. He swallowed and tried to back away from the heavy tone he'd unwittingly introduced. "I'd be more than happy to help you with that decision." This time the tone of his voice was teasing, but he was dead serious.

She sighed deeply, drawing her hand away. "I have friends in Seattle . . . and a nice town house."

"But no job."

She gnawed her lower lip. "I'll need to polish my résumé. But something will turn up."

"Damn, you're stubborn."

She stood up so quickly that her chair almost tipped over. "I can't think straight in the midst of all this forced Christmas cheer."

He frowned. "Forced?"

She cleared the table with quick, jerky movements.

She motioned toward the other part of the house. "Don't you get it? Christmas has a dark side. People spend a lot of time pretending." She slammed the refrigerator door and knocked a moose magnet to the floor. Her face was flushed, her eyes too bright. "Poor Timothy is being shipped off to Iraq or Afghanistan or who knows where in January, and they're all in there playing Yahtzee and pretending that everything is just fine."

Daniel didn't think of himself as the most perceptive man on the planet, but it was plain to see Hallie was hurting.

He wanted to take her in his arms and comfort her, but her body language said, *Back off*. So he leaned back in his chair and folded his arms across his chest. "I'm sorry your mother is gone, Hallie. And I know I'm a piss-poor substitute, but talk to me . . . please. What kinds of little things did the two of you do to make the holidays special?"

She swiped a hand at her damp eyes and sat back down, almost deflating, it seemed. Her bottom lip began to tremble, but she managed to get herself in hand. "We always made candy-cane cookies. And we watched *It's a Wonderful Life*. Sometimes we took little gifts to the nursing home in our neighborhood."

He smiled at her. "Sounds pretty special. She must have been very proud of you."

Color returned to her cheeks. "I was lucky. She was a great mom."

"You will be, too, someday." He shocked the hell out of himself. Where had those words come from?

Now he had embarrassed her. She looked down at the table, her silky hair shielding her expression.

He got to his feet and stretched, bidding adios to his dream of hot sex and an early night. "On your feet, Prentiss. We've got a houseful of guests who—I'm willing to bet—would love to chow down on Christmas cookies while they watch Jimmy Stewart."

Her head snapped up, her expression equal parts hope and uncertainty. "Do we have time?"

He opened one of the recipe books and thumbed to the back. "Hazel has a few 'cheating' recipes. Stuff she throws together in a hurry. These sugar cookies will do the trick. Add some red and green sprinkles and they'll think you're Martha Stewart."

An hour later, Hallie was curled up on the sofa with Daniel's arm tucked around her shoulders. The scent of freshly baked cookies filled the air, but the only remaining evidence of their existence was a smattering of sprinkles stuck to the empty plates sitting on the coffee table.

On the TV screen, townspeople were dumping baskets of money in George Bailey's living room to save him from financial ruin.

And all around Hallie and Daniel, the Denmans, Timothy included, were sprawled in chairs and sofas and on the floor, enjoying the evening.

Hallie stared pensively at the television as the classic movie wound to a close. George Bailey was a man who had everything that was important . . . a loving wife, sweet children, a boatload of friends. But when something went terribly wrong in his life, it took a dramatic experience to make him realize that his life was worth something.

Braving winter in Alaska wasn't quite the same as having an angel send you into an "alternate ending" life experience, but even so, this unexpected trip was a pretty drastic change from Hallie's normal life. And she had to admit . . . being here, especially with Daniel and the Denmans, was causing her to do some hard thinking.

She closed her eyes and absorbed the moment. None of the people in this room were related to her by blood. But she had welcomed them, had provided a home away from home for them so that they could share the holidays with their son.

And Daniel. His family was far away, but he seemed comfortable and happy here. He was everything a man should be. Honorable. Caring. Not to mention sexy as hell.

She stirred restlessly and felt him press a kiss to the top of her head. Was it really so simple? Could she start something new amidst the ashes of the life that had once seemed so complete?

And what if Daniel changed his mind? What if his interest in her was fleeting? It would be foolish to base a decision on the romance of northern lights.

The credits rolled, and the grown-ups made a united push to get the kids upstairs to bed. In the resulting commotion, Hallie and Daniel picked up plates and straightened the room. They bade their guests good night, and Daniel began turning off lights.

When Hallie finished loading the dishwasher, she turned to find Daniel staring at her.

Her heart skipped two beats. "Are you headed to bed?"

He reached for her hand, smiling a crooked smile. "Not alone."

He tugged her down the hallway toward her room, passing his on the way. Her suite was at the far back corner of the house, and there would be no reason for any guests to wander this way.

Daniel reached for the doorknob and matter-of-factly locked the door behind them as they entered. The quick snick of the mechanism sounded abnormally loud to Hallie. She could feel her heart beating in her ears.

He faced her, no longer smiling. The planes and angles of his face seemed sharper, more defined. Nothing was left of the jovial Santa from earlier in the week. This man looked predatory . . . determined.

He slid his hands into her hair, cupped her head, and ravaged her mouth in a hungry, desperate kiss. Her knees lost their starch. She leaned into him, matching him kiss for kiss.

He muttered as he teased the shell of her ear with his tongue, "I had a hard time keeping you out of my head when I was supposed to be working. You've bewitched me, Hallie Prentiss."

"The house seemed empty without you." She shivered as she made the confession. It was true. This exile in Alaska wouldn't have been nearly as much fun without Daniel.

He chuckled. "I doubt that." He removed her clothes with stunning speed and helped her do the same to his. Then he handed her a condom with a dare in his eyes.

She felt herself flush, but she opened the packet with shaking hands and rolled the protection onto Daniel's ready-for-action erection.

When she was done, he lifted her up and urged her legs

around his waist. "Are you getting used to the cold in Alaska?" he asked hoarsely.

She sucked in a sharp breath, feeling every inch of his considerable length and girth fill her completely from this new angle. "I'm never cold when you're here, Daniel," she whispered. She tightened her arms around his neck.

His arms rippled with muscle, and he made her feel dainty and sexy, even though she was far from petite.

He flexed his hips, causing them both to gasp. "You're perfect, Hallie. In every way."

Her throat tightened, and she wanted so badly to believe him. Was Daniel her own personal Christmas miracle? Or was he a bright, shiny toy that would lose its sparkle in the light of day?

He pressed her back and butt against the door and pumped with firm steady strokes. She buried her face in his neck and held on, not sure if the sensation of vulnerability was exciting or disturbing. She had lost so much this year. She didn't want to set herself up for more pain . . . more disappointment.

But with Daniel making love to her as if she were the only woman in the world that mattered, her heart beat an extra stroke or two in hopes that this crazy, unexpected relationship was not as ephemeral as the aurora borealis. She needed desperately to know that some things lasted.

His fingers bit into the yielding flesh of her ass. He drove into her relentlessly, the shaft of his cock stroking her clit in wild, sharp bursts of pleasure. Their bodies were slick with sweat. His breathing was labored, and hers had long since deteriorated into oxygen-starved whimpers.

He was hot and hard, all over. She was boneless in his embrace, totally dependent upon his strength.

Just when she thought she would die if she didn't come, he backed away from the door, carried her toward the bed, and dropped her on her back. "Roll over," he commanded hoarsely. "On your hands and knees."

She obeyed mindlessly and felt him fill her in this new position. His thighs were warm behind her legs. His hands stroked down from her shoulders, over the length of her spine. He toyed with her ass, kneading the flesh and deliberately slowing the speed of his strokes.

He reached one hand between her legs and found the spot that begged for attention. His touch was like a match to tinder. Hallie cried out, feeling an unstoppable orgasm swell from between her thighs and engulf her entire body in waves of pleasure.

Daniel wasn't done with her yet.

He gave her barely a second to recover. With a sleight of hand worthy of the finest magician, he rearranged their damp, heated bodies one more time, and soon he had her spread-eagled on the bed with his face buried between her thighs.

She tried to push him away. It was too much, too soon. But he wasn't to be stopped. His mouth was diabolical, no quarter given. His lips and his tongue combined to drive her senseless. She arched her back in a shocked, ragged cry of completion, and before she could catch her breath, Daniel was inside her again.

This time, his mighty control unraveled rapidly. His thrusts were jerky, unrestrained. He took her wildly and shook all over as he came. He groaned loudly in her ear and slumped on top of her.

His weight was not unpleasant. She liked it, in fact. In bed with Daniel she felt secure. She believed, in the intimacy of their embrace, that nothing bad could happen. Sex with Daniel was perfect and comfortable.

Right up until the moment when he nuzzled her neck and whispered in her ear, his words barely audible, "I think I'm falling in love with you, Hallie."

Chapter Six

The days on the calendar tumbled by rapidly, like reindeer scrambling across the sky to meet their December 25 deadline. Hallie cooked, shopped, cleaned, and then started the cycle all over again.

The Denmans soon tired of eating out, and since they were the B&B's only guests, Robbie cajoled Hallie into letting them take over the kitchen for lunches and dinners. Soon, the smells of lasagna, pork roast, spaghetti, and fried chicken filled the air.

The refrigerator was overflowing with all sorts of goodies, and when Robbie bought a dozen Christmas tins and began filling them with cookies of every size and shape, Hallie wondered if her waistline would ever recover.

Hallie and Daniel were in a holding pattern, no pun intended. The evening he mentioned "love," and she pointedly didn't respond, things between them became strained. But they still made love every night, sometimes in his bed, sometimes in hers.

It stunned her that he had learned her body so quickly. He could bring her to a gasping, desperate peak in bare moments, or he could drag out the anticipation of release with long, slow, achingly wonderful lovemaking that made her melt in his arms.

She'd stopped telling herself that she wasn't crazy about him. Daniel was the man she had been looking for all her life . . . at least when she wasn't too busy trying to climb the corporate ladder. But he'd shown up at the wrong place, the wrong time.

Her life was in chaos, the future murky and uncertain. She had to decide where to go next. She had to rewrite her five-year life plan.

One morning, when the house was amazingly empty and quiet, Hallie collapsed on the sofa and stared balefully at the two-foot-tall ceramic Santa on the coffee table. His arms were stretched over his head supporting a candy dish filled with peppermints. His red-suit-clad belly was appropriately rotund, and his black, painted eyes sparkled with mischief.

Hallie propped her ankles near him and leaned back, feeling the pleasant ache of well-used muscles. She had just finished scrubbing bathrooms and making beds, and she realized, much to her surprise, that she actually enjoyed the hands-on labor.

At the hotel in Seattle, her job had been more managerial—arbitrating disputes, juggling crises. But here at the Dancing Elves B&B, she was the whole staff . . . from maintenance to housekeeping to concierge and everything in between.

Her tenure was almost over. Tomorrow night was Christmas Eve. Robbie and Hallie had coordinated plans for a big evening meal. Timothy would be in attendance, but unfortunately Daniel was slated to work until nine.

A tight knot of panic crowded Hallie's chest. Nothing had been resolved between her and Daniel. She knew he was still waiting for some concrete sign that she returned his feelings. But she was too damned scared to admit the truth.

The fifteen Denmans were booked on a flight for eleven a.m. Christmas morning. Timothy had to work on the holiday, so all the tearful hugs would happen late on the twenty-fourth.

Hallie was due to fly out at two p.m. on the twenty-fifth. She planned to be up early on Christmas morning and spend the time after the Denmans departed making sure everything was spotless and well organized for Hazel and Roy's return.

Her head was achy and heavy with confusion. She glared at Santa, resenting his unrelenting cheer. She'd grown up knowing she was always on Santa's "nice" list. The girl who never made waves. Who always toed the line. Who believed in hard work and dedication.

And where had it gotten her?

She poked Santa's belly with her big toe. Of course, there was always another way to look at it. Maybe she was still on the "nice" list and Daniel was her present. "Is that it?" she asked, not expecting an answer. "Is Daniel my compensation for being unemployed?"

She grimaced, knowing that her situation was outside Santa's jurisdiction. And losing her job was the least of it, really.

Nothing could compare to losing her mom. The Prentiss family wasn't like the Denmans. They didn't have people to spare. Why did it have to be *Hallie's* mother?

No answers from the jolly man. Big life questions were not his territory.

She glared at him anyway, no longer seeing his image, but instead talking aloud, searching for answers. "And if I had to lose my mom, why did I have to lose my job, too? That's a lot to handle in one year."

Old St. Nick smiled genially. Was that a note of disappointment she saw behind the painted smile? Was there some big lesson Hallie was supposed to be learning?

The fictional George Bailey had been ready to commit suicide before he'd been rescued from himself. He'd been as full of self-pity as Hallie had for the last month. Shame twisted in her stomach. What did she really have to complain about? People died. All the time. It was the price of living. And at least she had had a job to lose.

She was young and strong and healthy—there would be other jobs. And in the meantime, she was blessed with friends. Friends like Julie, who had arranged this "working" vacation in Alaska. And like Robbie, who could have bitched about Hallie's incompetence in the kitchen, but instead had pitched in with grace and enthusiasm.

And Daniel. Daniel, who loved handing out presents at an elementary school. Daniel, who took pride in the important job he was doing. Daniel, who had treated her like a princess since the first day she set foot in the Land of the Midnight Sun.

She bit her lip and sat up suddenly. Father Christmas nodded his approval. She shook her head to clear it. All the sleepless nights in Daniel's bed were catching up with her. Was she really carrying on a conversation with a portly figurine?

She took a deep breath and let it out, her heart feeling lighter than it had felt in months. "Okay, Santa. I get the message. I'm a lucky woman. And I'm not ready for tomorrow. Not by a long shot."

She jumped to her feet and grabbed her coat and keys. Soon she was on the road headed toward Fairbanks to do some shopping. She'd already decided what to get her guests at the inn. A photography shop in town carried beautiful Alaska photo albums. Hallie bought four . . . one for each of the individual Denman families.

With no new job in sight, it made sense to guard her savings account. But Christmas was about love and generosity and giving. The joy the Denmans had shared with her couldn't be measured in dollars and cents. Though it wasn't strictly necessary, she purchased inexpensive toys for all the little kids and iTunes gift cards for the older ones. For Timothy, she selected a restaurant gift certificate. Playing Santa was exhilarating and fun.

That left only Daniel. What did you get a man you met two weeks ago? She didn't even know what his hobbies were. Between his job and the inn and the time the two of them had spent in bed, there was still a lot they didn't know about each other. And then it dawned on her.

With her backseat loaded with packages, including two

rolls of Christmas paper and tape and bows, and with the precious daylight waning rapidly, she headed for home. She had a lot of wrapping to do.

Daniel sat at his desk late on Christmas Eve and doodled a dancing elf on the edge of his notepad. The post was quiet tonight, everyone tucked in for the holiday. He wanted badly to be at the inn with Hallie and all the Denmans, but as a single man, he couldn't deprive a young dad of the chance to tuck his kids in bed on the most important night of the year.

His second-in-command had a two-year-old, so when the little boy was asleep, the other man was going to relieve Daniel. And one of the other single men had offered to cover the holiday tomorrow.

Daniel brooded as the hours passed slowly. Hallie was going to fly home tomorrow, and there wasn't a thing he could do about it. He had a gut feeling that if he didn't get her to admit she loved him before she left, he'd never see her again.

And it hurt. He was convinced she loved him. At least a little. But she was so damned focused on figuring out the future, she wasn't able to see the gift that life had dropped in their laps.

He and Hallie were made for each other. He knew it. And he had one last shot this evening at convincing her.

They were a perfect match in bed. Despite the string of nights they had spent together, his body ached for her all over again. She was hot as hell between the sheets. For the first time in his life, he could imagine waking up to the same face year after year. The thought was comforting.

Hallie was his, damn it.

He glared at the clock as it ticked away the final precious hours of Hallie's stay in Alaska. What was going on at the inn? Was Hallie in a good mood? Did she miss him?

Glumly, he pulled up a required report on the computer and started filling in statistics. He was stuck for the moment. Might as well get some work done. . . .

Hallie stared at the mound of presents under the tree and grinned. Dinner was now nothing more than a fond memory. They had all devoured enough calories in one sitting to make a grizzly bear comatose. And even though there was a huge plate tucked away in the refrigerator for Daniel, she wished he had been there to be part of the fun.

The kids were riding a sugar high, and the kitchen was a shambles. Hallie had planned to clean everything up while the Denmans had their family time around the tree, but surprisingly, the four fathers, plus Timothy, had declared the kitchen a "no female" zone and were now elbow deep in dishwater and dirty pots and pans.

Robbie and the other three moms were going through one last checklist to make sure all the presents were in place. They'd had to do some creative shopping to guarantee nothing was too big to ship home, but even so, Hallie was pretty sure there were going to be some overage charges on heavy suitcases.

Hallie was preparing to slip down the hall to go to her room when Robbie grabbed her arm.

The older woman grinned. "Where do you think you're going?"

Hallie shrugged, feeling awkward. "This is family time. I don't want to intrude."

"Bull crap. You're not running out on this circus, honey. You're an honorary Denman. . . . We all voted."

Robbie was kind enough to ignore the two tears that wet Hallie's cheeks.

Hallie cleared her throat. "Thank you for including me, Robbie."

Timothy was tapped to play Santa. There was a strict system in place for the distribution of gifts. The children each received one present first to take the edge off their excitement. Then the women opened a package.

Hallie was taken aback when a large, beautifully wrapped box was placed in her lap. Everyone paused in the mad frenzy of paper ripping, and suddenly all eyes were focused on Hallie. She felt herself blush. "What's this?"

Robbie, standing behind the sofa, brushed her hand over Hallie's head in a maternal caress. "All four families went in together to get you something special. You've made these two weeks really wonderful, Hallie. You have an extraordinary gift for hospitality. And we all really appreciate what you've done for us."

Timothy grinned, his face looking more like a kid's than an adult's at the moment. "Open it, Hallie."

She loosened the tape and carefully folded the paper to a chorus of disapproving groans. When she lifted the lid from the box, she caught her breath.

Inside was a lightweight, extremely luxurious cashmere robe in soft gray. She lifted it free of the thick tissue and held it to her cheek. "It's lovely," she said softly. "Thank you all."

Stanley patted her knee. "You're one of us now. Don't you forget it."

They were all kind enough to divert their attention from a choked-up Hallie as "Santa" continued handing out gifts.

When it came time for all the Denmans to open Hallie's presents, she could tell from their expressions that they were genuinely pleased. And the kids crawled in her lap for kisses and hugs.

Despite the festivities, Hallie couldn't help but wish Daniel were there. She missed him with a deep ache that had nothing to do with Christmas and everything to do with the fact that she could no longer deny her feelings. She loved him. Madly. And for the long run.

But she hadn't a clue what to do about it.

Julie's parents were paying her for only two weeks. Hallie couldn't exactly crash in Daniel's room like a college kid nabbing a couch.

When the front door opened and Daniel entered in a swirl of snowflakes and icy air, everyone greeted him with gusto. Santa found one last present under the tree, and soon a laughing Daniel was stripped of his coat and ensconced on the sofa beside Hallie.

He stole a kiss in front of their audience. "Merry Christmas, Hallie."

She grinned at him, feeling her world settle into its orbit at last. "Merry Christmas, yourself."

Daniel's gift from the Denmans was a fishing pole, top-of-the-line, to use the following summer. They had all heard him wax poetic about the streams in Alaska and wanted him to be ready.

By ten thirty, Daniel had eaten a plate of leftovers, and the merrymaking was beginning to subside. The Denmans were well aware that they all had to say good-bye to Timothy, who had to be back on post by midnight. Hallie and Daniel escaped to the kitchen to give the family some privacy.

He brushed a strand of hair from her cheek. "I have a present for you, my girl. Do you want it now or in the morning?"

She bit her lip. "Don't you have to work tomorrow?"

He shook his head. "I did some swapping. I'll be here to help you clean, and I'll take you to the airport if you still insist on leaving."

She bent her head, hearing his gentle rebuke. "I guess I want it now," she said softly. "I've never been a patient person."

He pulled a velvet-covered box from his pocket, and her heart stopped.

"It's not a ring," he said quickly. "Not yet anyway."

He handed it to her, and she opened it. Inside was a necklace, a delicate platinum chain with a small charm, a lovely sapphire representation of a flower. It was clearly expensive, and she wondered when he had found the time to shop for such an exquisite gift.

He took it from her and unfastened the latch, placing the necklace around her neck. He turned her to face a small mirror on the opposite wall. "It's a forget-me-not," he said gruffly, "the state flower of Alaska. I hope it does its job. I'm counting on it, in fact."

Her skin quivered when his fingers brushed her throat. She touched the jeweled blossom. "I love it, Daniel. Thank you."

He turned her in his arms and kissed her gently. "It's a start."

She smiled at him. "I have something for you, but I think I'll make you wait till the morning."

"How is that fair?"

She shrugged. "I'll make it up to you later."

He lifted an eyebrow. "I think I just found my second wind. Is it too early to say good night to our guests?"

Before Hallie could answer, Timothy eased the door open and poked his head into the kitchen. "I've got to head out," he said gruffly. Misery darkened his eyes, and it was all Hallie could do not to bawl. She gave him a kiss on the cheek, and the two men embraced briefly.

Daniel clapped him on the back. "I'll be keeping an eye out for you, Denman. Maybe we can grab dinner once in a while."

Timothy cleared his throat. "I'd like that." He smiled at Hallie, but his big puppy dog eyes made it clear that he was sad to be saying good-bye. "You've been wonderful to my mom and the whole family. We can't thank you enough."

"It was my pleasure," she said. "I hope we'll stay in touch."

Hallie and Daniel went out on the front porch with the rest of the crew to say good-bye and to watch Timothy drive off down the street.

After that, no one had much Christmas spirit left. Except for the children, of course, who were anxious to get to sleep so Santa would come. Hallie knew that, despite the early flight, everyone would be up with the roosters for the kids' benefit.

When the activity downstairs had quieted down, Daniel squeezed Hallie's hand. "Let's go to bed, sweetheart." About then the grandfather clock chimed the hour. They looked at each other and smiled.

She took his hand as they walked down the hall. "Merry Christmas, Daniel."

Their lovemaking was subdued. Daniel was exhausted, and Hallie was overly emotional from the evening that had made her aware of so many mixed feelings. He entered her slowly, and moved inside her for what seemed like hours. Her legs were twined tightly around his waist, as if clinging to him gave her the power to stop the clock. To keep the weak Alaskan sun from rising.

When it was over, they cuddled drowsily, wrapped in each other's arms. It was well into the night before Hallie slept.

When the alarm went off, she rose in a fog of fatigue, stumbling into the kitchen to prepare one last breakfast. Daniel was dead to the world, and she let him sleep. In the living room she could hear the childish squeals of glee as the little ones discovered their Santa presents.

The next couple of hours were a blur. Everyone ate, including Daniel, who showed up in the kitchen heavy-eyed and rumpled. Last-minute items were stuffed into already bulging suitcases. Occasionally someone snapped bad-temperedly, the result of too little sleep and the stress of leaving Timothy behind.

At nine thirty, all fifteen of the Denmans lined up by the front door for hugs and kisses from Hallie and Daniel. Robbie cried unashamedly as the big family went outside and loaded up in three rental vehicles. Despite the temperature, the older woman rolled down her window and leaned her head out. "Don't be a stranger, Hallie. I left you my e-mail address and phone numbers. Don't make me hunt you down."

Hallie squeezed her hand. "I'll be in touch."

Daniel rested a hand on top of the car and kissed Robbie's cheek one last time. "I'll keep an eye on him until he ships out. And I'll e-mail, too. Try not to worry."

And then they were gone.

Daniel put his arm around Hallie, who was shaking from the cold. "Come back inside before you turn into an icicle."

In the house, they stood awkwardly.

Daniel's scruffy one-day beard gave him a rakish look, but there were dark circles beneath his eyes.

She had entertained the notion that they might go back to bed for a quickie before tackling the four guest rooms, but Daniel didn't look like a man in the mood for fun and games. His mouth was set in a grim line, and his expression was an odd combination of resignation and aggression.

He thrust out his jaw. "What's the schedule?"

Frustration made her head hurt. What did he expect her to do? Julie's parents would be back tomorrow. Was Hallie supposed to rent one of the upstairs rooms so she could hang out with Daniel? And how did he think she'd entertain herself while he was working?

She reached in the closet for the vacuum. "I'll handle the laundry if you'll do the floors."

. . .

Daniel worked mindlessly. Would it help matters if he flung her down on the nearest mattress and screwed her senseless? Would it make a difference if he begged? If he told her he wasn't *falling* in love with her . . . but that he was already head over heels?

A man had his pride. He'd made it more than clear that he wanted her to stay. So yeah, maybe that would be hard for a woman like Hallie. There sure as hell weren't any hotel jobs available this time of year.

Did he expect her to stay in his bed, warm and willing, until he had the chance to join her? Put like that, it sounded a bit selfish, even if the visual *did* make him hard and horny.

Oh, hell. He tried to ignore the voice deep in his gut that said he'd be able to tolerate this parting a heck of a lot better if she had at least given him some indication of what she was feeling.

By noon, the B&B was spotless, every room ready for a new guest. All traces of the Denman family Christmas were gone. Only Hazel and Roy's Christmas decorations remained.

Daniel sprawled on the sofa and waited for Hallie to finish packing her bags. All he wanted now was to get this over with.

Hallie refused to cry. She was a grown woman. She and Daniel could work something out . . . maybe . . . if he was serious about his feelings. And if she didn't hear from him when she was back in Seattle, well then, she'd know she had done the right thing.

She glanced around the room and checked the dresser drawers one last time. Looking at the bed was a mistake. All she could see was an X-rated movie she and Daniel had made in her memory.

Her throat tightened, and she blinked rapidly. Her chest hurt, but she refused to let him see her get all teary and emotional. She owed it to Daniel to let him know how she felt, but it was scary. If she said the words out loud, fate might decide she needed to lose one more thing.

It was irrational. She knew that. But she couldn't shake the feeling.

She found Daniel in the living room, drumming his fingers on his knees. His entire posture said he was ready to be done with this good-bye.

His gift was tucked in her roomy purse. She planned to give it to him when they got to the airport.

He didn't say anything, and neither did she.

She picked up her coat, but before she could put it on, her cell phone rang. Hallie flipped open the phone, giving Daniel an apologetic glance. "This is Julie. I'll just be a minute. She probably wants to know what time to pick me up."

Hallie walked down the hall as she talked. It always made her nervous to carry on a conversation with someone else in the room. . . .

Daniel sighed and stood up to pace. He should have gone to work and let Hallie take a cab. This was killing him.

Minutes later, she was back, a look of excitement on her face.

He shoved his hands in his pockets. "What is it?"

Hallie grinned. "That was Hazel calling on Julie's phone. She and Roy want to stay in Seattle a little longer. And they've decided they may be ready to retire and put the B and B on the market. She wanted to know if I would mind working a few more weeks while they think about it."

"I'd be sorry to see them go." Daniel had become very fond of the couple who had given him a home.

"Well, it will take time. In this market, it could be a while before they find a buyer. But Julie's wedding is coming up next spring, and I guess they're already thinking about being grand-parents in the not-too-distant future."

Daniel smiled faintly. "Makes sense."

Hallie flung out her arms, her face alight with excitement. "Isn't it wonderful? I don't have to leave Alaska."

His stomach clenched. This was not exactly the way he'd envisioned things playing out in his fantasies.

Hallie's face fell, and distress creased her forehead. "I thought you'd be happy about this."

He shrugged. "I wanted you to stay because you needed *me*, not a job. But now I know where I stand." He felt ridiculously hurt, and the unaccustomed sensation made him surly.

She approached him, her eyes pleading. "I love you, Daniel. But I've been afraid to say it. I didn't trust what's been happen-ing between us. I was afraid to be happy for fear it would be snatched away."

"Convenient," he snarled. "The truth is, you were ready to get on a plane and never see me again. If Julie hadn't called, you would never have told me you loved me—right?"

"No," she cried. "That's not true. I was going to tell you at the airport when I gave you your Christmas present, I swear."

A leaden feeling settled in his stomach. "Well, I guess we'll never know."

She shook her head vigorously. "You're wrong, Daniel. I'm telling you the truth. Here." She reached into her huge purse and pulled out a small package. "Open this and you'll see."

The narrow flat box was wrapped in holly paper. The tag said "To my dearest Daniel . . . from Hallie."

He ripped into it with his heart beating and his mouth dry. Was Santa coming through for him after all?

He stared at the contents. "It's a ticket."

She put her arms around his waist and laid her head on his shoulder. "An open-ended, round-trip airfare to Seattle from Fairbanks. I knew I had to get my life in order, but I didn't want to lose you."

"You didn't?" he asked, hardly daring to believe that his Christmas wish was about to come true.

She pulled his head down for a kiss. "I didn't."

He grabbed her up in a bear hug, her feet dangling above the floor. "I think I have another gift for you."

She kissed his nose. "Where is it?"

"It's too big to wrap."

"Ooh . . . intriguing. Don't keep me in suspense."

He paused, suddenly unsure. Was Hallie really ready to stay in Alaska indefinitely? He cleared his throat. "I've never been married. Don't have kids. I lead a pretty simple lifestyle."

A frown line appeared between her brows. "Okkkaaayyy."

He set her away from him and took a deep breath. He couldn't think straight with her breasts crushed against his chest. "I've got a pretty significant nest egg built up."

She was staring at him in total confusion. "You lost me."

He shrugged and went for broke. "What if I buy the Dancing Elves B and B and give it to you for a wedding present?"

Hallie went perfectly still, her eyes wide and her mouth hanging open in an oval of pure astonishment.

Her silence scraped at his nerves. "Hallie?" He waved his hand in front of her face.

She swallowed hard. "Was that a marriage proposal or a real estate offer?"

The light in her eyes made him grin. "Either . . . both . . . I'll let you decide."

She launched herself into his arms and scattered kisses all over his face. "This is a totally underhanded way to get me to stay in Alaska."

He kissed her hard, holding her tightly. "A man's gotta do what a man's gotta do. Is there an answer anywhere in that fascinating brain of yours, or do I have to get down on my knees and beg?"

Her eyes were dreamy, her cheeks flushed. "Yes and yes. No begging required. I love you, Daniel. You're going to get sick of hearing it."

He swung her in a circle. "Do you know what this means?"

She giggled, her breasts smashed against his chest. "Tell me."

He sighed, a great, big, starting-down-in-the-gut exhale that summed up his cartwheeling emotions. "It means that you're no longer a Christmas Scrooge."

"Hey," she pulled away, pretending to be insulted. "I was never that bad."

He kissed her again, still shaky from nearly losing her. "You turned up your nose at every decoration and Christmas song when I first met you. Admit it."

She smiled, her blue eyes filled with joy. "I *may* have been a little conflicted about the holiday, but I always knew how I felt about you. You've made this the best Christmas ever, Daniel. And considering the circumstances, you deserve a medal."

He started unbuttoning her blouse.

She cocked her head, her expression curious. "I take it we're not going to the airport?"

He frowned, still rattled at how close he had come to putting her on a plane. "No damn way."

"Then what exactly did you have in mind?"

He sighed in approval at the sight of her red satin bra, wondering if her panties matched. "It's Christmas Day. We're all alone. And we've just agreed to purchase the Dancing Elves B and B. I think we should christen our new venture."

"With daytime sex?"

"Don't laugh. Daytime sex in December is hard to come by in Alaska. We have to make hay while the sun shines."

"So that's where the saying comes from?"

He put his hands on her breasts and caressed the gooseflesh he found there. The necklace he'd given her was nestled tantalizingly in her cleavage. "Do you think we could stop talking now?"

She caressed him boldly, making him see spots in front of his eyes. "Men really do have only one thing on their minds, don't they?"

His knees buckled. He pulled her down to the sofa, tucking her beneath him. "Marry me, Hallie."

The ceramic Santa on the coffee table smirked. And was Hallie winking at the guy?

She wrapped her arms around his neck. "Whatever you say, Daniel. I like the sound of a honeymoon where the nights are twenty hours long."

He finished undressing them both and settled into her warm, welcoming body with a groan. "Lord, I hope I can keep up."

She squeezed him with her inner muscles. "But on the other hand, I hear that Alaska is spectacular in the summer. . . ."

He would have laughed, but he was too far gone. He shut her up by the simple expedient of kissing her until they both gasped for air.

"Merry Christmas, Hallie," he muttered, trying to last a few seconds longer.

She moaned and shivered as she came. "Merry Christmas, Daniel," she whispered breathlessly. "It's going to be a wonderful life."

About the Authors

LuAnn McLane lives in Florence, Kentucky, just outside of Cincinnati, Ohio. When she takes breaks from writing, she enjoys watching chick flicks with her daughter and trying to keep up with her three active sons. Visit her Web site at www.luannmclane.com.

Susanna Carr lives in the Pacific Northwest. Visit her Web site at www.susannacarr.com.

Janice Maynard left a fifteen-year career as an elementary school teacher to write full-time. Since then, she has published more than a dozen books and novellas. She lives with her husband in Tennessee. Visit her Web site at www.janicemaynard.com.